Naked Came the Leaf Peeper

A Novel by

Brian Lee Knopp
John P. McAfee
Susan Reinhardt
Vicki Lane
Tommy Hays
Wayne Caldwell
Fred Chappell
Alan Gratz
Annette Saunooke Clapsaddle
Gene Cheek
Linda Marie Barrett
Tony Earley

Burning Bush Press of Asheville

Published by Burning Bush Press of Asheville,
a division of Renaissance Bookfarm, Inc.
Inquiries to Malaprop's Bookstore/Cafe
55 Haywood St., Asheville, NC 28801
www.malaprops.com

Printed in the United States of America
Cover and interior illustrations by Julie Armbruster
Design by Kasey Gruen

ISBN-13: 978-0-9658657-7-7

To Emöke—your extraordinary life and good deeds have proved that one can judge a book by its lover

A Note from The Authors

~~~~~~

T his is a remarkable work of fiction, if we do say so ourselves. With the current state of the publishing industry in mind, it appears that we must.

However, as a work of fiction, this book is populated by creatures human and nonhuman who never actually existed in real life. Take a breath. Accept this. It is irredeemably so.

The book also mentions places and things that do exist in real life—but these places and things are incapable of hiring legal counsel, and so they are not vexatious to us.

Know this: any resemblance between persons, institutions, corporations, or animals described in this book and those same entities existing outside this book—is purely coincidental.

Contents

"There are some 'dark corners' of the mountains, mostly on or near state boundary lines, where there are bands of desperadoes who defy the law. But elsewhere anyone of tact and common sense can go as he pleases through Appalachia without being molested. Tact, however, implies the will and the insight to put yourself truly in the other man's place."

—Horace Kephart, *Our Southern Highlanders*

Gravity

by Brian Lee Knopp

T o the casual observer, it would have looked like a man suddenly stretching his back, losing his balance, and then falling off the stout wooden guardrail that kept most cars and many fools from plunging off the Blue Ridge Parkway's scenic overlooks.

But there were no casual observers.

Even if there had been a witness—a good witness, say, like an elderly person who didn't relish their role as a random voyeur to violent death, someone whose ability to observe, recollect and narrate sequential events hadn't been destroyed in their youth by television or corrupted in their adulthood by arterial degeneration—it still wouldn't have made a difference. They couldn't have processed what they'd actually seen.

Which was this: a tourist being shot in the small of his back with a potato, and then falling silently to his death from the Beacon Heights overlook.

The detectives wouldn't be able to process it, either. They would shake their heads and snort and repeat, with rising scorn, the key elements that excited their overworked incredulity.

Shot in the back.

With a potato.

No sound. No gunshot. No scream.

Just a thud.

Death by spud.

"But that's what I saw!" the strong hypothetical eyewitness would insist.

And justly so. Because that's exactly what happened.

There had been a huff, a phantom *phoot* sound that barely disturbed the cold crisp autumn air at 4200 feet above sea level. Then a muffled *thoomp* from the impact of the improbable projectile. The starchy missile had disintegrated upon impact, but not before propelling the man off the guardrail on which he had perched. The tourist had arched his back in shock and pain. His arms first reached back in response to the tater's punch, then flailed reflexively, wildly, ineffectually, to stop his headfirst flight and subsequent fatal landing onto the rocky outcropping below.

Yet even that account, howsoever factually correct, would have been a couple of steps away from the truth. Because the heavy-set man dressed in the silver Helly Hansen rain jacket, khaki hiking pants, and LL Bean moose boots was not a tourist at all. And there was one person who knew the truth, knew exactly who had died and why he had to, knew that there had been a tell-tale sound, a very damning one.

If the perfect fantasy star witness had not been so riveted by the whole potato-splattered-disappearing-man weirdness, they might have heard . . . some snickering.

Or not. Maybe it was just the windblown leaves scuffling along the forest floor?

But then they would have been shocked to hear a female voice singing! And the mythical old bystander surely would have recognized the lyrics of Dee Dee Sharp's hit tune "Mashed Potato Time" fading into the thick forest.

*****

She had left nothing to chance. She had worked out all the details. That's what she was known for.

Her focus was calm and meditative as she drove towards the abandoned goat cheese factory a few miles outside of West Jefferson. There she would switch vehicles and dump some of the potato gun components. A couple of dull gray machined and threaded metal tubes and a can of starting fluid would not be conspicuous among the flotsam and jetsam of steel tubs, pipes, cutoff valves, cream separators, containers of sterilizing agents. She allowed herself some appreciative glances at the scenery unfolding all around her: tangerine beams of sunset that burned between the trees and melded the mountain foliage to a mauve glow.

It would take her another three hours just to drive her crusty old Toyota pickup on the back roads to the three rural dumpsters she had selected weeks before, each more than ten miles apart from the other. The dumpsters would swallow the remaining gun parts, a few potatoes, and finally the gooey pile of her nitrile gloves and nylon beanie that she had melted with a lighter and hidden inside a discarded Happy Meal container. The camouflaged canvas blind she had used was rolled up expertly and inserted inside a large thermos that lived behind the truck's bench seat. Her camouflaged sniper suit was stuffed in the bottom sleeping bag compartment of her backpack.

It was well after the time the sun went off the clock. When the mountains formed an unbroken chain of dark humps that twinkled here and there with houselights—only then had she allowed herself to relax. She relaxed even more once she was off the Parkway and on her way back to her campsite at Linville Falls.

She had done a good job, that she knew. But she had cursed at her reflection in the rearview mirror when she recalled her singing. Singing was another worthy talent of hers, one that she struggled—and usually failed—to keep from springing forth at the oddest moments. An ill-timed tune on the job could earn her a state-ordered, all-expenses-paid, lifetime lockup in a ten by ten cell. Or a chemical cocktail that she wouldn't have to drink, a cocktail that would surge through her veins and explode her much-broken heart once and for all.

She shivered from the possibilities, then shrugged them off. She stared at her headlight beams bouncing off corduroy tree trunks and marveled at the luminous lichens clinging to the exposed rock that walled in the highway. Hell, no one was perfect, she mused. She breathed a sigh of acceptance when she recalled that it had been a beautiful day, a great shot with the potato gun, a superb fall with no discernible witnesses, and no bad facts to deal with in the aftermath.

The potato shards would be scarfed up by rodents and crows.

The crime scene would have no solvents, metal shavings, lubricating oil, gunpowder, or any other typical artifacts and residues associated with a firearm.

The target's Lexus would eventually catch the eye of a passing Parkway ranger, but not until the wee hours of the morning. Car camping and hunting were prohibited along the Parkway, so the ranger would spotlight the vehicle for signs of both and for evidence of theft. If he found nothing and received no calls about the vehicle, he would leave it for the next shift. By then the body would be cold and critter-picked. The steepness of the drop-off below the overlook parking area and the seemingly impenetrable thicket of deadfall trees and limbs—these features would obscure the broken body's path as it bounced off the boulders and tumbled through the woods. Physics stepped in and tucked the accelerating remains under the patchwork quilt of leaf fall and erosion debris. The body could hide out there for weeks until scavengers came and spoiled it all.

Garnell Lee Ray was a tiny freckle-faced perky-nosed pigeon-toed assassin who went unnoticed and preferred it that way. She swirled her thick auburn hair into an uncharitable bun and hid her root beer colored eyes behind thick glasses and gave off an insular vibe. As a contract killer, she was one of the best in the trade.

And if humanly possible, she preferred to have her targets die by falling.

Garnell liked falls for many reasons. When done right, they appeared to be accidents, and therefore contained the magical element of reasonable doubt. Falls were the number two cause of accidental deaths behind car wrecks. Oh, yes, Garnell liked those, too, especially single vehicle accidents like rollovers and runaways off of switchbacks and blind curves. But they were so technical to pull off and too noisy, attracting attention even in remote areas of the Pisgah and Nantahala national forests. And Garnell was all about avoiding attention.

No, death by falling was a natural death, she reasoned, because of all the forces that were insurmountable in this life, gravity was certainly the most prominent.

Garnell was a mountain girl born and raised, and she had an abiding faith in the two irresistible mysteries that ruled every aspect of mountain living:

What will it take to get it up there?

What will happen when it comes down?

When people plummeted and passed on, as Garnell liked to convince herself, you didn't have to worry about hiding the body and the forensic riches it held onto despite all of the killer's efforts to the contrary. A country girl knew how fiercely animals held onto life, and people were animals—just more ornery, better armed, and with bigger homes. Body disposal was the biggest headache for murderers and the primary source of evidence with which to convict them.

Garnell thought it was just flat-out foolish to risk it.

What a mess they were, you know? Bodies begging, twitching, spurting, frothing, gasping; bodies torn open by gunshots and knives, busted by bludgeons, poisoned by chemicals; bodies pumping out fluids and gases and eerie noises far longer than anyone ever wanted to remember.

Hell, you never could get shed of it, she reckoned, nor sleep at night, if you dealt with it much.

And then when the drama ended, you had to deal with the corpse, which was a most stubborn thing. Bones didn't burn easily. Creatures would unearth them and then the show-and-tell would start with the law. Skulls popped up like daffodils after winter's heave and thaw, gawking at their discoverer and grinning with delight at their perseverance for years, decades, even centuries after their demise, getting the last laugh at their slayer: "Ta-da! I'm still here!"

Nossir, Garnell didn't fool with the dead at all.

So she did falls. True, they required much more work on the front end to set up, and they weren't 100% guaranteed, but then neither were bullets. With falls, the rare times there were witnesses, well, all they could say was "he fell" or "she fell" or "we heard them hit." There was something so mesmerizing about watching somebody falling that the witnesses forgot about every other detail. Their minds seized up and their bodies stalled; their instincts paralyzed by the sight of a diminishing object progressing swiftly and irrevocably towards a looming destination.

Garnell counted on this fascination for falling objects. That's how she took out her first target of the year.

The dude had been a prominent real estate attorney. He had so long and so often distorted logic and reason to evade cause-and-effect and thus prevail in his field—that he had forgotten that he was not immune to the higher laws of the universe.

It had been relatively easy for her to hit him with an oak tree.

Technically, he had not died from his own fall, but rather that of a five-ton chestnut oak. Garnell had mapped the lawyer's daily travels. She had noted that he encountered a railroad crossing near an isolated bend in the Swannanoa River over in Buncombe County. The tracks were on an elevated bump in the pavement surface at the railroad grade and the crossbuck gates came down to headlight level on most cars. There was no painless way to drive around or through the intersection once the warning lights began to blink and the alarm sounded and the black and white arms lowered with authority.

She had picked her way along the tracks one full moon June. The night air was heady with honeysuckle and creosoted railroad ties and she tried not to hum a tune while she attached a jumper cable to the rails about a hundred feet away from the crossing. The copper jaws and twisted wires of the jumper completed the circuit of the weak electrical current that flowed along the parallel steel rails, mimicking the effect of an arriving train and triggering the flashing lights and dinging bell and dropping the twin gates . . . and stopping the lawyer's car.

The lawyer waited.

No train came.

Several minutes passed.

But no train was heard or seen.

What the hell? he wondered. He jumped out of the plush confines of his cologne-soaked SUV and stood in the middle of . . . nowhere, really.

His shoes were sticking to the sun-softened, moon-washed asphalt. He was distracted and annoyed. The sultry summer night fractured his attention and scattered it among the lurid red strobes, the throbbing full moon, the beckoning blossoms, the cacophony of peepers, crickets, clanging railroad bells, nagging warning pings from his open door, thumping bass line from the SUV's stereo and . . . no . . . no, that *couldn't* be . . . was someone *singing* off down there in the bushes along the tracks?

He had scanned the ghostly gravel berms of the railroad right-of-way. The tangles of briars and vines that bordered the tracks were strange topiaries that billowed out from under the moon shadows cast by the taller tree line that flanked the Norfolk-Southern rails. Under the bright lunar lamp, he could see everything . . . and nothing.

While the lawyer stood there, puzzled and pissed off, Garnell used the awl blade on her Swiss Army knife to puncture the rubber inflatable logger's wedge that had kept the oak upright after she had patiently beaver-notched and sawn the trunk with her commando wire saw two nights before.

The forty-foot tree groaned and crackled as it discovered momentum. Woody sinews slivered, frayed, gave way. Heavy limbs swayed from the tree's swansong experience of travel. The tree, simultaneously animated and dying, seemed to stutter a hasty goodbye to the moon and the screech owls while it rapidly closed its angle to the ground.

The lawyer heard not the tree's death chant. He did not appreciate the fleeting shadow crossing the moon's face for what it was; he did not comprehend the consequences of the strange and growing silhouette reaching out for his own.

Wags at the courthouse would speculate darkly that they knew a high-pressure real estate practice would sneak up and kill a lawyer like him someday, when they least expected it. But not like that.

Garnell had worried about that gig. She couldn't really hide the fact that the tree had been deliberately cut, unless she could somehow pin it on a diabolically clever beaver. She had also wondered why Bob Dylan's "A Hard Rain's A-Gonna Fall" went through her head and out her mouth at the time, when she had meant to sing Amii Stewart's version of the Eddy Floyd hit "Knock on Wood."

Garnell didn't worry about ole Mr. Potato Dead on the Parkway, though. He had been easy, too. All she had to do was follow him as he made his weekly trips back and forth between the Pristine Hills golf resort and the A-frame cabin up in Blowing Rock he kept for his mistress. He had always stopped at the Beacon Heights overlook along the way and performed the same stupid stunt. He would jump up on the guardrail and spread his arms wide and do a solo, more manly version of the "I'm flying!" moment from the movie *Titanic*. Then he would attempt to yodel.

Garnell was pondering her dislike for yodeling, at least the Americanized version, as she drove up to the gatehouse to the Linville Falls campground. The glitter of bifocals appeared at the sliding window, followed by the friendly flapping jowls of Daniel, the seventy-something nighttime camp host on duty.

"Hello there, little Missy. 'Bout had to call curfew on you," he said with mock seriousness as he pointed at the gatehouse clock: 10:50 PM. Ten minutes to gate closure.

"Sorry. Didn't mean to worry you, Daniel. Got tied up with things and couldn't break away."

Daniel felt protective of Garnell ever since she had first rolled into the campground two years ago. He worried to no end about her being a lone female camping in the middle of a wilderness area. He hoped she carried a gun, then worried that she did and didn't know how to use it, and then worried some more that she might get scared and not come back if he asked about the whole gun thing.

But he would ask her, for the umpteenth time, if she needed extra flashlights or batteries; a police whistle; a better cell phone; more firewood; and a campsite closer to the road. He always concluded their conversational gambits with the same cautionary question.

"Ain't you scared of stayin' in these woods of a night, all by yourself?"

She always gave the same answer that made him belly laugh.

"A woman can do just fine in the woods . . . by *herself*. It's when visitors show up on her—that's when the trouble starts, Daniel. "

She smiled self-consciously at her gumption, and Daniel cackled appreciatively, then quickly clapped his blotchy old hand over his mouth, mindful of the camp's rules for quiet hours. She shifted the truck into gear again and cut her lights so only the amber parking bulbs shone, to keep from blinding campers. The gesture was courteous but wasted, she mused, because most of the campsites had either blazing campfires or battery-powered lights going. She drove at a crawl down the gravel path, past the RV's and pop-up trailers and lighted restroom shelters and toward the secluded row of primitive tent sites. She viewed the familiar outline of her dome tent with relief and fatigue and excitement—the usual emotions surrounding all backcountry experiences.

When she stepped out of the truck, the air was savory from woodsmoke. She felt the night's chill creep into her, its invasive grip taking her by surprise. She was an experienced three-season camper who had even enjoyed a few extended winter hiking trips. She had on a black knitted wool cap—or "boggan," as Daniel called them; a purple plaid Woolrich shirt with a white thermal layer t-shirt and white sports bra underneath; black nylon fleece hiker's pants; a trail runner's lightweight fanny pack; and thick woolen socks snug inside trail running shoes.

She believed it would likely freeze during the night. But it felt to her like it was freezing right then.

She considered that maybe a breeze had sucked some moisture off the falls and dribbled it onto her, making her shiver. She couldn't account for the deep tremble that started within her and surfaced as goosebumps on the back of her neck.

For some reason she turned her head over her shoulder, in the direction of the campground entrance.

Whether she had jerked her head away and jumped to the side before she saw the tongue of white-orange flame flicker in the distance or *after*—well, it didn't really matter in the end.

She thought she had heard a *pop!* like a balloon busting, but couldn't tell because there was a thrum of urgency all around her and the arrival of imminent danger filled her ears with a high-pitched whine that sounded like an old TV set warming up.

She remembered dropping down on all threes—her one hand frantically probing the pinch pain surging between her upper back and lower neck. The pain was like Spock's Vulcan death grip, and it grew stronger and spread through her torso like a burning zeppelin and the proverbial lead balloon at the same time. All she cared about first was scrambling behind some shelter until she could fish out her CZ-75 9mm compact pistol from the fanny pack. She crouched behind a dying hemlock and waited . . . one thousand two thousand three thousand . . . before resting one suddenly sweaty cheek on the scaly bark and poking one foggy eyeglass lens around the edge of the trunk.

There was no movement among the tents, except for campfires dancing inside the metal fire rings.

No people.

No dogs barking their queries from afar.

No shouts of "What was that?" or "Omigod!" or "Call the police!" or the usual litany of emergency phrases that one would expect after a shooting took place at a packed campground.

Because make no mistake. Garnell had been shot.

She was stunned at first. But when the blood poured down the valley between her breasts, soaking her liner shirt and bra, trickling hotly down her back, she felt a rising sense of—no, not panic. She wasn't locked in that airtight room yet. But she was definitely in the dark and narrowing hallway leading towards it.

The radiance of peril surrounded her. An unnatural heat spread over her upper body, as if she had stepped under one of those timer-activated heat lamps found in cheap motel bathrooms. The dark images before her were sporadically spotting up and bronzing over; the tall pickets of pines and hemlocks turned pale and doubled up. She was seeing the woods through a double-exposed film negative.

Garnell fought for focus, inhaling deeply through her nose. She stood up behind a trunk as big as her waist, trying to scan the campground through her increasingly unreliable vision. She thought she saw a dark shape moving erratically, wiggling upright, a metallic glint coming from a crooked stick or broken piece of camping equipment the figure seemed to be carrying. She blinked rapidly and the fuzzy figure cleared for a second or two before disappearing into a dense thicket of rhododendrons and young hemlocks. The figure was human, not animal. And it wore a dark hoodie and a backpack.

She lurched forward to give chase—and that's when some joker tilted the world and spun it around like a carnival ride that lifted her up and away from herself and then crashed her back down to ground. She was pretty sure she couldn't drive; even more sure that she had better get the hell out of Dodge, somehow. She wobbled toward the same thicket that had swallowed up the hoodie backpack individual. Now even her Woolrich shirt was sodden with blood, and her garments felt plastic and alien next to her skin.

Garnell could visualize the red puckered hole in her back just above the right shoulder blade and felt with her left hand the font that gushed dark fluid from the other side of her neck. She tried to stop the frantic flow but it made her probing fingers slippery and useless at first, then glued them together when she tried to squeeze shut the exit wound that was located just above her collar bone.

She was running, still. Or whatever it was that she was trying to do. Dash and collapse. Dart and stumble. Weave from one tall wooden crutch to the next. She veered wildly off her intended course and headed toward the far end of the primitive tent site area, because it was downhill and the going was easier. Gravity again.

She was outraged by her growing enfeeblement—so unfair, shot in the back, damn straight she was bitter about it—and wanted to scream something, anything. But she couldn't think of what to say. She didn't see anyone to say it to.

She tried to remember her wilderness first aid training. She could only come up with what not to do, like "Never keep a tourniquet on a neck wound for any length of time."

Garnell was sinking into the murk of an unknown land. Time and space were collapsing all around her. Her thoughts were standing apart from her like the hemlocks and the pines were apart from her. She could see her predicament through her own eyes but she was watching her awareness like a movie trailer someone else had made.

She didn't think she was dying. She kept noticing things and noticed her thoughts ruminating over what she had noticed: her one shoe gone (how did that happen?); someone's bandana tied to a branch (oh, I wonder if it belonged to a dog?); the worrisome feeling of emptiness in her front pants pocket where her truck keys should have been (oh no! I'll never find them at night!); the weight of the pistol in her all but useless right hand (better ditch the gun before I pass out).

All of this circumspection meant . . . she wasn't going down for the count. Right?

And if she was, well, she chose not to comfort herself with memories of lullabies and church hymns and scratchy old-timey tunes with high lonesome voices keening about unclouded days and seeing your momma and daddy once again and the surcease of toil and sorrow. Bizarre as it seemed, her internal playback mechanism selected a Southern Culture on the Skids tune to ease her passage to wherever it was she was going. Downhill, most likely.

Before she blacked out, she tried to sing the words to "Whole Lotta Things" but could not. This made her tear up and feel sorry for herself.

There were so many undone things she'd wanted to do. The ground came up and knocked her viselike-hold on her neck wound. She felt her eyelids droop. She willed them open, but the lids were heavy and unwieldy. She was gulping air like it was sweet tea served on the 4th of July and still she couldn't sing. She could only watch the song's lyrics fade in her closing mind's eye, like newsprint burning in a stove.

*****

Detective John Daniel "J.D." Klontz broke into a horse-toothed grin when he read the incident report. It was just this kind of case that he had dreamt about all those years he spent patrolling the frozen, axle-breaking streets of Buffalo.

A pair of rogue goats had eaten 5,000 Fraser fir seedlings in one night.

He inclined his head and gazed at the ceiling, lost in appreciation. Chucking softly, he rocked backwards in the worn-out office chair, which complained loudly underneath his bulk. He reiterated to no one in particular the same conclusion he had arrived at several years earlier: it was better to serve in paradise than reign in Hell.

Here he was, living the dream: a former Yankee cop getting paid half his previous salary to investigate true crimes of nature amid Southern mountain splendor.

Oh, he knew it wasn't a laughing matter here in Avery County, North Carolina. This was Christmas tree country, and such a loss would not go unavenged. As a Sheriff's detective in the major crimes unit, J.D. was certain this case would require much more than tracking down some bloated goats hiding in a laurel thicket, identifying their owner, and dismissing the whole thing as the civil matter it was.

No, the fun part would come when the aggrieved grower tried to collect compensation for the goat-gobbling—and the negligent goat-herd refused. When that happened, J.D. would become ensnared by the concatenation of 911 calls concerning dead goats, burned barns, and gunshot wounds.

He was lost in his reverie about the remarkable accomplishment of greedy goats and the inevitability of getback in these parts. His eyes wandered first towards the missing children alerts, then to the improvised weapons chart taped onto the locked filing cabinet containing open cases. He read for the hundredth time the hand-made poster tacked on the wall above a fellow detective's desk:

Before you make love, you undress each other;
After you make love, you get dressed by yourself.
MORAL: Once you're screwed, nobody helps you.

He pondered the county of his jurisdiction, and the insider/outsider status he enjoyed there.

Avery County had a sparse permanent population of only 17,000, but the transient population in the summer months could swell to 50,000 or more. The Blue Ridge Parkway ran throughout the county's breathtaking scenery. This scenic route would slow to a crawl in the fall with leaf peepers; in the summer, with RV creepers. Avery was the home to the Grandfather Mountain Highland Games, the largest gathering of the Scottish clans and Gaelic wannabes in the world. It was home to some of the South's best storytellers, Christmas tree farms, trout fishing, golfing, and high-end real estate developments. Resort communities and Floridians' luxury vacation homes perched conspicuously along the cliffs and ridges overlooking the tiny towns of Banner Elk, Elk Park, Sugar Mountain, Beech Mountain, Linville, and Newland, the county seat. Seemingly everyone wanted to be here, if only for a few weeks or months out of the year.

And J.D. was one of them now. He thought of his personal background in the stark, declarative statements found in police reports.

Age: fifty-two. Previous residence: born and raised in Buffalo, NY.

Employment: police officer for a total of twenty-four years, eight months, twenty-two days.

Physical description: six foot six inches, two hundred and ninety pounds.

Identifying features/markings: buzz cut dark gray hair; blue eyes that still didn't need glasses, thankfully.

Marital status: twice divorced.

And then he strayed from the report format towards some mental op ed about his past failures.

Regarding his divorces, he would talk only about the first if asked because it had been so long ago. Both parties had been too young. She had married a cop for all the same wrong reasons he became one.

13

The second one he wouldn't talk about at all. It had only been five years ago. He had fled to the mountains in the aftermath, trying to forget about it all while under the hypnotic spell that dimpling streams and clear swirling rivers cast upon many inveterate trout fishermen like him.

All he cared to recall was that he had worked first shift and did the night school grind for three years to receive his B.S. in criminal justice. He had barely passed his detective's exam. He had come home to celebrate his promotion with two bottles of thirty dollar champagne and a dozen roses topped with a stuffed bumblebee sitting on a plastic floret that urged her to "Bee Mine!" Instead, he found their house unlit, their bedroom ransacked of his wife's belongings, and their bathroom completely cleaned out except for his razor, toothbrush, and one estranged dress sock. On the refrigerator he had found the goodbye note written on a hot pink post-it that had "Urgent!" inked on the bottom margin.

The reasons for her leaving were unknown to this day.

It was the only puzzle he never cared to solve.

He resumed his police report on himself.

Habits and associations: quiet, mild-mannered loner, no known friends or associates outside of fellow law enforcement officers. Enjoyed trout fishing and bow hunting. Had two pets . . .

Here he broke off again from this game and thought fondly of his animal companions: Mister Pibb the beagle, and Pecker the raven.

Both had been adoptions, a fact which had a nice symmetry to it because J.D. himself had been orphaned. Mister Pibb's previous owners had been killed two years ago in a head-on MVA on US 19 up near Cranberry. J.D. was a city kid who had never owned a dog before and so completely doted on this one. At first his normal pursuit call or "voice" alarmed J.D., as it sounded like the dog was being electrocuted repeatedly. And J.D. had to rescue his sweet-natured, though somewhat inept little rabbit hunter on a weekly basis when it became briar-wrapped in the overgrown creek banks or stuck in drainage pipes, immobilized by the fear of its own distorted beagle bark bouncing off the dank metal tunnel surrounding him.

Pecker was a fierce, ill-tempered common raven. He had earned his moniker by his fanatic devotion to the practice of sending some kind of avian Morse code—or maybe he was a frustrated pileated woodpecker?—by rapping violently with his onyx beak on windows, mirrors, police car "fruitjar" light racks—and most painfully of all, on J.D.'s shoulder and chest.

The raven had been found by an SAR team looking for a missing rock climber almost five years ago in the Linville Gorge Wilderness Area. They had found the bird hopping around blindly, fumbling its pathetic attempts to flee. He couldn't fly away. Instead, he pinwheeled into branches and caromed off of tree trunks and then flopped in circles, scattering glossy, iridescent blue-black feathers everywhere. J.D. had been with the SAR crew at the time, and he had thrown a burlap bag over the stricken bird and brought him to the animal hospital near Crossnore. There a young vet who wasn't afraid to tackle something other than her small animal clientele made the diagnosis of lead poisoning, possibly from eating gut piles discarded by hunters and envenomed by lead bullet fragments.

Her weeklong treatment of purgatives, IV injections, and chelating agents had worked. Within three days, the first thing Pecker would see was J.D., and the first thing he would do was fly to the huge man's massive shoulder and puncture it with a beak as strong as needle-nosed pliers and as sharp as an ice pick. Then he had perched possessively on that same shoulder.

Their bond was established.

Pecker came and went as he pleased, like a feral cat. Being a raven, he could always scrounge up a meal. But he preferred to roost in a beech tree in J.D.'s backyard, and he could miraculously locate J.D. anywhere in the county whenever he felt like it. Which was daily.

Cops would rib him about Mister Pibb and Pecker. But they showed a rare restraint, and didn't go too far. They were mindful of J.D.'s subdued, genial nature, respectful of his professional reputation and skills, grateful for his surprising fluency in Spanish—and spooked by his relationship with a bird of omen and folklore. But more to the point, they were most impressed by his great size and strength, and by his astonishing reflexes that were quick and unpredictable as those of a sow bear with her cubs. They had seen his fingers, thick and hard as shotgun shells, catch an unruly suspect's swung fist and crush it like an egg, and never frown or break a sweat doing it.

But he still received anonymous, hateful notes about Pecker. Avery County was a small world, after all. A detective who had a large ebony bird following him and hammering away on his county-issued Dodge Intrepid—could not avoid the gossip.

The ungrammatical, misspelled taunts usually came from the county detention facility.

"Everbody tell me u got a bird Pecker. That goes with ur Birdbrain. Big stoopid ASS!"

"It just dont make senc. Why do a white pig like u have a black Pecker?"

The more literate complaints came from the disgruntled family of defendants who were in the process of becoming convicts.

You're nothing but a heathen Yankee and you should know that it is illegal to make a pet of a wild bird. Some example you set for the law-abiding citizens of this county!

And some true believers found Pecker to be a sign from God, and his Sheriff's detective consort to be blessed.

Thanks be to the High Sheriff and Praise God! Avery County has finally hired a man who can command one of the Lord's Messengers! 'And he sent forth a raven, which went forth to and fro, until the waters were dried up from the earth' – Genesis 8:7

The radio scanner's squawk and jargon intruded upon his musings and grabbed his attention:

10-21 BRP ranger at 828-737-2560; 10-60 suspicious vehicle on Parkway, 10-20 Beacon Heights, BRP marker 304.4, Linn Cove office. Time: oh nine thirty-five.

Comm, repeat the number?

Standby for number: 828-737-2560

Roger that, comm. BRP request 10-28 on 2010 Lexus, standby for NC Tag: personal plate, spelling N-Nancy, O-Opal, S-Sam, W-Winter, E-Edward, A-Apple, T-Tom . . .

And then he had been summoned directly by the dispatcher:

Avery CID-Two, you copy?

J.D. fumbled for his Motorola radio, punched in the county Emergency Operations Command direct line and responded to the police dispatcher:

"This is Avery CID-Two, go ahead comm."

"10-21 Avery-Patrol Four, arrange for 10-25 at Gannon Memorial regarding white female, 30's, 10-94'd last night at Linville Falls campground. Patrol-Four advised no 10-82 at this time."

"10-4, Comm . . . did Patrol-Four 10-14 the women's condition?"

"Avery CID-Two, that's a negative."

"10-4, Comm. Avery CID-Two out."

The gourmand goats would have to wait. After calling the patrol deputy in question from his cell phone, J.D. grabbed his pager, clipboard, legal pad, and field interview forms. He unfolded his great body from the crippled and potentially crippling chair and lumbered out of the office, waving in acknowledgment of the watchful eyes belonging to the unseen CID administrator who was lurking somewhere among the cubicles.

"You be careful, now, hon," her disembodied voice called out after him.

He was on his way to Gannon Memorial Hospital to talk to a young woman who had been found last night in a porta-potty located at the Linville Falls campground.

At the time of her discovery, the woman was trying to close a gunshot wound in her neck with duct tape and a large office binder clip.

There were no suspects at the time.

Mountain Lights

by John P. McAfee

Why is it in a hospital everybody smells of rubbing alcohol? J.D. knew Gannon Memorial was on its last legs financially and couldn't afford that much alcohol. But the place reeked. Maybe the alcohol smell hid the stench of a corpse?

It seemed to J.D. there must always be someone peeking out of the hospital, waiting for him, and just before he got out of the unmarked police vehicle, that person would give a sign and some orderly would quickly spread rubbing alcohol all over the floor. It was the only explanation. Any flesh-eating bacteria left in the hospital had to be an alcoholic by now. The doctors that remained out of loyalty, not profit, came to the hospital on Mondays, Wednesdays, and Fridays. Well, really just a half-day on Wednesday, since those who traveled up the mountain took the afternoon off to play golf at 4,000 feet. It was Friday night so the "gunshot girl," for that is how he thought of her, was lucky. The duct tape over the wound showed the ability to function under extreme duress. Not many would stay calm enough to roll out the tape, tear it off, and try to put it over a spurting wound.

The reception room looked like every other hospital reception room. Dripping noses on the left, high blood pressures on the right. And right in the middle, Nurse Rachel de la Fuente, open blouse, buttons and all, was bending over a chart at the reception desk, pretending to read it.

"Sign in, please," she said without looking up.

Her red hair spilled over her shoulders and neatly framed blue-veined globes that clung to her bra like a dying man clinging to the edge of a burning building. Her hips just—well, J.D. never got to the hips part. He was sure they were as nice, though. Most twenty-four-year-old hips are. He watched her shift her weight. One little nudge on the straining bra and it would be an X-rated hospital.

"What you lookin' at, J.D.?" Her voice snapped him out of his fantasy.

"Perfection." The word just slipped out.

The definition of old age: when you spend your time flirting with young girls but hoping like hell you don't catch one. Nurse Rachel was worth the risk. Still, two divorces made him as cautious as a coyote approaching a chicken coop. Besides, when she would be hitting her sexual stride at forty-two, he would be sliding towards seventy, scratching and clawing to stay on this side of the dirt.

"If you think that's perfection, I could show you paradise. But I bet you came down to check on the gunshot girl, didn't ya? It's never me." Her lips tried to pout but the sexy smile won out again.

"Just doing what I'm paid to do. How is she doing?"

"For someone with a hole in the neck, better than most. The duct tape kept enough of her blood where it belonged." Nurse Rachel flipped through some paperwork, then handed him a chart with particulars. NAME: Garnell L. Ray, ADDRESS: Linville Campground, INSUR-ANCE: none, NEXT OF KIN (actually hospitals didn't care, they just wanted to know who they could bill if the customer croaked): none, EMAIL ADDRESS: none, DRIVER'S LICENSE: none, U.S. GOV'T FEDERAL ID: Garnell Lee Ray, Department of Topographic Mapping.

"You ever done any topographic mapping, Detective Klontz? Figuring out the heights and valleys of some place?"

Her voice startled him. Nurse Rachel was standing disturbingly close to J.D. when she said this, and just for a moment he thought, "I will lift my eyes unto the hills from which cometh my strength." He frowned away temptation, handed the chart back to the poster girl for Victoria's Secret, and asked to see the wounded woman.

Nurse Rachel led the way, her squeaking nurse shoes showing her irritation with J.D. and her swinging hips reminding him of what he was missing. Watching that white skirt sway reminded J.D. of those sensual women washing their clothes in the creek in the movie, *O Brother, Where Art Thou?* He tried to look at the lime green walls but his eyes drifted back to the skirt.

Sometimes this job was really, really hard.

His radio crackled to life.

"Hey, J.D.?"

It was Deputy Marshall Harris who hailed from Marshall, North Carolina. If J.D. had to explain Deputy Marshall Harris in one sentence, it would be: he will forever be pulling on "push only" doors.

Simian in build and thought, Deputy Marshall Harris was living proof that the Neanderthal had not died out but existed in isolated places such as Marshall. His family tree had no branches. Somehow he had passed all the necessary law enforcement courses at Asheville-Buncombe Community College with minimal grades over a seven-year course of study—which was amazingly quick, considering.

Trying to remind Harris of professional protocol, J.D. spoke into the radio.

"This is Avery CID-2, go."

"Hey, J.D., guess what? We found an abandoned Lexus in the parking lot up at Beacon Heights overlook, and a body lying down the hill. Well, we didn't find it, me and the Ranger here, but a mother and her daughter saw a pair of binoculars hangin' off a tree about a hundred feet down and then the little girl spotted a sock a little further along, so we're gittin' ready to rappel down and see if the guy's still alive."

"Negative on helping the Feds. That's out of our jurisdiction."

"Not really. He fell far enough down that it looks like he fell back into Avery County." He could hear Harris chuckle. "From the Blue Ridge Parkway clean into Avery County. The boy was flyin'."

"How far down do you reckon the body is?" J.D. decided to slip into Harris-speak.

"250 feet, 300 maybe. Yep, he's back in our jurisdiction by a good twenty feet."

"We don't know positively if the body is a 'he' yet, do we?"

"No, not yet. But we ran the plates on the Lexus, and the owner's name is Sweatt. Richard Sweatt. Think he's alive?"

"At an acceleration of thirty-two feet per second per second, the body hit the side of that rock face going about seventy miles an hour. Whoever it is, they are not alive."

There was a long pause from Harris as J.D. imagined him trying to figure out the math.

"What?"

"Have you secured the area?"

"What?" Harris was still working out the math.

J.D. sighed and pushed the talk button. "Is there a suicide note, a folded jacket, signs of a disturbance around the vehicle?"

"Wait a minute, let me look." Harris kept the talk button on so J.D. could hear him looking around. "Nope. Nothing but some busted potato pieces. Guy musta' been getting' ready to cook something for dinner."

J.D. looked at his radio. He knew he shouldn't ask but he had to. "How do you know they're potato pieces?"

"Tasted like it."

"Harris, you might be eating evidence."

"Naw, it's just a potato."

J.D. hoped the rope would break as Harris bounded down the side of the overlook.

Harris had been hired by Avery County on a grant from the state trying to bolster small town law enforcement numbers. Candidates had to be dirt poor or "impoverished" and from an "impoverished-impacted" area with chronic unemployment. Marshall was made for the grant. Some idiot from the county manager's office had signed him, obviously sight-unseen, to a three-year contract. Harris had been working for J.D. for a year and a half and it was a race between J.D.'s ulcer and Harris's contract which would win. He could feel his stomach muscles twinge from each inquiry phoned or mailed into the Avery County Sheriff's Department addressed to "Marshall" Marshall Harris from sales agents trying to sell the latest law enforcement tool. Every sample from socks to Tasers was sent to "Marshall" Marshall Harris.

Nurse Rachel stopped at Room 7. There was an old man sitting in a chair beside the door, his dirty tennis shoes, rumpled jeans and torn red sweater had served as pajamas and house shoes through the night. Both of the shoes were untied.

"This is Daniel Puckett, the caretaker at the campground. He brought her in and refuses to leave her side. Mr. Puckett?" Nurse Rachel gently shook the old man awake.

He slowly opened his eyes and looked directly into Nurse Rachel's valley of delight.

"I'm in heaven, right?"

She patted his cheek. "Sweet." Then, glancing pointedly at J.D., as if to say, "well, somebody appreciates me," she left the two of them alone.

J.D. glanced through the little window in the door at Room 7. He could see a slight young woman propped up on some pillows, an IV running into her arm.

"Tell me what you know."

The old man studied the large man in front of him. "You ain't from these parts, are you?"

J.D. shifted his gaze to the old man. Daniel swallowed hard.

"Didn't hear no gunshot, just saw her runnin, fallin, and runnin again towards the woods. Finally, I was able to catch up to her. Never saw so much blood."

Daniel shook his head. "Didn't have no dressin'. Just used what I could find. Korea taught me that."

J.D. smiled, which made the old man relax.

"War makes us all improvisers."

The old man nodded knowingly. "Improvise or die."

His old hands reached into a paper sack on the floor beside his chair. "Might want to take a look at this."

J.D. tensed as Daniel withdrew a pistol. "Found it beside her."

J.D. grabbed some exam gloves off a nearby nurse's cart before handling the weapon. He turned the pistol over in his hand.

"CZ-75 9mm pistol," he muttered to himself. He glanced at the woman through the window, then inspected the gun.

That was a lot of pistol for a camper. He couldn't find a serial number. Curious.

"This hers?" He turned the dark weapon over in his hand, noting some details: custom grip for a small hand, fully loaded maximum capacity magazine, filed trigger.

"Never saw her with no weapon in the two years I knowed her." Daniel ran a shaky hand through his long silver hair. "Nossir, sweetest little girl. Stays to herself mostly, sometimes goes out and just disappears for a few days but always comes back."

"Where she from?"

Daniel shrugged his shoulders. "You know, I don't know. We talk all the time but the more I study on it, the more I realize don't know nuthin' about her."

He glanced up at J.D. "I mean, if she had died, who would I have called?"

"She have any enemies, get into any arguments with others in the campground?"

"Lord, no. Keeps to herself," The old man smiled. "Doesn't mind having a sip of some branch water now and then with an old coot like me."

"Can she hold her 'branch water'?"

Daniel nodded. "Better n' me. 'Course at my age, I'm having trouble holding any kind of water. Pee more than a waterfall every day and night. Old age ain't for the timid."

J.D. pushed open the door to the woman's room. Daniel rose to follow him.

"Let me talk to her first, then you can come on in." Nodding his head, Daniel sat back down and J.D. stepped towards the room. Her singing of Aretha Franklin's "Chain of Fools" stopped him.

Her voice trailed off as she glanced at the huge figure filling the doorway.

"Now, that's some good dope shit that can make me see Sequatchie in my room." She frowned, realizing that wasn't the right word.

"Sasquatch." Yeah, that was it. She smiled at her little victory.

J.D. stood by the bed, holding the pistol.

"This yours, Garnell?"

She looked away, stared out the window.

"Nope. Never saw it before. Is it yours?"

Pulling up a chair, J.D. eased his large frame down. He placed the pistol on the table beside the water pitcher and cup and studied the woman.

Attractive, a bit on the tomboy side, with, what color would those eyes be? Root beer, brown and frosty. That was it. Her slight frame was heavily bandaged all the way from her left shoulder to the right side of her neck. Her auburn hair was still matted from blood.

He patted the pistol.

"Unusual tool for a camping lady."

She ignored him.

"When I find a weapon with the serial number gone, makes me curious. When I get curious, I pay more attention to things." J.D. knew this sounded lame, but his size usually scared people into talking.

"Got any idea who shot you?"

"Drunk redneck deer hunter full of Jesus and booze." She turned and studied the seated man. Little bit of a paunch but still in shape enough to get the job done; scars on his knuckles from hitting teeth or walls; muscles in places where most people didn't even have places. That said, she could take him. She noticed he favored his right leg when he sat down. Bad knee, and that was one place you couldn't build muscle. It still took just twenty pounds of pressure applied the right way to snap it clean. Once somebody as big as this lug hit the ground, you could take your time finishing the job.

She glanced at his crotch. There was more than one way to bring this big guy down.

J.D. felt uncomfortable under her direct gaze. So he stared back until she turned away.

"It's not deer season. The line of sight in a campground is pretty clear. Somebody was hunting something, and that something was you. I don't suppose you could make my job easier and tell me who?"

"Sorry, but I have no idea." Her voice was softer and resonated with J.D. "And I have no enemies in this area that I know of."

"What brought you to these parts?"

"Researching the Brown Mountain Lights."

"The what?"

"Strange lights appear in the passes and tree tops of the Brown Mountains near Linville Gorge. The phenomenon has been noted from the time of the Cherokee up to today. I wanted to research the legend and see if there's anything to it."

24

"Is this where my federal tax dollars go, for a university grant to see whether or not the supernatural exists in Avery County?"

He could see that touched a nerve. Her face hardened into granite, as hard to read as the mountains outside the window.

"Sure as hell beats my tax dollar going to a fat ass cop using DEA drug money to bust people for smoking something that's been growing in these mountains forever."

J.D. smiled. "What would you suggest I do?"

"Kiss my ass?"

"I don't take advantage of wounded women, especially those investigating something as special as the Brown Mountain Lights. Which school you working with?"

"None. I was doing some topography work up here when I was an undergraduate and had a summer intern job with the Forest Service."

"And?" Outside, clouds clotted the sky and the wind picked up.

"That's when I first saw them." She glanced at J.D. "They're real, alright, maybe too real. First time I saw them, I was sitting on a rock ledge near the Beacon Heights overlook drinking a glass of Cabernet. I like to do that of an evening. I expected to see something like Tinker Bell floating through the trees."

She gave a rueful laugh. "Boy, was I wrong."

"What did you see?"

"A goddamn freight train headlight coming at me about thirty feet below my rock ledge. It lit up the whole damn mountain side. Scared the shit out of me. Made me spill my wine. There's nothing silly about the Brown Mountain Lights."

"So you've stayed around for, what, eight, maybe ten years trying to figure out what you saw?"

"Might stay another ten years or so if people quit shooting me."

J.D. stood up.

"I'm going out to the campground and see what I can find but before I do, I'm driving over to the Beacon Heights overlook to see about a dead body belonging to somebody named Sweatt. "Ever hear of him?"

She turned away, but not before giving J. D. a "tell."

She knew of the body. Curious.

He paused a bit to see if she had anything to say. But he gave up when she began humming an old tune, "I shot the sheriff, but I did not shoot his deputy . . . "

He stood and picked up the pistol.

"I'm going to have the state boys run this weapon. And I hope for your sake, I don't find a ballistics match with a dead Mr. Sweatt, or your fingerprints all over the gun."

She actually stopped singing and giggled when he said that. Curious.

"Let me know if you see any Brown Mountain Lights," she said as he shut the door.

Daniel stood up when J.D. came out.

"How is she?"

"She's doing fine. You ever talk about the Brown Mountain Lights at the campground?"

Daniel nodded. "Damn straight, we did. I told her about my family livin' up here in the Brown Mountains. We go back four generations. A lot of stories about the lights have been passed down. Why one time . . ."

J.D. held up his hand. "Love to hear it sometime but I got some business to do. She's all yours, Daniel. I suggest you keep an eye on her and let me know if she starts packing to leave the campground. She drive a vehicle?"

"I brung her in it. Beat up ol' Toyota. Don't have a car of my own. Gave that up years ago. Too expensive, gas, insurance. Hell, the damn things worry you to death."

"Where'd you park it?"

Daniel handed him a parking ticket with a slot number on it. As J.D. walked away, he called after him, "When you have a look, mind getting' this thing stamped? Don't know how long me and missy here gotta' stay."

J.D. thought the line about her research of the Brown Mountain Lights was a cover for something else. While he was reviewing all he knew so far, he almost missed the people running out the front of the hospital. After a particularly portly lady bounced off him, not even apologizing, he looked up.

There was a black spiral of smoke lifting up from the parking lot. As he exited the front door, he realized it was coming from a vehicle. Quickly, he called it in. Sirens went off all over town. When you have a volunteer fire department manned by bored shopkeepers and seniors in high school just waiting for the opportunity to hop up in class, run out to their trucks, and put those flashing red lights on their dashboard to impress little girls looking out school windows—the response was always noisy and quick.

He hurried towards the fire, telling everybody to step back and watch out for the fire trucks. He could make out the outline of an old beat-up Toyota pickup now a dingy gray-black soot color. So much for any evidence there. There was an imploded gasoline can next to the truck, its color a perfect accessory match to the charred vehicle. He glanced at his ticket stub. Guess Daniel wouldn't owe anything on it now.

As he turned over the scene to the arriving firefighters, he vaguely wondered how Daniel and Garnell were going to get back to the campground. Should he post a guard at her room? No, she could take care of herself, bullet hole and all. Besides, now she had to stay at the hospital unless she wanted to walk the twenty miles back. For some reason, as he put the unmarked Dodge on the road to Beacon Heights, he had this image of ducks in a shooting gallery.

It was almost dusk. The early October air chilled his exposed skin as he drove with open windows towards the Beacon Heights overlook. When he arrived and stepped out of his vehicle, he could hear the soothing sigh of the wind through the treetops, a consistent rhythm like waves breaking along a shoreline. He took a deep breath. This was why he had come south. In Buffalo, it was the sound of rushing traffic, here the sound of gentle winds.

"Glad you got here, J.D. The Ranger left about an hour ago. He said the feds don't pay overtime and just file a report with them in the morning."

"Did you have to leave the bag out scaring tourists? Just call in an ambulance to haul it away."

"Nobody been by to scare away. This place gets a little creepy this time of an evening. I did try to call the girls but the ambulance was busy, it bein' Friday night and all, couple of fights, couple of wrecks so far."

The two evening shift EMTs, Gladys and Janet, were a pair of roommates who were friends with benefits. Competent and steady in a crisis, they had taken some medical courses while at Appalachian State University, did an internship with Avery County, and just stayed on when they graduated. They liked tattoos. In the past, Harris had fantasized about where some of their tattoos led. He had tried to engage J.D. in speculation about the complete tattoo picture.

"Where you reckon that tiger's tail goes?" or "Okay, if the peacock's feathers on Janet's chest fan out, do you reckon it covers . . . ?"

"Harris, your curiosity borders on obsession. I suggest you drop it and do your job. Besides, they go for each other, not for you."

Harris pondered this for a least twenty minutes and J.D. forgot he'd even mentioned it. He began doing some tagging of evidence when he felt like someone was staring at him. Harris was looking at him through the steel bars of the evidence room.

"What do you want, Harris?"

Harris gave this little kid grin. "Think they'd let me just watch and take pictures?"

"Damn it, Harris!" J.D. said, but Harris had fled.

Mountain religion suppressed much too much of the human character and after years of repression, what happened was people like Marshall Harris. As they say in the mountains, "That boy ain't right."

"Why not put the body in your patrol car?"

Harris pointed to the bag. "Be my guest."

J.D. bent down to pick up the bag. He got it off the ground okay, but to carry to the patrol car, not a chance.

Deputy Marshall Harris grinned. "I told the Ranger you'd get it up. It took two of us and this is as far as we got. He bet me a Hindenburg sub that you wouldn't be able to get the body up and standing. Damn, that sub's gonna' taste fine."

There was a local college hangout up in Boone, NC, famous for its Hindenburg sub which supposedly could feed five. Harris usually ordered two when his paycheck came in. The man could flat put it away.

The wind changed from a soft breeze to a low moan, like some kind of wounded animal deep in the ravine. The temperature fell quickly.

Steadying the corpse on his shoulder, J.D. found some cloth handles along the side of the body bag.

"Give me a hand, Harris. We'll put it in the trunk and get on home."

Harris gave a nervous look around, then hurried over to help Detective Klontz.

"The sooner we're out of here, the better. This place gives me the willies."

The two of them struggled with the body bag and unceremoniously dumped it into the trunk of Harris's patrol car, the springs protesting the sudden increase in weight.

J.D. smiled at the image of two men putting a dark body-shaped bag in the trunk of a car while the wind was howling around them.

"Igor! It lives!" he muttered to himself, smiling.

"What did you sa—?" Harris was looking past J.D. back towards the overlook. "What the hell is that?"

Floating along the tree line on the mountain next to the overlook, now just a darker outline of shadows, was a ball of light dipping here, appearing there, then darkness, only to blaze again an impossible distance from its last sighting.

J.D. stared in disbelief.

Slowly, the two of them walked to the edge of the overlook and watched as the light descended quickly into the bottom of the canyon, only to appear on the far side as two balls of light moving up towards Hawksbill, a mountain with a jagged stone edge for a top resembling, well, a hawk's bill. The wind chilled them both to the bone.

"Lord a'mighty!" cried Harris. "Ain't never seen somethin' like that!"

"I believe, Harris," said J.D., trying to sound a lot calmer than he felt, "we are being introduced to the Brown Mountain Lights."

The two lights then merged into one that began to grow larger and larger. Suddenly, it shot across the canyon and up towards the overlook, its blue eerie light outlining all in a supernatural glow. The lights stopped and hovered over Beacon Heights. A cold night wind brushed the trees clean of summer and promised death to the leaves.

Harris sprinted for his patrol car and dived in, locking the door behind him. Giving one frightened glance over the shoulder, he started the car and put it in gear. J.D. turned from looking at the lights to see two smaller red lights disappearing down the dirt road leading back to the main highway.

"Loyalty goes a long way in these mountains," he said underneath his breath. The lights blinked out and J.D. Klontz was alone in the dark.

"Curious," he said.

Some People Just Need to Die

by Susan Reinhardt

The pain had become unbearable; her gunshot wound pulsing as if a too-tight blood pressure cuff wrapped itself around her neck. Garnell Lee Ray pressed the button for the nurse. She could take a lot of pain, had her share during childhood when daddy would beat the shit out of her. But this was different. This was pain inflicted by someone she didn't know. Or maybe not. She had a clue. And it wasn't going to be bloodless when revenge slipped upon her.

It was a her. A she shot her, and Garnell had a pretty good idea who it was. She hummed a tune from the Dixie Chicks, something about riding on the sin wagon, but her voice cracked from the bullet's damage.

She punched the button for the nurse again.

And again.

The nurse, Genevieve, scuffled in. Not the sexy one from last night with the huge Hooters' boobs and Kim Kardashian ass, but a frumpy thing with her red and yellow crocheting efforts blooming from her little teddy bear smock.

"I need more Dilaudid. Now."

"What's the magic word?" the grandmotherly nurse asked.

"Actually, there are two magic words: Fucking! Now!" Garnell smiled so big the nurse could see one of her back molars was missing.

30

"Now there's no need for a pretty little thing like you to go and cuss like these other mountain fools. I'm sure your mother raised you better'n that."

"My mother was a whore."

Genevieve gave up. She smelled like ancient Estée Lauder perfume and hand sanitizer. She snapped on gloves, tapped a syringe, and injected the pain-easing juice through Garnell's veins. Garnell felt the cold fluid spreading throughout her body. She inhaled and wished someone would wash her wounds. She smelled like road kill.

Relief from the injection washed across her like the haze over the mountains after two merlots and the Virginia Slims menthols she sometimes sneaked. "Jesus, that's good. I never had a lover treat me this damned good."

"Now, now," Genevieve counseled, "I had a son who had a mouth on him like yours and he never amounted to nothing. Only manners can make a person do good in this life. You gotta live for Jesus, young lady. The Lord is where all your answers lay."

Was it the Lord who was going to show her the woman at Linville Campgrounds who chicken-shit shot her? A bitch who caused her to end up in a shit-filled porta-potty?

"I got a Bible up at the nurses' station and don't mind reading you some Psalms or Proverbs. Will relax you better than that poison shooting through your veins."

Garnell thought about her father, member of the Yancey County Board of Commissioners, and how he'd pour three fingers of Maker's Mark and then begin shouting stuff from his open Bible. Seemed to Garnell that Jesus and "The Juice" went hand in hand in some people's lives.

Her daddy sipped from a tall tea glass, and lay in his green recliner in the ranch house on top of one of the most gorgeous vistas in Burnsville. Every Sunday morning, they sat like a normal family in the second pew to the left at the First Baptist Church, her daddy being a deacon and all. It was Garnell, Ruby, her younger sister by two years, and a brother born ten years later. The "accident," they called him.

She'd read the Bible. Enough of it. She knew what she was doing, all the killings, put her straight in line with the Devil's black beard. She tried for years to be a good Christian girl, washing and ironing her daddy's clothes when her mother wouldn't show up for days. She never let a boy touch her privates until college, while most of the girls in rural western North Carolina were already raising their second or third babies.

"No Bible," Garnell said. "Didn't work the first time, so I don't expect it to hit home the second go-round."

The nurse threw her gloves in the trashcan. "God is always ready. When you are. Now you just let me know if you need a thing. I'm a good listener."

Maybe that's what Garnell needed. A heart-to-heart with this woman to clear the sin webs from those parts of her that couldn't forget all the men she'd killed and those coming up on her list. They deserved it. All of it after what the bastards had done to her family.

Her mama had said it best years ago. "Garnell, some men just need killing." How prophetic those words would later become.

"I smell food," she said. "I don't eat meat. You got anything here that's not fried from something that once had a face?"

This seemed to stump Genevieve. "No meat? No yummy meat loafs or fried chicken on Sundays?"

Garnell once ate meat. Was the McDonald's personal hamburger hussy. Then it all changed. She hated meat-eaters. She hated developers. Realtors. Real estate attorneys. She burned at the thought of people raping the mountains just for another golf course or gated community. She hated it enough to kill. And got good money doing it. She thought of The Potato Man cold in the morgue, those oddball cops scratching their heads and coming up with nothing but a sliver of Idaho skin or a bit of pulp.

That's why they paid her to kill. Nothing there. She was good at leaving zilch to go on.

She thought of Dawn Reindeer, the phony Indian woman at the campgrounds. Dawn and her herbs, her strange-smelling fires brewing with tonics or toxins, her spying on Garnell's comings and goings. Dawn had about as much Cherokee in her blood as Garnell had conscience. No need for regrets.

What had she done to set Dawn off? Garnell was about fifty percent sure that Dawn Reindeer had fired the bullet that had seared a hole in her neck. But why?

She closed her eyes to wash them of Dawn Reindeer, then that Klontz detective dude stretched across her mind like a movie. He'd taken her gun. Shit. Something could turn up, even though the people who hired her assured her she was covered.

"You know, Genevieve, I wouldn't mind talking to you after you get me something to eat," Garnell said.

Genevieve smiled, as if she were about to catch and convert a sinner and lasso her over to Jesus. "I'll be right back. How's grilled cheese?"

"Fine."

The nurse paused. "May I asked you something?"

Dilaudid worked its magic and Garnell's tongue was getting loose. "Go ahead."

"How old are you?"

"Thirty-one tomorrow."

"Cute little thing like you should be home with a husband and babies. Not shot up here in this broken-down hospital."

"Ha! I'm not the playground-mother type," she said, feeling phantom pain, that torn spot in her womb where life had once grown. She didn't mind talking to this nurse, but she wasn't going there. That baby never had a chance from the time it was conceived on a boat seat at Lake James. Born with Trisomy 18, head too small, limbs flipper-like, heart riddled with holes and twisted valves. That's the baby God gave her. Five hours she lived. There would be no more.

Genevieve departed with a swish of her scrubs and a cloud of old Estée behind her.

*****

Years ago everything had been so different. Garnell Ray, living in middle-class America on top of primo land every developer wanted. She was both swamped and cradled in the emotional quilts of the good but nosy people of a God-fearing town in a dry county.

She had gone to Mountain Heritage High School and played soccer so well two colleges offered her scholarships. She even spent a couple years as a peppy little cheerleader, shaking her tiny ass and pom poms as the Cougars lost about all their games.

The student body loved her so much, that feistiness, that fuck-you attitude, they voted her Homecoming Queen.

Even though everyone knew the hell that festered in her brick rancher: the mother, built like Raquel Welch, who felt it her duty to screw half the town and even into the next county over, and the father who would beat them both just shy of needing hospitalization.

"Whores. The two of you," he'd yell when the Maker's Mark and Bible verses wrestled his rational mind and took over. "All I want is a decent family and this is what I get? A wife who fornicates like it's her daily exercise class and a daughter who . . . who . . . dresses like a lesbian lately. A whore and a homo. Why can't you be like Ruby?" Ah, Ruby. Ruby who grew up perfect and graduated from Queen's College, later working as a nurse anesthetist over in Asheville. Even a member of the fucking Junior League.

After Garnell's college sweetheart took her virginity at the lake and left her with a dividend that didn't survive, she had changed. She felt it coming on slowly, like something in a crock pot that takes forever to cook. Her heart grew spots rough as eczema, finally folding into itself like a napkin no longer needed.

She traded her skirts for trousers and hiking pants. She tossed her high heels for boots. She took her long auburn hair and cut it just past her ears. Worst of all, according to her father, she became a "goddamn Democrat. Nothing but a liberal piece of trash."

She took the scholarship and played soccer at Appalachian State in Boone. After the second season, one of promise, she broke her shin and quit the team. She changed her major from teaching to environmental studies and decided her mission in life would be to save the mountains— the mountains someone was so eager to develop that her family, for all its dysfunction, had become the target of greed. If only their land hadn't been so desirable.

The killings came later. Her parents never had a chance.

The first time The Agency paid her to assassinate she threw up and didn't get out of bed for three days. It had been gruesome, a gunshot wound to the chest and a man who writhed and spit up bubbles of blood until she'd aimed better and between the eyes. That's what scared her now. That it was so easy. Like shooting clay pigeons. While her family was as flawed as any, they didn't deserve what had happened. She would avenge their deaths and continue with her mission.

Genevieve returned with a plate of food. Garnell couldn't believe her hunger as she consumed the grilled cheese in about four bites and downed the carton of milk without a breath. The smells of the meal comforted her, reminding her of a time when her mother wasn't out trolling and instead baked sourdough bread and tended her family.

"Are you ready to talk now, honey?" Genevieve asked in a tiny voice reserved for the frailest of patients.

"No. I changed my mind."

"I got a call and those nice police officers are on their way. Head nurse said you were stable enough for questioning. Oh, I got a piece of juicy gossip. Wanna hear it?"

"Couldn't hurt."

"They found a man dead. He apparently fell off some overlook nearby. Couldn't say much more than that. Strange, huh, that it was the same day you got shot."

Garnell felt the milk rise up like steam in her throat. With the shooting and the drugs, she'd forgotten about the man. She ran over the entire scene in her mind. No. No. She couldn't have left a clue. Not unless . . . God, what if . . . ?

"Do you want me to call your parents?" the nurse asked.

Garnell felt dizzy and gagged. The nurse rushed for the plastic puke tub.

"Honey, are you okay?"

"They're dead. I'm sure you remember the whole sordid story. Jean and Lawson Ray. Shot to death execution-style seven years ago?"

Genevieve clutched her big bosom. "Mercy, oh I do. I'm so sorry, child."

"Why are you sorry? Did you kill them?" Bitterness oozed from her like the blood under bandages.

"Why, no . . . I just meant—"

"Never caught 'em." But I know who did it, Garnell dare not add. And two were already stiff as rocks and rotting in their graves. She prayed The Potato Man was on his way to hell and not hooked to life support, waiting to regain consciousness and talk about the singing woman behind him prior to his fall and cracked bones.

"I knew your mother," Genevieve admitted. "She was the sweetest woman, and I never listened to the gossip."

"I'm sure you didn't."

"That's a deadly sin. Gossip."

"I'm sure it is."

"The Lord will make it right one day. It's all in the Bible's promises."

No, Garnell thought. I'm making it right. One killing at a time. They may not have been much as parents, but for someone to go in and kill them while they ate supper—fried grouper, over-cooked broccoli and coleslaw? Nobody had a right to do that.

A knock on the door interrupted Nurse Genevieve. "Come on in," she said to the young Candy Striper holding a bouquet of wild flowers that smelled of earth and dirt, not perfume. "These are for you," announced the young girl in the candy-cane smock, and she had placed them on the windowsill.

"You want me to read the card?" Genevieve asked, itching to know who they were from.

"No. That's not necessary. I know who sent them." Daniel. Who else could it have been?

*****

J.D. Klontz saw something in the girl's eyes that bothered him. He'd seen it before in those who were scared and running. And in those who were guilty. Two wives and two divorces had given him an inner instrument to gauge women. Garnell was a beauty beneath those rock-sharp edges. Those brown, almost snow-capped eyes. That lean and taut body of someone who ate sparsely and lived on the land. He usually went for curvy women, but wanted to kick himself for lusting after Garnell. Shit, he couldn't help it. He hadn't been laid in three years.

J.D. was an unlucky man in the romance department. He signed up last year for Match.com, and the women who bit his stupid-ass bait were . . . well . . . Jesus, they were awful. His last date looked like J. Edgar Hoover and spat her gum on the ground, just before lighting a stogie.

He worked as carefully on his Match.com profile as he did before getting the job as a detective. Every word counted.

Tall and built well. Muscular. Kind and quiet. Loves unusual animals.

Eyes like gray clouds with the sun peeking through just before a thunderstorm.

Loves God. All gods.

Sports are my thing, but I can go to a ballet and be happy. Okay, that was a lie but sounded pretty darned good.

Maybe it was his profile picture. Too bulky or threatening. Only the freaky women responded, seemed to him, but he was horny. Especially tonight after a shooting and a murder. He needed release. He could just Instant Message some gal and get laid. Lot of women want to sleep with a cop.

He wanted something meaningful, someone soft and skilled enough to take his mind off his second wife who left without explanation or provocation. She was like a cat. She'd come to him purring and rubbing. Then one day up and vanished. Klontz tried hard not to think of her, but couldn't stop wondering where she went. Maybe once all this death and shooting were solved, he'd have someone put a trace on her. Just to see. Couldn't hurt.

He woke up to a white sun that spread across the sky like an explosion. He could see the mountains from his house, a small rondette he rented for $700 in the hills. Not far from his kitchen window, a trout pond glistened like crushed stars.

He wished he could take the day off and catch a few fish, but too much was going on and it was his job to solve things. None of the other idiots in his office knew what to do. Hell, one was even tasting the evidence off yesterday's corpse.

"Caveman Cop" is what he called Harris.

J.D. finished his third cup of coffee, ran a smear of Colgate over his teeth and wet his buzz cut. He grabbed a banana and jumped into his Dodge Intrepid. Lots to do today. Murders, shootings. Nothing like those good old days of goats and Christmas tree seedlings. This was crime. Real crime.

He knew the sheriff, Ed Laws, was nearing retirement and he had a good chance at the job.

He took the curving roads leading to Gannon Memorial Hospital where the petite woman—was that guilt in her eyes?—could do some more talking. The more they talked, the more they gave away. Keep 'em chatting and the noose would fall and bam!

Up ahead, a car crossed the center line. Again and again. Weaving like some Appalachian granny. Suddenly, the car veered to the edge of the highway and crashed into the guardrail. Oh, Jeez. What choice did he have but to pull it over. He flipped on his blue lights but the car kept going. He switched his police radio to speaker function and yelled a warning to stop immediately.

The car, an old Ford Focus, struggling to maintain its red paint job and ripped front bumper, eased onto the grass at one of the overlooks.

"Do not exit the vehicle," J.D. commanded, instinctively checking the gun at his waist. He moved in closer and what he saw floored him.

In all his years, this was a first.

Holy shit.

He was eye-to-crotch with a woman trying to cover up her privates with an empty six-pack carton. Next to her was a tattooed man, smooshed by an airbag.

"What in God's name are you doing?" he asked the woman, a washed-out dope-faced blonde who'd lost her beauty a decade ago from hard living, he figured. She reeked of alcohol and blood drops dotted her upper thighs, and she was clutching something. What?

A pink lady's razor. Lying on the floorboard was the entire shaving kit complete with foam for that extra close shave.

He wondered if he should call for backup, then figured horny Harris would be the one who responded. He decided to handle this himself.

"Driver's license?" he said.

"I don't have it with me," the woman said.

He noticed she wasn't wearing pants. "Are you *naked*?"

"I was just doing a little grooming and things got out of hand."

"Grooming? Are you saying you've been shaving—"

"Look, I'm not getting any prettier up top, say from the chest up, so I needed to be nice and shave down around my pretty patch."

J.D. tried to take that in. He bit his cheek hard to stop the laughter building within him. This wasn't funny. But no one was going to believe this in a million years.

"Who's the man next to you?"

"That's my ex-husband. He was steering while I shaved my . . . cooter . . . and he wrecked the damned car."

"I'm going to run a check on your tags. Stay put. And put on some clothes. I could get you for indecent exposure."

The charges mounted in his head. Reckless driving. DWI. Endangerment by vehicle . . .

J.D. ran the plates, found them belonging to a woman named Vicki Adele Chapman, 37, of 16 Happy Valley Mobile Home Park in Weaverville. Revoked license. Expired tag. Had been charged with a DWI within the past twenty-four hours.

He took them in for booking. Within two hours the media went wild. The Associated Press caught wind of the story and spread it across the nation.

Why did this have to happen when so much was going on more important than an alcoholic crackhead shaving her crotch while driving?

He had a standard line for reporters.

"My phone has been ringing off the hook all day, and I know there's a funny side to this, but it's also deadly serious. This is a scary road and a lot of bad wrecks are caused by dumb stuff like this. Well, not exactly like this, but you know . . . people thinking they're safe out here in the boonies and can perform sex acts while driving. We have to stop this reckless, dangerous behavior."

He was really pissed that this took precious time away from interviewing the shot girl and figuring out more on the deceased, Mr. Sweatt.

"Harris, you handle this one from here on out." The man beamed like a toddler given a Happy Meal.

It was after lunch when he made it to Gannon Memorial Hospital.

The corridors still smelled like death and cleaning solution. Where was that super hot nurse?

Instead, some old granny nurse was cruising the halls, seemingly flustered and mumbling to herself.

"I don't know where she went. I gave her lunch and some medication and—"

J.D. stopped. "What? Where *who* went, ma'am?"

Nurse Granny gulped the air as if there wasn't quite enough to go around.

"Her. Garnell Ray, the little woman who'd been shot. All I did was obey her wish for a nap and now she's gone. She's not healed up enough to take off. Didn't get her meds or antibiotics or clothes. Just left with her jacket over her hospital gown."

No point in taking bloody clothes, J.D. thought.

"Do you know how she left? As in transportation?"

"No. I . . . uh . . . you know there aren't cabs all the way out here."

J.D. pondered this for a minute, hoping instinct would kick in. Where would a shot girl, a suspicious shot girl, go after leaving a hospital?

"Am I in trouble?" the Nurse Granny asked. "I promise you I didn't—"

"Not your fault. Did anyone see her escape? Have you questioned everyone?"

"Everyone I can think of. Hardly anyone on staff today."

"Anything unusual?"

"She got flowers from somebody. They're over there. She forgot to take the card with her so maybe the name will help you with leads."

He read the card. "Heal quickly. We need you back in the game. Yours truly."

Back in the game. He'd think about that one. He turned towards the nurse.

"I'm going to interview every person in this hospital immediately. I want you to get the supervisor on the phone and ask for a lockdown. Now."

*****

Garnell had walked out of the hospital as easily as if she'd been a ghost. She'd lost so much blood she felt she might topple like one of her stiffs. Should have stayed long enough for another bag of blood or two, she thought.

She swiveled her head, looking in all directions. No one had seen her. She hoped.

Outside, Dawn Reindeer waited in her decrepit Subaru wagon. Jesus, no.

Daniel wouldn't have sent a killer to get me, she thought. She considered turning around and going back to Room 7 and all of its wretchedness. No. This is the choice Daniel sent, so Garnell ducked into the grumbling car, pain so intense she nearly passed out.

The interior smelled of rosemary and cilantro and maybe sandlewood. Incense burned in a tiny Buddha pot in the cup holder.

They were silent in the car, until Garnell began singing "Amazing Grace." It was the only church hymn she knew in its entirety.

It calmed her and unfrayed her nerves enough to ask the question she needed answers to.

"I'm not going to be too mad, chickie, but did you shoot me?"

Dawn angled her head at Garnell in surprise.

"Why would I spring you from the hospital if I was the one who tried to kill you?"

"I don't know. Maybe you wanted to finish me off."

"Daniel said you called him. He had no transportation, said someone blew up your truck so he asked me if I'd get you. Don't get me wrong. I don't like you. I think you're a snob and up to something out here. But I'm no murderer. I'm a healer, which you could use for sure.

"And how are you going to keep me from dying of infection?" Garnell asked.

"There are so many types of Native American healing practices dealing with a variety of ills. I can use herbal remedies, purifying rituals and symbolic healing to help you. If all else fails, I can call on a shaman to treat you."

"Why the fuck didn't I just stay in the hospital?"

Dawn Reindeer considered this a question, not just rhetoric.

"Because you're running. Hiding. Your karma is way off kilter." Dawn wanted to add: *I know more than you think. I see you sneaking around this place like some sort of weirdo. I see you loading up that old truck with bizarre equipment.* But she kept silent.

"Shit. And here I thought it was you. Now I'm at square one."

"If I'd wanted to kill you, you'd be dead. Believe me. Let's get you well, then we can try to put all this together. Pray to all gods he or she doesn't return to finish the job."

After about twenty minutes of bumpy driving and pains shooting through her shoulder and neck, Dawn Reindeer pulled into her digs on a hill above the campground.

"I have valerian root with chamomile tea and a shot of whiskey. You will sleep six hours and then we'll try the salve."

Dawn helped Garnell into the foul-smelling camper and put her on one of the back bunks that reeked of mold. She held a clay cup to her mouth that was brimming with a sulfurous concoction.

"Drink," she said. "Sleep."

Within ten minutes, Garnell was dreaming about her parents, a recurring nightmare that fueled her missions. She was supposed to call The Agency the next day to get her new assignment. That wasn't going to happen unless Dawn pulled off a miracle with her fake Indian self and her potions.

*****

Daniel Puckett was torn. He had a fatherly protectiveness for the girl, but he knew she was in some sort of trouble. People don't get shot in campgrounds for nothing.

He heard the detective's Intrepid coming. Gravel churning, dust rising, and then pulling in too fast into the campground and stopping in front of the caretaker's hut.

Daniel didn't want to deal with this. He was the caretaker. It was his job to make sure everything worked and was in good shape. He wanted no part of an investigation. His entire past could come up and he'd be the one doing time.

He polished off his BLT, drank the rest of the Miller, already lukewarm, and waited at the door of his ramshackle dwelling.

The big detective greeted Daniel with "I need to talk to you."

Daniel nodded but didn't move. He could feel gas recoiling in his stomach from a case of nerves. He prided himself on not getting too close to the campers and residents, but it wasn't a matter of not wanting to get to know them. He didn't want them to know him. One wrong word and it would all come out. He'd get life in prison for sure.

"May I come in?"

"Sure, c'mon in," Daniel said, putting his empty beer can in a recycling bag. "Want a beer? Oh, sorry. You're on duty."

J.D. really could use a beer after this morning's events. The cooter shaver, the girl escaping from the hospital . . . then the gun with no serial number, the dead man at the overlook, the shooting at the campground.

He reconsidered, then remembered he was going for the sheriff's job.

"Here," Daniel said, pulling out a straw-woven chair at his makeshift kitchen table.

J.D. sat and wondered what the peculiar odor was coming from a stained crock pot on the man's stove. Groundhog? Coon?

"Let's get right to it. Where's the girl?"

Daniel was a great liar. He had to be.

"No idea. Last I saw her was last night at the hospital."

"I'm not buying it."

"Then don't."

"Mind if I check around the campground?"

"Most of the campground ain't in Avery County, detective."

"Maybe so. But I have probable cause and I'm in pursuit of a suspect for a crime committed in Avery County. That work for you?"

Daniel worried about Dawn Reindeer's campsite, up the hill overlooking the other campsites and over the Burke County line. This cop was no dummy. He'd find Garnell within half an hour, with or without the help of Burke County deputies. And when he did, Daniel would be an accomplice.

He decided to talk.

"All right. She came here this morning. Staying with some Indian medicine woman up on the hill. It's no crime. Some people hate hospitals."

J.D. scooted out of his chair and walked to the window. Dozens of sites. He'd need more to go on.

"Where is she? This Indian woman?"

Daniel swallowed hard. He didn't want to rat them out, but he had to look out for Number One. If he became a suspect, his life on the outside was over.

"She's in lot 45, up behind the community showers. You can't miss it. You'll smell it before coming to it."

"Thanks. Maybe you and me can have that beer later."

"Sure thing."

J.D. set out combing the Linville Falls campground. He wondered how people could live in a tent or camper on a permanent basis. He picked his way through the maze and started up the hill. Yes, there was a smell. And here it was, lot 45 with a lopsided camper leaning into the earth.

He took some deep breaths. That Garnell woman did something to him. He both suspected her and lusted after her, throwing blankets of guilt all over him.

He knocked on the little metal door.

He waited a few minutes and knocked again. The door opened. Standing there was a tall woman, say thirty-five, with long black hair. His nose, far too sensitive to smells, got a good whiff of something earthy and powerful. He cleared his throat and spoke.

"Detective Klontz, Avery County Sheriff's Department"

She opened the door wider. "What can I do for you?"

"I'm told a woman named Garnell Ray, who was shot last night, is here."

"She's resting."

"Wake her up."

"Don't think I will. She came here to heal and I've given her something to sleep."

"Do you want to be under arrest for obstruction of justice?"

"I just want to obstruct waking someone who's just been shot and needs the sleep."

J.D. rubbed the bridge of his nose. He wondered how far he'd overstepped, being out of his jurisdiction. He better go back to headquarters and follow protocol. "You don't have authority to give her prescriptions. That's a felony, Miss."

"No worries. It's an herbal tea with valerian root and natural healing."

"I'll come back in a little bit. If you try to hide her, I'll take you into custody."

Dawn raked her raven hair back. "I'm not into custody. I'm a free bird. Come back whenever you want."

After Dawn shut the door, she could feel the pulse beating in her neck. Why, she wondered? She wasn't a criminal. So what if she used black hair dye and tanning cream to look Indian or had taken an Indian name. No crimes there.

She remembered her mom, a great beauty who suffered from breast cancer and who managed to live an additional five years because Dawn took her to the Cherokee reservation for successful alternative treatments following the chemo and radiation.

Those with cancer and other incurable ills knew where Dawn was. They would show up at her camper, just like this little shot woman did.

After cracking her own neck a few times, Dawn had walked into the tiny living area and was shocked to see Garnell sitting up on the cushions.

"What's the deal? You didn't sleep but two hours?"

Garnell winced with pain. "I need to be somewhere by six tonight and don't have a car. What do you say I give you cash and use yours? It's important. Life or death."

Dawn laughed. "My car? You come to me like a half-dead bird, riddled with infection, and now you want to go for a joy ride in my Subaru?"

"Yes. I'll come back late tonight. I promise."

"That car is all I have—"

"How much is a 1989 rattle trap like that worth?"

"That's not the point. It's—"

"Excuse me. I'll be right back."

Garnell fished around in her backpack for a wad of cash she'd earned for her latest assignment. She peeled off ten one hundred dollar bills.

"Here's $1,000. If I'm not back, it's all yours."

"I'll be damned. Where did you get that kind of money? Never mind, sister. Best I don't know."

Garnell leaned into the cushions. "Is it a deal or not?"

"Deal."

"Give me some of your hocus-pocus pain remedies, and I'll see you later tonight. I'm going to hang with you until I find out who's trying to kill me."

Garnell reached again for her backpack, ignoring the searing burning in her chest and neck.

"Take this. In case."

She handed Dawn a gun. A small .22 revolver. Not a 9mm, but it would do the job if she needed it.

Dawn handled it as if it were coated with the plague. "I have a bow and some arrows."

"Quit fucking playing Pocahontas and get a real clue."

Dawn breathed deeply and thought of what she'd witnessed earlier from the Grandmother Mountain area close to the Beacon Heights overlook. Garnell had no idea Dawn had been in the woods hunting ginseng.

Sound carried far in the mountains. She could still hear Garnell's song in her mind. She could still see the man falling like a cliff diver to his death.

She tried to piece the two together. But something, a tiny something, was missing.

Safe House in Sodom

by Vicki Lane

The dreamcatcher with its beads and phony-ass turquoise and pink feathers swung like a pendulum as the Subaru navigated the mountain curves. Garnell frowned at it. The tacky piece of Native American/New Age shit was getting on her nerves but she resisted the urge to toss it out the window. Making an effort, she focused all her attention on the road. If nothing went wrong, she'd make it to her appointment in Marshall by six and be back to the campground before midnight. With any luck.

Luck had been running her way ever since the frumpy nurse—Genevieve, that was the name—had helped Garnell slide out of the hospital before that big cop came back with more of his inconvenient questions and hungry, leering looks. Genevieve had claimed to know Garnell's mama and around here knowing someone's family was enough to know whose side you were on. Who you gonna believe anyway—someone from around here whose own mama used to go to the same beauty parlor as you or a big old Yankee cop who talks funny? Nurse Genevieve hadn't had a problem answering that question. She'd helped Garnell slip out unseen and promised to cover for her if—or more likely when—the big cop returned.

"Don't you worry, Garnell, honey." The grandmotherly nurse had patted her gently on the shoulder and flashed a conspiratorial grin. "That big feller'll just think I'm several bricks shy of a load to let one of my patients get away from me—he ain't going to credit I could be lying to him."

Probably true, thought Garnell, slowing as she hit the outskirts of Burnsville. But had the big cop bought her own story about the Brown Mountain Lights? Maybe—but in case he hadn't, she could show him two published articles with her name on them, as well as an impressive mass of research. Research done in the down time of her day job.

Odd, how the two dovetailed so neatly—contract killer/phenomenological researcher. She wondered idly about some of the other 'researchers' she'd encountered in the mountains—that skinny guy wading the branches looking for salamanders—*salamanders*! What was *his* game, really?

Garnell looked at the clock on the Subaru's dashboard—almost five. She'd be in Marshall, as directed, by six. So much for the R and R she'd promised herself. She'd only managed to grab a couple hours of much needed sleep back in Dawn's camper when the insistent vibration of her cell phone in the knapsack pillowing her head had wakened her. The call had been brief, as calls from the Agency always were. The familiar voice on the other end had directed her to get her ass to Marshall—a tiny county seat halfway between Burnsville and Asheville.

"There's some kind of festival going on," the voice had said, "costumes, parades, dancing in the streets. You go to the middle of the bridge and wait on the downstream side. Your contact will be dressed as a scarecrow and will be carrying a folded *Wall Street Journal*. Got it?"

At first Garnell had thought it was just a drug-induced dream—but as the voice kept on, she'd become painfully aware of her current reality—the camper with its pervasive smell of patchouli and mildew and the throbbing pain in her neck.

"Do you people realize I just sprung myself from the fucking hospital? I've got a gunshot wound and I—"

"We are, of course, aware of your situation. Are you withdrawing from the contract?" the impersonal voice had inquired.

That was The Agency. Cold.

Burnsville behind her, she was coming up on the turnoff that led to her family home . . . and to the mountaintop with its fields and pastures, woods and waterfalls that had developers from six states and three foreign countries practically pissing their pants at the thought of how they could turn pristine natural beauty into an expensive playground for fools with money to burn.

Garnell tightened her hands on the wheel and bit her lip. With every fiber of her being she wanted to turn the Subaru up the road and head for home—if she pushed the old rattle trap, she could be atop Raven Ridge just in time to watch the sun slip behind the blue and violet haze of the western mountains. She could sit there atop the bald, listening to the owls calling, waiting for moonrise. She could sleep in the lean-to, as she had so many times before, curled up in a sleeping bag and breathing the clean night air.

There'd be no need to open the locked gate, no need to follow the road that led to the boarded-up house on the lower ridge, no need to go inside, no need to see again the green recliner, the overturned rocking chair, the stains . . .

When death has come and
Taken our loved ones,
It leaves our home so
Lonely and drear . . .

She sang herself past the alluring turn off and headed for the highway to Mars Hill, her thoughts revolving like a hamster on an endless wheel.

Death has come and taken my loved ones, but did I love them? Not really, at least not Daddy, not after all the preaching and all the beatings . . . Mama, yes, I guess I loved her—even with half the town whispering about all her running around. At least she tried to keep him off me . . .

Garnell dragged the back of her hand across her eyes. Shit. Why did she care about her father, the sick fucker? She'd hoped long ago to take her revenge on him. But the way things had gone down, the son of a bitch probably died praying for mercy and was likely singing his head off in some Baptist heaven right now.

They were crappy parents . . . but they were my parents and those fuckers who wanted the land bad enough to kill them like that . . .

When law enforcement and the justice system had failed to punish the four sorry individuals thought to be behind the murder of her parents, Garnell had moved in. She'd taken out the first one on her own—hardly knowing what she was doing and lucky as hell not to have been caught.

Except, she *had* been caught—by The Agency. An anonymous-looking man had knocked on her apartment door the day after that poorly planned, almost botched killing and presented her with a bouquet of red roses.

"Congratulations," he'd said, "on your first removal. May I come in?"

He'd quickly established that he knew exactly what she'd done but had just as quickly assured her that he was not with law enforcement—"not technically."

"I'm with a firm that specializes in . . . removals, as we prefer to call them," he had said, leaning back on her dingy sofa and looking around the room. "I've been authorized to offer you an interesting job and a chance to improve on your natural talents."

When she was able to breathe again, Garnell had been tempted to make a getaway by going out the window—but something about the man's semi-amused expression as he went on to make a clinical assessment of her execution of the first . . . well . . . execution, had intrigued her. She'd stayed to listen to his proposition. Just as well, considering her apartment was on the fifth floor.

Mr. Black, if that was actually his name, and Garnell was pretty sure that it wasn't, had assured her that his employers were only interested in the 'removal' of individuals who were adjudged to have escaped the law due to their own wealth and power. People whose removal would be a benefit to society and, more particularly, to the environment.

"My . . . principals are passionate about protecting the environment," Mr. Black had explained. "And sometimes that necessitates the removal of those who have no regard for fragile natural balance. That, of course, would include the individual you just dealt with as well as the . . ." he paused to consult his Blackberry, "the other three that we presume you intend to act against."

Garnell had opened her mouth to speak but no words came out. Mr. Black smiled.

"Ms. Ray—or may I call you Garnell?—please, rest assured that your secret is safe with us. In fact, we applaud your efforts and wish you continued success in your endeavors. We understand that you are acting for personal reasons with these four—now three—individuals responsible for the death of your parents. But if you decide to work for us, you'll be paid retroactively for last night's removal and then for the other three. The pay is delivered in cash, within twenty-four hours of verification."

He glanced again around the little room and its shabby furnishings and lifted an eyebrow. "You might find the compensation . . . useful. And if you choose, there would be more opportunities. The legal system is, alas, so flawed . . ."

Then he named a sum, per removal, that made her gasp.

In the end, it was the money that convinced her. That and the fact that, like her mama had always said, some people just needed killing.

As Garnell turned off I-26 at the Mars Hill exit, she wondered if her brother—Little Law aka Lawson Junior aka The Accident—was still trying to get their sister Ruby to agree that a quick sale of the family property would be best for all of them. If Little Law and Ruby both pushed for it, she didn't have a chance . . .

Shit, all Little Law cares about is having money for weed and getting a better car. And more of those stupid video games.

Slowing the Subaru to the crawl necessitated by crosswalks swarming with Mars Hill College students on their way to whatever the evening held, Garnell scanned the various groups, wondering if she would see her brother among them. Little Law was, as he described it, "a third semester junior" and, she suspected, as far as ever from the degree in whatever it was he pretended to be studying.

Weed and World of Warcraft—that's his double major. What a fuckup.

Little Law was the problem. By patient talk, Garnell had pretty much convinced Ruby that it made sense to hang on to the property till the current unpleasantness of the real estate market improved. Ruby was doing well—good job, nice apartment, and a fiancé who was a doctor with a lucrative practice. She was willing to wait. But Ruby could be such a pushover when Little Law started his pathetic orphan act.

Garnell stopped for the oblivious gaggle of guys spilling off the sidewalk to lumber across the street. Despite the chill air, all wore huge baggy shirts and droopy shorts; all had iPods in, and most seemed to be texting, thumbs dancing madly. *Probably texting each other.* She shook her head, suddenly feeling old.

If she could keep her brother in playthings and in school a while longer and if the removal market held up, within a year or at most two, she would have the money to buy out her siblings, bulldoze into oblivion the haunted rancher with the green recliner and the rocking chair and build her own little place on Raven Ridge.

That was her hope. That was her dream.

That was what made her a contract killer.

*****

J.D. Klontz leaned back in his creaking desk chair, shaping a mental list as he stared unseeing at the missing children reports. For the first time since moving to this little backwater, he had some doubts . . . Things hadn't gone well, he had to admit. Locking down the hospital and questioning everyone in it while Garnell Ray walked free probably hadn't been the best use of his time. Among other things, he'd pissed off a lot of people: most of the nurses, two women in sweaty, profane labor, a doctor sneaking a smoke, an administrator who'd been having a very private meeting with a nurse, and a Free Will Baptist pastor who'd been visiting a member of his flock but had taken advantage of J.D.'s walking into the room to fall to his knees and pray loudly for all the lost sinners out there.

And if that hadn't been bad enough, J.D.'d been forced to listen to one flatulent old man's medical history, "Of course, my bowels *pootpootpoot* have always given me a sight of *squee* trouble *brrrat*."

He'd exited that room, gasping for breath. His next interview had been with a wild-eyed woman who, on seeing his cop ID, had insisted that he arrest the doctor who'd done her breast implants.

"Just look at these!" she'd demanded, pulling open the flimsy hospital gown to reveal a pair of tits that made him think of his wall-eyed Aunt Edna back in Buffalo. "See there?" the aggrieved woman had whined. "This one's pointing straight on like it ought to but this other's all skee-jawed."

If "skee-jawed" meant aiming up and to the side, J.D. had to agree she had a point. So to speak.

The chair creaked derisively as J.D. shifted his weight, trying to decide on his next move. The only thing he had to show for all the time he'd wasted at the hospital was the card that came with the flowers the suspect had received. His next job was to get over to Florally Yours and find out who'd ordered the bouquet with the card about getting her 'back in the game.' Maybe they'd know where that foul-mouthed little thing was likely to go to ground next. And maybe he'd get some clue as to what she was up to anyway. *Brown Mountain Lights, my ass.*

J.D. was beginning to have his suspicions. The name Ray had rung a bell somewhere and a little rooting around in the cold case file had turned up Lawson and Jean Ray, victims of lead poisoning to the back of the head, survived by their three children, one of whom was named Garnell.

Also in the files were the records of numerous interviews with so-called 'persons of interest'—one of whom was named Sweatt.

Just like the dead man at Beacon Heights.

Coincidence? J.D. thought not.

He'd as good as had her, back there at the campground, if that Indian woman hadn't stonewalled him. Like the mess at the hospital, it hadn't been his finest hour. If he'd just stayed put and kept an eye on the camper . . . It had, and he'd be the first to admit it, been a mistake to go for coffee and donuts. When he'd returned, the camper had been dark and silent and the old Subaru, plastered with all those tree-hugger, bleeding heart liberal stickers, was gone.

A bleak smile crept across his face and J.D.'s spirits lifted. Fortunately, he'd remembered the Subaru's vanity plate—HLR WMN—and had alerted the local units, as well as departments in neighboring counties, to report if the car turned up. With any luck, someone would spot the vehicle and let him know where she was. And then . . .

J.D. raised his hand and pointed his index finger at the poster of the missing teenager who looked eerily like the elusive Garnell Lee Ray.

"Pow," he whispered, then brought the finger to his lips to blow the imaginary smoke from the imaginary weapon.

*****

Well, fuck me! thought Garnell. *Looks like the culture wars are over and the hippies won.*

Marshall's Main Street lay before her, thronged with prancing, danc-ing, wildly-clad figures of all ages. Decorated bicycles, dogs with bandanas, a rag-tag marching band of sorts, and two homemade-looking floats added to the carnival effect. A bearded man in overalls sported a top hat as he strode on stilts behind the float carrying a bevy of little girls dressed like mermaids. There was music; there was laughter; there were dreadlocks and strange costumes as far as the eye could see.

Garnell blinked, wondering if she'd dropped through some time/space wormhole and landed in New Orleans at Mardi Gras. But a second look told her that it was indeed Marshall, proud county seat of Madison County, NC—all two and a half blocks of it.

She'd been through the quiet little town almost twenty years before, back when she was in eighth grade. She could still remember the preacher standing on a box in front of the red brick courthouse, hollering till the spit flew. And the old men in overalls sitting on benches and whittling and the ancient-looking stores that were mostly closed. There'd been a stoplight but it had evidently been for show as there had been almost no traffic and it had just blinked yellow, high above the empty street. She remembered . . .

But now the blinking was the blue bar lights on a police cruiser parked just ahead, blocking the street to accommodate the parade. A sudden instinct for caution came over Garnell and she pulled into one of the few available parking spaces by a bright red caboose. The map on her Blackberry showed the bridge about two blocks away.

Her luck was still in. The crowds would hide her—if anyone was looking. She was even dressed for the occasion.

Garnell looked down at the clothes she'd borrowed from Dawn—a pair of black leggings that only bagged slightly, as long as she kept them pulled up high on her chest, and a fake beaded and fringed buckskin shirt that fell almost to her knees. Perfect.

She released her hair from its usual knot and plaited it into two braids, securing the ends with thin strips of rawhide from the dreamcatcher. *Good thing I didn't toss it out back there*, she thought as she tucked the bright feathers into her braids.

It'd be better if I had a mask . . . Tilting the rearview mirror, she frowned at her reflection, still so recognizably Garnell. A thought struck her. Thrusting her hand deep in her trusty knapsack, she pulled out her makeup kit and, using lipstick and eye shadow, laid three horizontal strips across her face. As she painted, she hummed a tune from Disney's *Pocahontas*.

The transformation to Indian princess complete, Garnell grabbed her knapsack, slipped out of the Subaru, and raced for the bridge, blending unnoticed into the jostling throng.

At the silver-domed courthouse, she broke away from the rowdy crowd second-lining the official parade. Music and laughter died away behind her as she turned left, down the sidewalk leading to the bridge. At once she spotted the strange-looking figure leaning over the railing at the center of the span and picked up her pace.

Then she stopped. Just ahead, parked in front of an anonymous looking white building, were three cars, all with flasher lights across their roofs. A large gold star decorated the door of the nearest.

Shit! That's either a donut place or the fucking sheriff's department! What if . . .

The figure on the bridge looked her way. Garnell hesitated, thinking furiously.

This is Madison County, she reassured herself, *different jurisdiction. That big guy who came looking for me was Avery County law. No worries. Still . . . I think I'll cross the street so I don't have to walk right by the sheriff's front door.*

I shot the sheriff, she sang under her breath as she headed toward a sprawl of customer-filled chairs and tables outside the coffee shop across the street.

The town sure has changed. Garnell took in the scene with a sweeping glance, remembering the overall-clad farmers of her long ago visit. *The only overalls on this crowd are being worn ironically. The food of choice is lattes and wraps instead of meat and three and Mountain Dew. And there's not a whittler in the bunch—they're all talking on their cells.*

Just at that moment, two uniformed men, both with heavy-laden gun belts, came out the door of the coffee shop. One was sipping from a travel mug, the other had a cell phone to his ear.

"Subaru?" he was saying. "Do you know how many old Subarus there *are* around here? And they've every one of them got those stickers. Well, then gimme the plate—"

Without waiting to hear the rest, Garnell turned away and hurried down the narrow sidewalk, past a dread-locked young woman shepherding two tiny wailing girls in mermaid costumes toward the festivities.

"Madison, Nevaeh! I need you to be quiet now and put on your mermaid smiles. You'll get to be in the parade—it's going to turn around in a minute and go back the other way . . ."

Garnell strode on, toward the bridge. The white-fronted building, which did, indeed, have a modest sign on the door indicating that this was the sheriff's department, seemed deserted but she held her breath till she was safely past.

The odd figure at the top of the span straightened as Garnell approached. It was a stereotypical scarecrow, almost comforting in its familiarity. Faded overalls, patched at the knees with red checked fabric, an equally faded long sleeved work shirt with wisps of straw protruding at the cuffs and a ragged straw hat—all that was lacking was the crow sitting on one shoulder. The face, however, was nightmarish. Painted bone white with black-rimmed eyes and a slash of red at the mouth, the face turned and watched her cautious approach. As she reached his—*her? its?*—side, the scarecrow took a folded newspaper from its back pocket and flapped it open.

The Wall Street Journal—yes!

Garnell paused and bent down as if adjusting her shoe. "Jesus saves," she said, repeating the first half of The Agency's recognition formula in a conversational tone.

"And Moses invests," replied the scarecrow, refolding the paper and turning again to look downstream. "You're late."

Garnell stayed down, fiddling with her shoes. "No fucking way," she protested. "It's not six yet—"

"The other kind of late," the scarecrow broke in. "I'll explain. Go on across the bridge. There's a gray Ford pickup in the parking lot to the right. The back bumper has an Eat More Possum sticker on the right, an NRA sticker on the left, and a there's a Number 3 with wings in the back window. Get in and wait. I'll be along directly. Gotta take care of your car first. They're looking for it."

*****

Not till they were twenty minutes out of Marshall did Garnell ask one of the many questions running through her mind.

"When you said you were going to take care of my car . . ."

She looked across at the erstwhile scarecrow behind the wheel of the gray pickup. Another of The Agency's many operatives she'd never met, he'd introduced himself as Marshall—like the town, he'd said.

The headlights of an oncoming car showed that the bizarre face paint had been wiped away, leaving only a trace of darkness around the eyes and a faint reddish stain on his lips. The straw at his wrists was gone, along with the gaudy knee patches. He looked—and sounded—like an ordinary product of the rural North Carolina mountains.

Marshall Harris flashed a toothy grin. "I hate to tell you this but you just had another vehicle burn up on you. Agency orders—they'll reimburse you."

Garnell shrugged. "Easy come, easy go, I guess." She yawned and hugged her knapsack to her. "So what does The Agency have in mind for me now?"

Marshall slowed the truck and turned off the highway onto a secondary road. *Lonesome Mountain*, the white sign read.

"You can't go back to the campground. And we aren't sure yet who it was shot you. So Mr. Black told me to take you to one of our safe houses. We've got a little something underway to make it look like you're dead. That ought to take the heat off."

A rich chuckle filled the dark cab. "So far, the whole thing's working out slicker 'n owl shit. I was already on your trail—trying to get up with you before old J.D. could."

"J.D.? As in Detective Klontz? That big Yankee fucker who came to the hospital?"

"That would be the one. But could you watch that language, Garnell? Granny purely hates a foul-mouthed female."

Garnell fought down her rising nausea. This twisting road and the strobe-like flashes of the headlights against rocks and trees were conspiring to make her feel carsick. Struggling to ignore the feeling in the pit of her stomach, she asked, "Granny? Is that some kind of code name for another operative? And where are we heading, anyhow?"

Marshall slowed to let a possum scuttle across the road. "Granny's what we all call her—but, matter of fact, she's my great aunt. She's been with the agency from the beginning. Granny's what they call a witchy woman—she can help you heal. And where we're going is the safe house in Sodom. Won't no one find you there."

*****

A piercing sound cut into Garnell's troubled dreams. *Ac arroo aroooo.* A siren? A fire alarm?

She opened a cautious eye and looked around the unfamiliar room. Pale flowered linoleum on the floor, dark brown bead board walls, decorated with a feed store calendar, turned to June 1967, and a picture of Jesus, opening his chest to display a luridly tinted and all too realistic heart. A window revealed gnarled branches with tarnished leaves and a few small red apples, a bedside table with a crocheted pink doily, on which rested a Bible and a kerosene lamp, a straight back chair with her knapsack, and the Indian princess outfit . . .

Aroo, aroo. The shrill cry seemed to be just outside the window. Something was moving in the branches—something large and black. Garnell wondered if this was all some weird dream—maybe if she closed her eyes.

"You sleep all right, young'un? Ol' Pilate out there says it's time to git up."

A tall, raw-boned old woman in loose jeans and a blue and brown plaid flannel shirt stood in the doorway, holding a stack of folded clothes. Her thin white hair was pulled back in an uncompromising bun and her bright blue eyes studied Garnell through thick lenses set in heavy black frames.

No, this was no nightmare. This was the safe house and that was Granny. Now she remembered.

Garnell threw back the layers of soft, faded quilts that covered the bed and sat up. A twinge at her neck reminded her of the wound and she explored the bandage with careful fingers.

"Yes, ma'am, I slept good," Garnell replied, wondering when she'd last called anyone *ma'am.* "That herbal tea or whatever it was knocked me out like a fu—. . . like a fine sleeping pill."

It had, too. Tasted like dishwater with a touch of lawn clippings but when Granny had told her to drink it down last night, it hadn't seemed

58

possible to argue. And that sweet-smelling ointment the old lady had insisted on applying to the gunshot wound—Garnell's fingers continued their probing of the bandage. It was dry; the seepage had stopped and the whole area was no longer painful to touch.

"Feels some better, I reckon." Granny crossed to the window and rapped on the glass. "Be gone from my apple tree, you black good-fer-nothing, less you aim to season my soup."

There was a flurry of feathers and Garnell laughed. "It was a rooster! But why do you call him Pilot?"

"On account of he's so proud, crowing all the time and such. Proud as Pompous Pilate."

Granny set the stack of clothing on the bed. "See can you find something that fits. I keep a closet of clothes for times like this." She gave Garnell a friendly smile and started for the door. "You get dressed, young'un; I've got your breakfast ready and then we got things to do."

Garnell chose a pair of worn Levis and an orange sweatshirt with GATLINBURG 2003 emblazoned across the chest. Both were a little large but a lot warmer than the fake Indian outfit Dawn had lent her.

Dawn . . . okay, so maybe it hadn't been Dawn who shot her; in fact, after a good night's sleep and with a clearer head, Garnell realized that the slight figure she'd seen just before the bullet had plowed through her, back to front, could have been almost anyone. Dawn was just another pathetic Native American wannabe. But she'd stood up to that creepy macho-man detective.

Garnell shuddered. The way he'd looked at her in the hospital—old enough to be her daddy but that never stopped them. Hell, it hadn't stopped her daddy—she'd had to be the one to do that . . .

The smell of coffee and baking biscuits wafted through the door. Garnell pulled her hairbrush from the knapsack and gave her hair a perfunctory brushing before pulling it back into a ponytail. Her thoughts ran on—questing like a beagle on a rabbit's trail.

But if it wasn't DawnfuckingReindeer—could the Agency be playing games with her? There'd been a hint that there was another operative, set to move into her place if she couldn't carry out the assignments. That was the thing about this business—they were all of them a bunch of cutthroats, herself not least.

There was something nagging at her—something that she'd over-looked the previous day first because of the meds, and then the pain, and then in her hurry to keep her appointment in Marshall. *In Marshall and with Marshall, as it turned out.*

"Daniel," she whispered to her reflection, "fucking Daniel, the help-ful old geezer . . ."

That was what didn't add up. Where did Daniel go? He'd taken her to the hospital in her truck and made a big point of staying near her. Then her truck had burned up and Daniel had gotten back to the camp-ground—how? He'd sent Dawn to pick her up. And had he then called the cops to tell them she was at the campground?

"Come on, honey; it's on the table." Granny's voice broke into Gar-nell's speculations just as she became aware that the enticing smell of bacon had joined the coffee aroma. *Oh, dear.*

The kitchen was comfortably warm, due, no doubt, to the big, white enameled cook stove to which Granny was just adding another stick of wood. On the plastic-topped table, a plate with three bacon biscuits sat waiting, along with a glass of milk, several jars of jelly and preserves, and a mug of coffee.

"Git you a chair, young'un," Granny directed. "You need some nour-ishments."

Garnell took her place. "Aren't you going to eat?"

"Why, honey, I done et two hours back of this, right after I did the milking."

Garnell pulled the top off the biscuit, slipped the bacon out, and set it to the side of her plate.

"I guess I should have told you—I'm a vegetarian."

Granny's wrinkled face creased into a tender smile and she reached out to pat Garnell's shoulder. "Why, honey, that don't matter. I reckon we're all of us Christians of one kind or another. But just you try that bacon—I cured it myself from last year's pig. He was a fine one—that's his lard in the biscuits too. Get you some of that blackberry jam to put on it."

Bowing to the inevitable, Garnell ate her bacon biscuits. All three.

"Granny," she said, as the old woman whisked her plate away to the pan of soapy water in the sink, "Marshall told me he's your nephew. I'd never met him before this. Do you know how long he's worked for The Agency?"

"Let me see now," Granny dried her hands on a dish towel and leaned against the sink. "If I remember right, he joined up right out of high school. Course, they didn't put him to work right off – nossir, first they sent him off to college – paid for every bit of it. He done good, too. It like to kill him when he found out that what they wanted him to do soon as he graduated was to go be a sheriff's deputy over in Avery County."

"What?" Garnell stared at Granny. "Avery—"

"Law, how he hated it at first. But now he's having fun playing the fool—got them thinking he's just some ignorant country feller. Marshall says they ain't a one of them over there got any idea that he's a groundhog."

"Do you mean a *mole*, Granny?"

The old woman considered. "Well, I disremember. But it was some kindly of a varmint."

A thought struck her. "Go look there on the wall in the front room— they's a picture of Marshall when he graduated college. Might be there's a date on it."

The front room wall was a gallery of school pictures of children, grandchildren and great-grandchildren, nieces and nephews—family pictures dating back to the fifties, posed in front of improbable studio backdrops, and a few sepia-toned pictures from a much earlier time.

As she scanned the photographs—all bearing a distinct and somehow familiar family resemblance, Garnell kept coming back to one handsome face—a dark-haired young man in standard gown and mortarboard. That same haunting familiarity—but this wasn't Marshall, this looked more like—

"That there's my least 'un."

Garnell jumped. She hadn't heard Granny enter the room, but the old woman was at her side, reaching out a gnarled finger to touch the picture. "That one was my heartstring. He come along when I had thought I was well past bearing—almost forty-three, I was. Oh, and he was the sweetest baby—it purely broke my heart how he changed. He took against me and the rest of his family and old Sodom and lit out of here right after he finished high school. He was the smartest boy around, but . . ."

Granny shook her head. "I hate to say it, but that boy got plumb above his raising."

There was a suspicion of moisture in the old woman's eye and she moved toward the kitchen. "Drat that old woodstove; it's awful bad to smoke. Worries me to death when it gets in my eyes."

Garnell continued to study the graduation picture—surely . . .

"Granny," she called out, "what was his name, your youngest son?"

A pot rattled on the woodstove and there was a silence. Then the old woman answered.

"We always called him Babe. But his right name was Lawson—Lawson Belvy Ray."

*****

"Okay, Harris, I'll ask the questions in here, you got it?"

J.D. paused at the doorway to the Madison County Sheriff's Department and fixed his deputy with what he felt was a steely glare. Harris snapped a fake salute. "Yessir, Detective Klontz, sir."

J.D. frowned, wishing that Harris would pronounce his name properly—it always came out sounding suspiciously like *Klutz*. But he had a feeling that Harris wasn't up to the finer points of pronunciation.

They had checked out the remains of the incinerated Subaru which was, indeed, the one Garnell had been last seen in. When they'd run the plate, it had turned out to be registered to a Debbie Jean Jones, whose place of residence had the same address as the Linville Campground. When Debbie Jean, aka Dawn Reindeer, had finally surfaced, she had eventually admitted that Garnell had gone off in her car.

Now they were on their way to follow up on a report that some female-type clothing and other belongings had been retrieved from the river, just below the remains of the Subaru. J.D. hated to think that someone had gotten to that pretty little thing before him. Had she been killed and dumped in the river? The French Broad didn't always give up its dead—or sometimes bodies made it as far as Tennessee before they were found.

Remembering the frosty root beer eyes and the taut little body, J.D. sighed. *What a waste, if that's what went down.*

The tiny waiting room of the Madison County Sheriff's Department was occupied by a gaunt, hollow-eyed woman who was helping a grizzled old fellow to fill out a form of some sort. They both looked up as Klontz and Harris entered and the old man broke into a delighted toothless grin.

"I'll be a summabitch! If it ain't that good fer nothing Harris boy. Marshall, where you been keeping yourself? We ain't seen you since Decoration Day."

Klontz groaned. Old home week with the yokels, he didn't need. He gave his name to the uniformed honey at the front desk whose friendly smile seemed beyond the line of duty. He could feel her eyes on him and was pretty sure she was checking out his butt as he started toward the door she indicated.

It occurred to him that he didn't need Deputy Doofus Harris with him, making the Avery force look bad in front of the Madison sheriff. Anyway, Harris was sitting in the plastic chair next to the old man, yammering away about someone or other.

"Harris," Klontz snapped, "you wait here. This won't take long and I believe I can dispense with your valuable services for the moment." He turned on his heel to go through the door that the honey was holding open for him.

"Son," the old man called out and J.D. stopped.

"You talking to me, sir?" he asked over his shoulder.

"Yes, I am, all right. I got something important to tell you."

The old fool grinned like an ape. "Son, do you know where that deputy of yourn is from?"

"Harris is from right here in Marshall, sir," J.D. replied, trying to sound patient with the old fool. The honey was watching and women went for that sensitive shit.

The toothless grin widened. "Nossir, if I don't mistake, that boy was brought up in Sodom. And you know what they always say . . ."

J.D. winked at the honey who seemed fascinated with him. "No sir, I guess I don't. What is it they always say?"

The old geezer elbowed Harris and shifted a plug of tobacco from one cheek to the other. "Son, don't you never turn your back on no one from Sodom."

Vertigo

by Tommy Hays

A ndy Michaux adjusted his stance, pulled back the club and swung
smoothly, meeting the ball, like he met all of life, head on. Savor-
ing the moment, and sensing another good photo op, the state
senator from Mitchell County lingered at the tee in his lime green shirt
and luminescent pink golf trousers, shading his eyes with his hand, and
watching his ball soar deep down the perfectly manicured fairway and
drop masterfully only a couple of yards from the green. He heard the
photographer from the *Asheville Gazette* snapping away, so he held his
pose a moment longer, imagining the picture in tomorrow's paper, "Up
and coming state legislator keeps his eye on the ball."

"Beautiful shot, Senator," said Bob Snideson, a red-faced, cigar-chew-
ing, fireplug of a fellow who was chairman of the North Carolina Republican Party. His drive right before Michaux's had hooked badly, cleared the
wrought iron fence that bordered the Grove Park Inn course and bounced
along Kimberly Avenue, nearly hitting a shapely mother in spandex pushing a two-baby jogging stroller up the hill who'd given their party the
finger and shouted something about Parks to Putts my ass.

"Very nice, Andy," said Gloria Gudger, the third member of their late
afternoon threesome and one of Michaux's wealthiest campaign contributors. Gloria, a widow in her mid-forties, who was magnificently endowed

in other ways as well, was often compared to Raquel Welch. They'd said the same about her older sister before her untimely end. Gloria had been far more discriminating about who she'd bedded and who she finally married. Gloria would've never married that abusive, alcoholic, holier-than-thou son of a bitch her sister had ended up with, much less had three children with him. Of course who was to say they were his? Her sister had given herself to half the men in the Tri-County area. Gloria had sworn off kids after seeing how her sister's had turned out, especially that Garnell. What a piece of work she was, with her stingy little figure, her squirrelly root beer eyes, those ridiculous Groucho Marx glasses she'd started wearing and that tight-ass bun she'd been putting her gorgeous hair up in ever since her parents were murdered. Most embarrassing of all were the bumper stickers that covered the tailgate on that old Japanese made pickup of hers. *I Still Think* and *If Bush Could Become President, Just Imagine What You Could Be!* and *Who Needs Hell, Reverend Falwell, When We've Got Global Warming?* and *Don't Hug the Goddamned Tree, Plant One!* Gloria was grateful her sister hadn't lived to see what a flaming liberal her daughter had become.

Unlike her impetuous sister, Gloria had bided her time, ruining only a handful of marriages. Ten years ago, she had finally settled down to marry Walter Gudger, an octogenarian feldspar magnate who'd made millions raping Mitchell County's mountainsides. However, even the best laid plans . . . and she'd laid him and laid him, but the old relic clung to life and to her ample bosom for another decade. He'd only given up the ghost last February. Rumor had it that Gloria, having had enough, took the old boy to bed for a week and literally loved the son of a bitch to death.

What a way to go, Michaux thought, admiring Gloria's assets as she swung her club back, which pulled her sweater tight across her chest. Michaux experienced a corresponding tightening in his nether region. She would be his reward tonight after his big speech to the fat cat donors. He imagined she'd be as good as her sister. Probably better. Gloria had an edge to her that her sister had lacked. Michaux, who in his previous life had been a developer, had switched to politics after the bottom fell out of real estate. Well, after that and after the very messy incident he'd gotten entangled in. Never ever mix business with pleasure he'd instructed himself in the bathroom mirror every day since that gruesome evening on

Raven Ridge. Michaux had never been one to waste much time trying to locate, much less listen to, his conscience. After all, he was planning to bang the sister of the woman he'd . . . How should he put this? Decommissioned? Phased out? Retired in that most permanent of ways? Even so he still felt bad about not letting her and that pathetic excuse of a husband finish their fried grouper and their coleslaw, although they hadn't missed anything when it came to the broccoli which, in his opinion, had been way overdone.

It was precisely because of his underdeveloped conscience that Michaux's transition from real estate to politics had been seamless. He'd only been a North Carolina senator for two years, but had taken to politics like a catfish to river bottom and had already been named Legislator of the Year. He'd spearheaded a revocation of the additional penny sales tax the Democrats had pushed through a couple of years earlier to bolster education. Michaux also introduced legislation that laid off thousands of overpaid, underperforming state employees who took summers off, for God's sake—aka "public school teachers." He authored bills that shuttered half the state's breeding grounds for leftwing propaganda, aka "state universities"; shut down the radical socialist media, aka "public radio and TV"; cut thousands of freeloading nut jobs, aka "the mentally ill" from state's coffers; and stripped away any and all impediments to private sector growth, aka "environmental regulations."

But Michaux wasn't just about taking away, he was also about giving. He created the Good-Student Firearms Program in which high school students with a B average or above were allowed to bring a concealed handgun to school. He introduced A Flat Screen for Every Room Initiative, a voucher program which entitled impoverished families to use food stamps toward the purchase of flat screen TVs. But of his many bills that he'd introduced he was proudest of his Parks to Putts Project in which North Carolina's many state parks were to be converted to finely groomed 18-hole golf courses. Not only would it create thousands of jobs, it would also collectively raise North Carolinians' golf game. He didn't understand why the environmentalists were so up in arms. It wasn't like he was proposing a Wal-Mart or a Home Depot in every park, although that wasn't a bad idea. Hell, he'd drawn on his own heritage, being the descendant of the great French botanist, Andre Michaux who'd come to these mountains in the 1700's collecting specimens and, like all good Frenchmen, had deposited a few of his own. With his Parks to Putts Project Michaux felt sure his ancestor would be proud of his descendant. After all, he was keeping the great out of doors, just organizing and smoothing it out a little bit.

"Amazing shot, Gloria," said Snideson.

Michaux had gotten so caught up reveling, as he often did, in his brief but already mythic political career, he'd missed Gloria's actual engagement with the ball. However, he saw now how her shot soared well past where his own ball lay and landed on the edge of the green, rolling within feet of the flag. For the first time in his life, Michaux had been out-driven by a woman and, instead of being upset or humiliated, he felt his lower self, which was always up for a challenge, stand to attention. He remembered his father's oft-repeated words of wisdom: son, always let your pecker be your guide.

"My God, what a shot, Gloria," said Michaux. "Just a hell of a shot." He almost patted her bottom but remembered which county he was in.

"Uh oh," Snideson said under his breath, watching Michaux watch Gloria walk back to the golf cart. Snideson had been the one to suggest this threesome in the first place. As Michaux had risen quickly to the top of the Republican party, Snideson had realized that if he wanted to remain party chair he needed to keep Michaux in women, preferably hot rich widows. No married women with living husbands. On this Michaux was insistent, as if he'd run into complications in the past. Snideson had come to think of the widows as mice fed to a snake, a poisonous snake, a copperhead, no a timber rattler or maybe a cobra except they didn't have those in the Appalachians . . .

The main thing was to keep Michaux satisfied so he didn't become irritated and strike out at an innocent bystander, like Snideson. Although Snideson had begun to worry about this pairing, since Gloria Gudger wasn't sucking up to Michaux the way the other grateful widows did. In fact, Snideson's instincts, and they were seldom wrong, told him that she might be as predatory and potentially poisonous as the senator. If Michaux was a big old rattler, she was a small but just as deadly coral snake . . . well a small snake with big breasts . . . oh, and coral snakes lived along the coast not around here . . . and were easy to get mixed up with the nonpoisonous king snake. What was that old saying? Red and yellow kills a fellow. Red and black is safe for Jack . . .

The three of them had climbed into the cart and with Michaux at the wheel, they started down the fairway. Michaux noted what a beautiful crisp fall day it was, the intense over-fertilized green of the fairway contrasting with the fiery maples along the edge of the course. Who said he didn't appreciate nature? He was a nature lover, as was his lower self, which had remained on high alert with Gloria sitting next to him in the cart. Michaux had attained a kind of meditative ego-induced reverie when something swooped over their heads. Michaux watched as an immense black bird flew down the fairway toward the green.

"Watch out!" cried Gloria.

At the last minute Michaux looked down to see a beagle streak in front of the cart, causing him to swerve off the path and run them into a giant pile of mulch.

"Where the hell did that dog come from?!" Michaux said, spitting out a mouthful of mulch.

"I don't know," said Gloria wiping mulch out of her lap.

"Look," Snideson said, pointing to where the bird had landed beside Michaux's ball.

"That's the biggest damned crow I've ever seen," Michaux said, guessing its wing span to be at least four feet.

"That's no crow, that's a raven," Gloria said.

"Well, technically, a raven is in the crow family," said Snideson. "But Gloria's right. It's a raven. You don't usually see them in town. They tend to be out in the woods, loners."

"Quoth the raven, nevermore," said Michaux, hoping to impress Gloria with his literary knowledge but she was preoccupied picking off a piece of mulch that clung desperately to her sweater. God, he thought, to be that piece of mulch.

"What's it doing to your ball, Senator?" Snideson asked.

Michaux looked down the fairway to see the raven pecking his golf ball repeatedly, causing it to roll and seeming to guide it across the fairway and ultimately into a sand trap. Then the beagle they'd nearly hit came bounding up behind, took the ball in its mouth and ran off, with the raven flying just ahead of it as if leading the way.

"Hey, what the f—," Michaux caught himself, noticing an elderly couple playing nearby. Then in a lower voice he said, "That dog took my ball."

"It was almost like they were working as a team," said Gloria, obviously suppressing a grin.

"I've never seen anything like it," said Snideson. "No one would ever believe it."

"Don't worry, Senator," a voice behind them said. Michaux had forgotten about the photographer from the *Asheville Gazette* who had pulled up behind them in his own cart. He was grinning and clicking away in the direction of the dog and the bird, which disappeared and then reappeared as they ran over bunker after bunker, getting smaller and smaller in the distance. "I've got the whole thing on film."

"Great," Michaux said with not a whole lot of enthusiasm, guessing tomorrow's front page picture would be a little different than what he'd hoped.

Having a beagle carry your ball off wasn't covered in the rule book, but Gloria and Snideson generously allowed Michaux to play on with a new ball and no extra strokes. Still, Michaux's heart wasn't in it anymore. His game fell apart. He hooked drives, missed two-foot putts and spent more time in sandtraps than on the green. The more he played, the deeper of a funk he sank into. And to make matters worse, more than once he'd thought he'd heard a woman singing just beyond the stark white line of birches on the other side of the course. He recognized the tune and a phrase or two of the words, something about somebody throwing himself off some bridge but couldn't quite remember the name of it. He got so distracted he ended up losing not only to Gloria but to Snideson as well, who Michaux knew had been doing his damnedest to let the Senator win. No, there was something unnerving about seeing that beagle and the Edgar Allan Poe bird run off with his ball. An omen is what it was, the most ill of omens.

He knew this to be true when he returned to the inn and his first floor room and found that his electric key didn't work. "These things always screw up," he'd said to himself. "What the hell was wrong with plain old metal keys? Probably invented by some Chinaman." He decided when he returned to Raleigh he'd introduce a bill to do away with these aggravating cards they had the nerve to call keys and reinstate the good old American metal key. He started to go back to the front desk to get a new key, but then he thought he heard someone inside his room. He put his ear to the door and sure enough he heard voices. He banged on the door, and in a minute the door opened part way, but the chain held it and a little boy stuck his head out. In the background the theme to Sesame Street blared on the TV.

Michaux double-checked the room number with the number on his key. "You're in my room," Michaux said.

The little boy just looked at him.

"Why are you in my room, little boy?"

"It's the room they give us," the boy said matter-of-factly.

"Where are your parents?"

"Mama's taking a shower. Daddy's playing tennis or leastways that's what he told her. Mama thinks he's probably down at the bar tying one on. What he's tying to what I can't rightly say. And me and my sister are watching Count Dracula count bats. Not the baseball kind, the cave kind, which Mama says have some white nose disease that's killing them off, and oh another thing she says is that I'm not supposed to talk to strangers." With that the boy shut the door.

Michaux was about to pound on the door again, but decided that would lead nowhere good. In a fury he went back to the front desk. The clerk, a young pretty African American woman he guessed to be in her late twenties, had just finished registering a guest. Michaux always felt a bit off balance around blacks. He'd grown up in Mitchell County where there were hardly any. That was one thing about Raleigh that had come as a shock to him, that he was surrounded by blacks. This woman, though, had roused his lower self.

"I'm Senator Michaux," he said, "and a family seems to have taken over my room."

"Oh yes, Senator Michaux," the clerk said, "your assistant called and said you wanted to be moved to the highest floor in the hotel. She said that you wanted a view and a nice balcony. So we gave you the best room in the house and moved all your things up there. She said she'd notify you. I'm sorry if she didn't get in touch with you about that change."

"That can't be. My office didn't call. Besides, my assistant isn't a she," Michaux said. "You'll have to move me back."

"I'm afraid that's impossible," the clerk said.

Michaux looked around, leaned toward her and in a low desperate voice said, "I'm afraid of heights. I get vertigo. You'll have to move me back."

"I'm sorry Senator, but there are no other rooms available," she said. "We've got the Arts and Crafts show going on all this weekend and people have come from all over the country," she said, brightening a bit. "My suggestion is that you just don't go out on the balcony and keep your curtains closed."

"Mother fuck," said the Senator his temper getting the best of him. "Mother fuck."

The clerk raised her eyebrows at him.

"Sir," she said in a loud voice, causing guests to turn in their direction. "I'll have you know that I have a mother, that I know many mothers personally, and in fact am considering becoming a mother myself, and that I find your remarks repulsive and obscene, especially coming from one of our most prominent legislators."

Aware that people were now staring, Michaux lowered his head. "I'm sorry," he said, in a very quiet voice. "I'm very sorry." Who had called to have his room changed? Somehow, word had gotten out about his fear of heights. It occurred to him that this was the Democrats ploy to get him to lose his cool before his big speech tonight. Well, he wasn't going to fall for it. No, he wasn't going to fall for it.

Taking a deep breath and mustering some semblance of a smile, he said, "I apologize for my outburst." Then he raised his voice for any and all to hear. "And I promise next session to introduce a bill to set aside a day just for North Carolina mothers. We'll call it Tar Heel Mothers Day."

The clerk didn't say another word, just gave him a new key to his new room. Reflexively Michaux grabbed a copy of this morning's *Asheville Gazette* from the stack on the desk. He hadn't a chance to read it this morning.

"Oh Senator," the clerk said.

"Yes?"

The clerk curled her finger for him to come back to the desk, which roused his lower region again and had Michaux feeling hopeful. Perhaps he'd have a couple of conquests after his speech.

"My 64-year-old mother with bad arthritis taught third grade for twenty-four years in Winston-Salem," the clerk said, "and was one year away from retirement but recently lost her job because of your legislation to cut school funding. Now she's a caddy in one of your state park golf courses."

He shrugged. "At least she gets outside now. They say exercise is good for arthritis . . ."

"One other thing," she said, a new cruel edge in the clerk's voice. "I've given you the Pink Lady's room."

"The Pink Lady?"

"The ghost of a young lady who in the 1920s fell to her death in the Palmetto Room, which your room overlooks. They say she jumped right about where your elevator will open. She's said to haunt the hotel to this day." She fixed Michaux with a withering gaze that shook him to the core.

As he stepped into the elevator, he was surprised the clerk had gotten to him so. After all, he was used to being hated. In fact he'd always figured that as developer or politician, he wasn't doing his job if somebody wasn't hating him somewhere. Still, the clerk's look had sent chills up his spine. What was happening to him? Was he losing his necessary edge? Could it be that doing in Gloria's sister and her sniveling cuckold of a husband was finally getting to him? And why now since that was nearly seven years ago? Lord God, could he be developing a fucking conscience? He sure as hell hoped not. He reassured himself, recalling that two of the guys who'd participated in the Fried Grouper Massacre were dead. One had run into some bad luck with a falling tree and the other had been shot, probably by one of the half dozen jealous women he'd fucked over. Michaux had considered their elimination from the scene a happy coincidence. Fewer mouths to spill the beans. That left only him and that yodeling fool Richard Sweatt and Sweatt was such an airhead, he'd probably forgotten all about it anyway.

Michaux took the elevator up to the top floor of the hotel and when the doors opened saw what the clerk had meant. His room, which was on the fifth floor, was in the old part of the hotel and faced an open atrium in the center that looked down upon a lounge area with antique couches and chairs. He stupidly glanced over the edge wondering if this was where the Pink Lady had jumped. As he looked out over the expanse he felt an almost irresistible urge to slip over the rail and hurl himself out into the open space. His fear of falling masked his deeper urge to fall. The world tilted and began to spin. He turned away, collapsing into one of the Arts and Crafts chairs that populated the landing. When his vertigo had subsided, grateful that it had since these attacks could sometimes go on for hours, even days, he patted the sweat from his forehead with his monogrammed handkerchief and then on unsteady legs sought out his new room.

He was relieved when he slid the key in the lock and the little light turned green. However, when he opened the door, he found himself confronted by what most others would've found absolutely breathtaking—an early evening view of the Grove Park Inn's lush golf course, with the city of Asheville in the distance and the purple waves of Blue Ridge Mountains beyond. Michaux ran over and shut the curtains before his vertigo started up again.

He took a long hot steamy shower and began to feel human, although every now and then the image of that beagle and that spooky bird running off with his ball intruded on his reverie.

What in the hell was that about?

After his shower, he dressed in the satin robe the hotel had provided in the closet. Tempted as he was to get a drink out of the mini-bar, he knew that alcohol sometimes precipitated his vertigo. There weren't any soft drinks in the mini-bar. He thought about calling the front desk to see if he could get a Coke delivered to his room but worried he might have to deal with that clerk and besides he could save the taxpayers a little money by getting it himself. So he went out in the hallway and keeping his eyes away from the open atrium (although he sensed the great chasm to be only a hop, skip and a jump away), located a vending machine. But when he went to push the buttons, the machine was out of everything but A&W. Root beer? He hadn't a root beer since he was a kid. His finger paused over the button. He remembered as a child, he and his father would go into Spruce Pine and get a root beer float at the Upper Street Cafe. He'd forgotten all about that. It was a tender memory and caught him off guard. He felt something wet streak down his face and wiped it away with the back of his hand. It took a moment for him to figure out what it was. A tear. A damned tear! He was definitely losing his edge.

He returned to his room pressing the cold root beer to his brow which felt a little fevered, then sat down at the little cramped hotel desk in his room and took out his notebook. As he read through his speech, he began to relax and even chuckle to himself between sips of the A&W. He'd forgotten what a damn good speech he'd written. He'd outdone himself. Positively inspired. It would have the magnolia-tree-saving Wiccans, the Warren Wilsonites, the drum circle morons, the street people and the street people wannabes, the Leaf Festival/Woodstock wannabes, the organic farmers and their cheery red-cheeked children, even the self righteous National Public Radio listeners positively apoplectic. By the time he was done this New Agey, Green Man-y, Womansong-y, Jubilee-y, Every-Other-Person-You-Meet-Is-Buddhist-y, crystal consulting-y town would be so angry, so beside itself, it would spontaneously combust.

In his speech he argued for the lifting of just about every significant environmental regulation in the state. "How is it that we've made pollution such a negative thing?" His deep rich baritone echoed in his room. "Pollution is a sign of prosperity, of an economy at full throttle. Productive factories pollute, cattle yards and big farms pollute, diesel tractor trailers toting all sorts of American-made goods all across this great country pollute, people driving to work, to the mall, and of course, to church, pollute. We must rethink how we think about pollution." His voice rose with conviction. "Pollution made this country great, and I believe if we put our hearts and minds to it, we can pollute our way out of this deficit." He paused and smiled out to his imaginary audience. "I propose that we change the state motto from some lame old Latin phrase about *being* rather than *seeming*. Latin's a dead language for Lord's sake. No, I propose we change the state motto to "North Carolina—Where Pollution isn't a Dirty Word."

But instead of applause, what he heard was singing. That same singing he'd heard out on the golf course. But this time it seemed to be coming from right out on his balcony. It was singing the same song in a sad, lonely voice. It hurt his heart to listen to. He felt goose bumps rise on his arms and he felt tears threatening again. What was happening to him? He thought about sneaking a peak through the closed curtains but worried his vertigo would start up and then he'd have to cancel his brilliant speech. So instead he called the front desk, which turned out to be that same clerk, who pretended not to know who he was and then finally said she'd send up security whenever she located them. Security didn't arrive for a good fifteen minutes, long enough for Michaux to nearly be driven out of his mind, listening to that singing which the longer it went on, the more tears he cried. He did finally remember the name of the damned song: "Ode to Billie Joe."

Finally there was a knock at the door and the singing stopped. Michaux, dabbing his eyes, answered the door. Security turned out to be a frail looking old guy, who Michaux guessed was in his seventies and who wore a security uniform that was several sizes too big for him. This guy would've made Barney Fife look positively capable.

"Not a soul out there," the old guy said, coming back in from the balcony. "Mighty nice view, though, this time of night."

"Would you close those curtains, please?" Michaux snapped, keeping his eyes away from the balcony. "I definitely heard somebody out there singing."

"Oh, I don't doubt that," the security guy said, closing the curtain. "You're in her room."

"Whose?"

"The Pink Lady's."

"I don't believe in ghosts."

"I didn't either," the security guard said, "till I started this job. I've come up on her a few times over the years and I'm not the only one. Most of the staff have seen her. She's always real nice. Never hurt a hair on anybody's head. One night not long after the wife died I was feeling particularly low. I was working the late night shift at the Gingerbread House Display, trying to keep out a family of raccoons that had been sneaking in the automatic doors and wreaking havoc, and I felt someone come up and give me a good long hug but there wasn't a soul there. I know it was the Pink Lady. I tell you I've never felt so peaceful in all my life . . ."

"Yeah well, I need to get back to my speech," Michaux said, taking the guard by the arm and leading him to the door. "Thanks for coming by." He put a five dollar bill in the old geezer's hand. Michaux was starting to close the door when the security guard stopped him and said, "You'll know for sure when the Pink Lady's around. She makes the temperature drop all of a sudden in whatever room she's in."

Democrats, Michaux reassured himself, as he sat back down to review his speech. Democrats have been piping in the singing somehow, making it sound like someone was out there and hoping to drive him to distraction. Well, he wasn't falling for it.

There was another knock at the door. With a sigh, he went to answer it. He opened the door saying, I'm fine now. But it wasn't the security guy. It was Gloria and she was wearing a tight silver shimmering dress that looked as if she'd been poured into it.

"Gloria," he said, self-consciously tugging on the tie to his robe. "I'm not dressed."

"Thought I'd come by and see if you were having pre-speech jitters," she said walking past him into the room. "If you might be in need of some distraction."

"I thought you were the security guy," he said closing the door behind her.

"Why do you need security?" she said, turning to him. "Can't keep the women off you?"

He laughed nervously, suddenly feeling out of his depth with this woman. His instincts told him there was something about her he needed to be careful about. But it wasn't helping matters that his lower self, now unrestrained by the confines of pants, was conspicuously attentive.

She came over to him, kissed him and then parted his robe, running her hand down his bare chest and heading lower still when there was what sounded like a loud caw from the direction of the balcony.

"What was that?" she said. "It sounded like it came from . . ."

"Oh please don't . . ." But before he could ask her not to, she'd swung open the balcony doors. A very large familiar bird sat on the rail, just looking at them.

"It's your raven," she said in a quiet voice. "From today."

For a moment, Michaux and Gloria didn't move. They just watched the bird which seemed to have fixed its avian gaze on Michaux. Michaux felt himself grow more and more uncomfortable under the bird's stare. It seemed to him that the bird was about to speak when off in the distance they heard the bay of a beagle. With a great flapping of wings it suddenly took flight, gliding out across the golf course and then disappearing in the oncoming night.

"How strange," Gloria said, looking in the direction the bird had disappeared. "That bird must have a thing for you." Then she said, "What a view you have up here." She leaned far out over the railing, showing her tight shimmery bottom.

"Yes," he said, feeling the stirrings not of his lower self but of his vertigo. He averted his eyes and retreated to the safety of the room.

"Don't you want to join me out here?" she asked.

"I'm not dressed," he said.

"So? It's getting dark. No one can see. I'll give you a little taste of what you can expect later, after you've slain them with your speech."

"Speaking of which," he said, keeping his eye on the carpet, "I better finish reviewing it."

"All right, spoil sport." Gloria came back, kissed him on the mouth, surprising him with a little playful tongue, then said she'd see him at the dinner and was gone. He waited till she'd left and then rushed over and closed the balcony doors and closed the curtain again. Realizing what time it was, he began to get dressed in the tux he wore for these big deal dinners. As he dressed, he found himself coming back into himself. As he buttoned his shirt, then slipped on his pants, he felt like a soldier, no, a general, putting on his armor, girding his loins for battle. By the time he pulled on his coat and was admiring his striking image in the mirror, he felt confident, at the full height of his power. He would do as Gloria said, he would slay them and then he would ravish the hell out of her.

He folded the copy of his speech and slid it into his inside coat pocket. He was just about to head out the door when his eye fell on the copy of the *Asheville Gazette* he'd picked up at the desk and he read the headline— *Prominent Dick Sweats to Death.*

Michaux rolled his eyes. The paper was notorious for botching headlines but they'd sunk to new lows with this one. They'd never live this one down. Michaux took the last swig of his A&W and picked up the paper, his curiosity piqued by the mangled headline, whatever it referred to. However, as he read, the mild amusement he'd been feeling gave way to a cold stab of fear. They'd finally identified the person who'd fallen from a Parkway overlook and it was Richard Sweatt. The same yodeling fool.

Michaux's hands began to shake as he set down the paper. Two might've been a coincidence, but three? Any idiot could see that someone was doing them in, one by fucking one. That's when he heard Bobbie Gentry or whoever the hell it was out on his balcony start back singing about Billie

Joe McAllister throwing himself off the goddamn Tallahatchie Bridge or did she say The Mile High Swinging Bridge?

Tongues of Fire

by Wayne Caldwell

A ndy Michaux had been a man of faith ever since he had given his life to Jesus at a revival when he was nine. That day, his pastor had said "Faith is like knowing a can labeled 'corn' really contains corn, not beans." Made perfect sense to young Andy.

His faith became unshakably grounded on a set of beliefs including, among other things, the conviction that Jesus was: (a) God's son, (b) a being who intended nothing but the best for His people (males, anyway), and (c) a Republican. Anything conflicting with these tenets was suspect. Andy was certain Jesus never allowed beans to hide in cans of corn. Unless, of course, it was succotash, in which case it would not be labeled "corn," so the rule still held.

This belief sustained Andy through high school, when he ignored Jesus's injunction to cut off his right hand when it offended him. (Obviously not an authentic word from the Master—see [b] above.) In fact, because his steady girlfriend did not let him past first base, his right hand afforded constant comfort.

By the time he finished college he had left behind all beliefs conflicting with (b) above, including a sub-part of (b) that might possibly include in "His people" anyone Not Like Andy. It simplified life considerably to eliminate the middleman, so to speak. If a person agreed with Andy, he or she was bound for the promised land—if not, he or she was headed for hell in a handcart.

This eliminated questions like "What would Jesus do," especially when biblical example might prove embarrassing. Jesus, for example, treated women as whole persons equal to men. Andy, on the other hand, viewed women as existing for man's pleasure and comfort, therefore (see [b] above) they had no particular rights over their bodies.

He had especially enjoyed science in college, because it represented verifiable beliefs. Gravity, for example, he understood, and also became convinced mountaineers knew it more intimately than flatlanders.

Over the years, however, he had become disappointed with science. To his mind, it had been politicized in a manner that set his Republican teeth on edge. Relativity? Gluons? Black holes? String theory? What happened to the fundamentals? Black-and-white, yes-and-no answers? Damn liberals had taken over everything—even the weather.

His weather radio told him today had been hot—ninety-two degrees. The record high for the day was ninety-six, set in 1916. The record low, forty-six, was set in 1999. Those were scientific facts which argued against global warming, climate change, whatever the press called it this week. Maybe, he thought, he'd throw a paragraph about that into his evening speech, and, on his way out, turned the air conditioning in his room down a couple of degrees.

In fact, he saw need for another bill when the legislature next convened. The weather in Western North Carolina came out of Greenville-Spartanburg, in South Carolina. Another example of government gone mad, of federal law trampling states' rights. He'd have his assistant compile a bill to have all North Carolina weather reported from within the state. If we don't do something about the National Weather Service, he thought, soon it will be run by the United Nations and we'll get our weather reports from Bangladesh or Bahrain or some damn where.

He'd seen an article in the Asheville *Excuse* (as he called it, for its liberal bias, sorry sports pages, and running "Mallard Fillmore" on the editorial page as if it weren't as blatantly biased as "Doonesbury") indicating that a recent spate of tornados substantiated global warming. Not so—storms and wars and turmoil were signs of Jesus' quick return.

Then People Like Andy would help Jesus rule the earth for a time, during which there would be no more crying, gnashing of teeth, or, for that matter, OSHA or EPA. Life would be abundant, good, and, eventually, eternal. He could stand it.

Especially if it included Gloria.

The people paying ten thousand dollars a plate to dine with their senator and listen to his speech had been arriving at the Inn all day. The parking garage was full of large, shiny vehicles, many of which still sported not only McCain/Palin stickers but also faded "W in 04" advertisements. Some hosted new banners referencing rampant socialism. Only one had an Obama sticker, but an evilly grinning Calvin pissed upon it. A pastel-colored sedan appropriate for a Mary Kay dealer boasted "Have you hugged your assault rifle today?"

Their cars were full of golf clubs, fly rods, and huge rollaround suitcases which had spent time in Pinehurst and Myrtle Beach. More than one vehicle harbored large-caliber handguns under seats or in glove boxes.

These people were, as a general rule, not liberal tippers.

Bartenders who, at various drink stations, listened to the contributors talk of raspberries and oak and various other bouquets, excused themselves to the kitchen to make fun of the rich dinner dummies and freshen carafes from boxes from the local grocery. Beer of choice was Heineken. Women tended toward Mojitos or white wine. By dinner several of the guests might be sozzled enough to leave by mistake a five- or ten-spot in a tip jar.

(The Baptists among them might or might not drink a discrete glass of wine with dinner, but room service planned a very busy evening.)

Snideson met Michaux in the hall outside the Heritage Ballroom. "Are you ready, Senator?"

Michaux was several floors removed from his acrophobia. "I was born ready, Bob. Born to run, too, while we're at it."

Snideson tried to escort Michaux toward the head table but the pair kept being sidelined by well-wishers, the odd lobbyist, and, in clothes not quite as nice as the wait staff wore, the reporter from the *Gazette*.

"Senator, here's a little something you might want," he said, holding up a slightly gnawed Titleist.

Michaux's forehead wrinkled like an accordion. "What in the world?"

81

"Take it, sir. It's yours." The reporter extended his hand as if Michaux might actually accept the ball.

Grabbing it from the reporter, Snideson snapped at him. "How do you know this is the Senator's?"

"Notice the toothmarks—terribly characteristic of a beagle. I know because I own one about the size of our ball thief."

"How did you find it?" demanded Michaux.

"I have my sources," he said, and smiled. "I'll be interested to hear you tonight, sir." With that he walked toward the rear of the room and sat in a straight chair.

"Let me see that," said Michaux. He eyeballed it, held it to the light, rolled it in his palm. "It's mine, all right. That damn dog chewed it so I'll never use it again."

Snideson glared at the reporter, who gave him a friendly wave.

Michaux grinned. "Bob, I'll take this as a good omen. Lookit."

Snideson examined the ball. "What?"

"See how the teeth marred the trademark? It says 'TITEIS."

Snideson seemed unimpressed.

"Titties, dummy. I have titties in my future."

"Good one, sir. Good one. Here come some now."

Gloria appeared, it seemed to Michaux, like magic, caressing his arm and fairly purring with healthy femininity. "You're going to score points with these people, Andy. Just remember, afterward" (here she whispered in his ear) "you'll score again." She pinched him on the butt. "You always carry your balls to dinner?"

He stowed the golf ball in his trouser pocket and grinned like a devil in one of those old separating-the-sheep-from-the-goats paintings.

They seated themselves on the podium and scanned the crowd. Maybe half the people were in their seats, drinking as if they were bored within an inch of their lives. Several men shook hands like momentous deals had been made. Wait staff with oversized trays began to emerge from the kitchen.

Snideson waved to an older, underdressed, white-haired man. "Come on up," he said. The man nearly ran into a waiter carrying an enormous tray filled with food, then ascended the podium. Snideson shook his hand. "Welcome, Reverend. Ready to bless this mess?"

Reverend Todd nodded. He spent weekends in the lobby of the Inn, on call in case a pair of guests might suddenly decide to marry.

Snideson went to the microphone and asked for the crowd's attention. "Folks, it's wonderful to see you all," he said. "While these fine young men and women bring the salad course I'd like silence. Reverend Todd will ask our blessing."

Todd, except for Michaux and Snideson the only sober male in that area of the room, nodded as people bowed. He blessed the food and the hands that prepared it and, while he was at it, the missionariesinthehome-andforeignfields. Snideson was about to yank Todd's jacket tail when he wound up the prayer. "Forgive us our many sins. In Jesus's name, amen." The crowd sighed like a balloon losing air.

Michaux, for his part, silently added, "And for what I'm about to receive I give you thanks," eyeing Gloria instead of his croutons.

Some say Michaux gave the best speech of his career that night—at least until things got out of hand. He certainly preached to the choir. For thirty minutes he stuck to his prepared text, excoriating everyone not in the room—people without means—and uplifting his audience—people with means. They applauded his position on pollution and gave him a series of standing O's, culminating with one reacting to his raking of the National Weather Service.

Encouraged, he ad-libbed about the Good Old Days, which he had heard about from his father's generation. Cheap gasoline, even cheaper cigarettes, days when you rode around in your gas-guzzler with no seat belt and threw butts out the window with perfect freedom. It was his legislative dream to restore that era. In a vision of pure inspiration he said if he were backed by "good people like you," he'd lead the fight to repeal tobacco taxes and all the stupid No Smoking legislation. "In fact," he shouted, "how many of you have cigars, cigarettes, pipes on you?"

The crowd's roar said he was running in the right direction.

"Do you have lighters?"

Another shout of acclamation.

"Then, by Nellie, smoke 'em if you got 'em."

Wait staff froze in horror. The reporter, however, seemed overjoyed as he lit a smoke and scribbled furiously in a notebook. The diners passed cigarettes and lighters like they were beginning a candlelight service in hell. Someone began a chorus of "For he's a jolly good fellow," and the crowd, lost below a blue haze, seemed on the verge of carrying Michaux around like he'd slain a dragon or stopped a world war.

Wait staff, having looked at each other for instructions or at least encouragement, conferred in the kitchen and decided to call upstairs. Management, not wanting to anger such high rollers, said bring more wine and coffee and open some doors.

About that time smoke alarms began screeching like demented soprano herons. Snideson, who did not smoke, said to Michaux, who usually did not but was addressing a Cuban cigar like it was an asthma inhaler, "Let's get out of here, Andy. I don't see a bit of good coming from this."

"I'm having too much fun," said Michaux.

"Think of tomorrow's headlines: SENATOR LAUNCHES TOBACCO RIOT—GROVE PARK INN BURNS DOWN. It might end your career."

"You might be right," said Michaux, as people pounded wine and smoked like tar kilns. They chanted "Don't Tread on Me" and "Remember the Alamo" and one booming bass voice belonging (one reckoned) to a native of New Hampshire sang "Live Free or Die" as if it were an aria in a surreal opera.

Fueled by alcohol and caffeine (a good formula for making wide-awake drunks), people began dancing and high-fiving. One young man set fire to the contents of a trash can. "Okay," Snideson said, "let's blow this popsicle stand. It's out of control."

"This what?" asked Michaux as Snideson led him off the dais toward an exit.

"It's a figure of speech, sir."

"Speaking of figures, where's Gloria?"

"Dunno. Maybe in your room."

Ducking into an elevator, they reeked of Cuban leaf, choice Virginia tobaccos, both burley and flue-cured, and Swisher Sweets (these sneaked in by the wait staff).

"Blindfold me," said Michaux.

"What?"

"You heard me. Here—use my handkerchief. Blindfold me and lead me to my room. That way I won't go nuts over the altitude."

"This is a little strange, sir," said Snideson as he tightened the monogrammed handkerchief and pushed the button for the top floor.

"Don't get any weird ideas, Bob. I mean, I don't want to know if you carry pink handcuffs in your pockets."

"Sir, are you suggesting I'm a . . . "

The door opened. "Not in the least. Here's what these hotel people call a key. Probably made in China. Just get me to my room on time."

The men entered the room slowly. Snideson looked around. "Just a second, sir. I want to see out your window."

"Damn it, Bob, where's Gloria?"

"Just stay still, sir." Bob pulled open the curtains. From town many red lights headed their way. Fire trucks, the whole city's worth, he figured. Then he heard sirens and saw Blue Mountain Lights heading up the hill. "Damn. We need to get out of here, Andy. The cops!"

"How'll we manage that?"

"No problem," cried a female voice as netted shrouds simultaneously enveloped both men.

"What the hell? Who are you?"

Two sets of hands tightened the shrouds and gagged the men. Michaux thought he recognized the scent of Fire from Heaven on the one binding him. "G-gloria?"

"Ask questions later, boys," said the other voice. "Now, march!"

Both men, feeling pistols aimed at their backs, obeyed.

*****

The next thirty minutes or so were very confusing to Michaux. He felt himself lifted into a laundry cart which rolled, it seemed, for miles, first on carpet and then, after an elevator ride, on concrete with deep expansion joints that jarred the cart enough to take his teeth out.

After a time he was dumped into the trunk of an automobile. His head was crammed with the sounds of sirens of all varieties (displacing the siren song of Gloria for the nonce) deluging the mountain with racket. People ran and shouted, screamed, hollered, automatic weapons chattered—or had the fire found fireworks in some kid's backpack?

Their vehicle was quiet, certainly no Detroit machine, likely a hybrid of some sort. Or maybe a Subaru. Sure, that was it. They rolled down Macon Avenue without, best he could tell, any pursuit.

Which, he reflected, was bad.

They turned onto Charlotte Street. Soon he heard a left signal, and figured they had entered I-240 through the Open Cut, a DOT project his father's generation had foisted upon Asheville. It had caused sharp, ill winds (especially in winter) to blow downtown, especially on College Street.

He heard music. A radio, maybe, or an iPod. Dylan, singing "Blowin' in the Wind," with a female voice in close harmony (if you called Dylan harmonic). Michaux tried to make enough racket to be noticed. Nothing doing.

As they left the expressway and headed east on Tunnel Road the music changed. Whoever was driving—the same woman who had arranged the music?—was clever. Next up was the Kingston Trio singing "MTA." The driver seemed gleeful as she joined the final line: *He's the man who never returned.*

Jesus save me, Michaux thought. She's turning up to the Parkway. Where that damned Sweatt was offed. Please, Jesus, get me out of here. She'll murder me for sure.

Then he heard the fine baritone of Johnny Cash singing "Long Black Veil." His driver sounded happy as she sang of that old killing and turned right. This, he thought, should be south, toward Mt. Pisgah. She sang along with the Man in Black.

Michaux wasn't sure how long it was from Cash through "Last Kiss" and "Lonesome Valley"or whether he'd soiled himself or even if he could believe his ears when he heard Tom Waits sing "Closing Time," a sweet, gentle song suitable for a hanging or shooting or worse.

Right-side car wheels on gravel as the car stopped. Waits and his piano unceremoniously clicked off. Front door open. Quick steps to the rear of the vehicle. Another car pulling behind. Another door opening and shutting. Low female voices. Then still as death.

He wasn't sure how long they had parked when he heard a screech owl cry. No evidence of his captor. Was she in cahoots with whomever kidnapped Bob Snideson? Was Snideson in the other vehicle? Would they get out of this alive? Feeling lightheaded, he realized he had eaten no dinner. The owl and his guts contrapuntal in the inky darkness.

Sometime past the middle of the night he heard two sets of footsteps. No talk. One set entered a vehicle, which started and headed around them into silence. The other opened the door and paused. He strained to hear music, a motor, anything to let him know he might make it through the night. All he heard distinctly were zips—perhaps the opening and closing of a flight bag. Perhaps.

Then the trunk opened and he heard a familiar voice. "Lord, what have we here? I swear, it looks like a body. Shoo. It doesn't smell like roses, either."

"Gloria?"

"Come out of there, handsome." Fine fingers undid his gag and loosened his shroud.

He wasn't sure he'd ever straighten up again. And, yes, now that he tried to unfold he knew he indeed had moved his bowels. If this were really Gloria, he might never be allowed to touch her again.

The hood came off. She wore an LED lamp on a headband, light from which bounced randomly off the round metal tubes of a guard rail. Her car was dark green, or maybe black. "Hello, Andy. Long night, huh?"

"Gloria, thank Jesus it's you. I didn't think . . . "

She held his chin and gave him a peck on the nose. "Don't think. It doesn't pay. Come out of there. You stink."

"I'm sorry. Couldn't help it." He stood, unsteady as a three-legged card table.

"Here," she said. "It's a change of clothes, some wet wipes, a hat, hiking shoes. Hurry. It'll be dawn soon. We need to be gone. I bet every cop in Christendom has an APB on you."

She shone her light on a guard rail. "Sit there. I'll be back in a minute."

He removed his tux and cleaned himself. The pile of clothes seemed if not to be his, at least his size. Soft cottons, flannels, nothing like his usual garb. He sat his butt on the rail—still a bit warm from the previous afternoon's heat—and put on socks, then stood and donned a pair of chinos.

She returned with a garbage bag. "Lay the nasty stuff in here, dear. We leave things as clean as we found them if not better."

A songbird began to trill. "We're within a half hour of sunup," she said. "Gray dawn. Birds wake to it."

"Where are we?" Michaux asked.

"On the Parkway. Specifically, the bridge over I-26."

Michaux's eyes grew as big as a lemur's. He knew he shouldn't look down, but instinct is powerful. He barely made out the outline of an interstate some two hundred feet below. When a transfer truck lit the highway his eyes immediately ordered his body to shut down. "Dear Lord," he said, and collapsed into Gloria's arms.

*****

He woke in the Subaru less than an hour later. Gloria drove on US 25-70, the new section of which locals called the "Ponder Parkway" after the Madison County political family, led by Zeno and E.Y. Ponder. Liston Ramsey, state senator of another generation, had ramrodded highway money to cause DOT to build an interstate-grade highway in the middle of nowhere. Michaux looked at Gloria. She chose not to glance his way, but smiled. "Where are we?" he asked. He felt in his pocket—no golf ball. Maybe it was in the garbage bag.

"Heading to Marshall. Then we're off to Hot Springs for a vacation, just me and you. And our bodyguard."

"Wait a minute, Gloria."

She looked at him and patted his thigh. "What, darling?"

"I can't take time off. I have work to do."

"Not even a week or two with Gloria?" she purred.

"People will miss me. I'm a politician, you know."

"We've thought of that. It's already out that you're hiking the Appalachian Trail, and I think since you don't have a wife people will believe it. Besides, this isn't South Carolina."

"What about that sleazeball John Edwards?"

"Ouch. Well, he might be a North Carolinian, but, dear, he is a Democrat."

"And what do you mean by 'we?' And what's this about a bodyguard?"

"Well, darling, there had to be more than just little old me to deal with your supercilious shadow, Bob. And somebody has to protect you from ravens and hounds and kidnappers."

"Isn't that what you did to me?"

"I'd call it removal of the senator for his own protection." She turned left off the bypass. "Hungry?"

"I'd eat the ass end of a ragdoll."

"They've probably got one at some little shop around here. But I was thinking of real breakfast."

"Sounds great. You say I might stay with you for a week or two?"

She rubbed his thigh vigorously. "With all manner of perks and privileges, Andy dear."

"Then I might like this situation. Say there's breakfast in Marshall?"

*****

Marshall, as locals said, was "a block wide, a mile long, sky high, and hell deep." (One suspects "block," a citified term.) The town, Michaux allowed, certainly had growth constraints—a long main street bounded on one side by the French Broad River and the other by a mountain.

Marshall was "coming back." Where it had been had to do with the bypass, which at first local businesses chose to ignore. But when they saw their livelihoods dissolve like salted slugs, they moved to the bypass or out of town entirely. Soon the bypass was crammed with tacky-built structures housing "tourist traps," gas stations, produce stands, and a couple of restaurants touting "home cooking." Except it never seemed anyone was home to cook.

Downtown Marshall, meantime, emptied. Municipal government even moved to an ex-grocery on the bypass, leaving the old courthouse empty save for one office, the duties of which included re-directing taxpayers and tourists to the bypass.

But lately the town had been discovered by the artsy set, and small businesses were moving back downtown. Gloria pulled into a parking space in front of a redbrick coffee house across the street from the nearly-vacant courthouse. "Here we are, dear," she said. "Let's eat."

They sat at a square butcher-block table in a spacious dining room, close to a large chrome catty-corner counter. Michaux scanned the menu for something familiar. "I don't see eggs and bacon," he said.

"Try the granola. It's the best anywhere."

"I've never eaten it."

She looked at him like he had just walked out of "Little Orphan Annie." "Try it. You'll like it."

He soon confronted a bowl of grains, nuts, dried fruit and, best he could tell, floor sweepings. He doused it with milk and took a bite. "Like munching rocks," he said.

"Eat your breakfast, Andy. I need a man with energy." She spread cream cheese on a bagel.

He ate. And found, to his surprise, it was good. He was about finished when a slump-shouldered, long-armed man entered the cafe and spotted Gloria.

Michaux watched him sidle up to her as if they knew each other from long ago and far away. An unfathomable easiness between them.

"Morning, Glory," the man said. He looked across the table to Michaux. "Mighty pleased to see you, Senator. You look right peart to have survived last night's fire." The last word rhymed with "car."

"Andy, meet Marshall Harris," said Gloria. "He'll be with us down the road."

The men shook hands. "You always eat that stuff?" Harris asked.

"Never had it before. But, you know, I kinda like it. Where are you from, Mr. Harris?"

"Call me Marshall, Senator. I'm from right down the road a piece." He looked at Gloria, then his watch. "Ain't we best be getting a move on?" She nodded. "We need provisions. Let's go."

The supermarket on the bypass—this would be the new grocery, across the road from the one which now held county offices—was one of the "super" stores, with a gas station adjacent. Before the town of Marshall passed beer sales, its beer and wine section had been forlorn, filled with both flavors of O'Doul's and sparkling grape juice, but now was quite respectable. They loaded up food and drink in cloth bags Gloria had fished from the Subaru. Harris, prone to motion sickness, scooted to the middle of the back seat to have a view of the road. "How do you like Madison, Senator?"

"Fine, Mr. . . . Marshall. It's beautiful country."

"It's pore as Job's turkey. Ain't but two ways to make decent money here."

"Which are . . . "

"Liquor and dope. You need either one, let me know."

Michaux was silent for the run by Walnut and through Hopewell and down the mountain to Hurricane, where they turned left and crossed the Laurel River. Harris pointed to a promotional sign for a development. "Just look at that, Senator," he said. "'Firefly Mountain.' Ain't that a crock of crap? Ain't nobody but Yankee California queer-baits calls a lightning bug a damn firefly."

Michaux, who knew the developer, offered no comment. At the gap Gloria pointed to a pedestrian overpass. "Andy, that's the trail you're walking this week. Just so you'll know."

As they headed down the mountain Michaux stomped the passenger side floorboard brakes. Harris grinned. "You should of seen this road before they built it. It was so twisty that if you got behind one of them Newport-bound tractor-trailers it'd have took you all morning to get to Hot Springs. Boy, I've puked many a time on that old bastard. This here ain't bad at all."

Just before the bridge over the French Broad they turned right and twisted by a large yellow house with a fine river rock porch. "Boy, that's a nice place," said Michaux.

"That house, Senator," said Harris, "was bought right out of a Sears, Roebuck catalog. They've took good care of it."

That was the last spectacular building Michaux noted. In front of one run-down house sat a rusted-out station wagon with "Jesus is Coming" crudely lettered on its side. This was, according to an equally unsophisticated sign, the Tongues of Fire Mission. Not Andy's idea of Jesus. Tourist cabins with empty driveways littered the roadside. Then the pavement ended.

"Where in the world are you taking me?" asked Michaux.

"A place where you can get away from it all," said Gloria.

The river lapped the roadside in places. "I suppose it floods often here," Michaux said.

"All the damn time," said Harris. "But where we're going's on high ground. If it floods there, you can expect old Noah to come by soon enough."

They passed a campground and kept going. "Senator, you like to fish?" asked Harris.

"Not much of a fisherman, I'm afraid."

"Too bad. There's a world of smallmouths in here."

"Here we are, boys," said Gloria, as she finally put the Subaru into an abbreviated driveway.

The house was, really, a shack, previously home to a bootlegger who ran two stills, one on the mountain behind and another on the island across the river. The house was old and gutterless and nearly devoid of paint but it had a long, narrow porch ten feet from the road and eighteen from the water. A man could throw a golf ball in the river with no effort at all.

"I think I'm going to like it here," said Michaux.

And he did. For a week he ate, drank, slept, and consorted with a willing and able Gloria. There was, really, nothing else to do. No television, no cell signal. They occasionally took walks and swatted away deer flies and no-see-ums. They played cards. Otherwise it was sit on the porch, listen to the music of the river, watch the tourists float by in rafts, kayaks, inner tubes.

Gloria delighted him and Harris kept a discreet distance. Life was very, very good.

After a week he had almost forgotten there was another world out there, one where surely someone had missed him. Representatives from that world floated by on the river or drove by, bound for Tennessee, just a mile down the road. But nothing motivated him to leave, not yet, anyway. He certainly had not had his fill of Gloria, who turned out to be as good a cook as lover. He even liked yogurt on his granola. For the first time in his adult life he was regular.

He loved watching the people on the river. They glided by mostly silently, except for college boys who thought it cool to have a boom box blaring while they towed a cooler in its own smaller raft. One afternoon a perfectly naked young woman lying in a yellow raft graced his vision. There were fishermen. And tourists in all shapes, sizes, ages, and colors. He'd not have been terribly surprised to see Huck and Jim heading to the Mississippi.

He learned the wildlife, too. Plenty of geese (which Harris called "flying possums") and ducks, solitary blue herons, buzzards, enough crows to populate a kingdom, kingfishers, hawks, doves, and a big crop of indigo buntings. Insects in the trees counterpointed the river's racket. He gave up trying to count the myriad species of butterflies.

One afternoon in the second week, when Gloria had taken a walk and Harris had gone to town for supplies, he lounged on the porch, more than half asleep. He was so still a blue-tailed skink ran under the chair to the other side of the porch. Suddenly Michaux realized the crows had quit gabbling. Like someone pressed a mute button. Michaux quickly felt about as alone as he had ever felt. And cold.

He looked around but saw nothing out of the ordinary around the cabin. A raft was parked upstream but that likely was a fisherman. As he leaned over to pick up Harris's binoculars something bounced off the tin roof. The noise was akin to a shotgun blast, and as Michaux hit the floor a golf ball landed in the narrow yard.

"What in hell?" he said. He trained the glasses on the river. When he found the anchored raft he saw looking back at him a large, horse-toothed man with binoculars. Beside him sat a beagle looking eager for dry ground and a chase.

He lowered the glasses. "I'm in a heap of shit," he muttered. Out of the corner of his eye he saw a dark shape light in a roadside catalpa. A large black bird, tail shaped like a wedge of pie, croaked three times in a hoarse, rusty voice. Michaux yelled "Gloria" with vigor and appreciable volume, but with little faith she would show up.

Yukon Gold Means Death!

by Fred Chappell

H arris was continually aggrieved. He considered that most folks, including especially his law enforcement superiors, including most particularly his immediate superior, J. D. Klontz, under-estimated his intellectual capacities. He phrased the thought in rather different terms:

"They think I got shit for brains, but they don't know shit."

He had been waiting for an opportunity to display his mental powers and now the moment had arrived. He had visited the scene of the murder and had got first look at the evidence. He had some knowledge of that evidence unknown to the other investigators because he had tasted the fatal potato. J. D. had raked him over for that, but Harris was used to J. D.'s insolence, understanding that it went along with the job. When they got an assistant deputy, Harris would give that old boy what-for too. Keep him on his toes. "It was a Yukon Gold," he said to himself. That would have meant little to J. D., who was not well versed in matters agricultural, but Harris knew it to be what they used to call a "Clue," though now he had to call it "forensic evidence."

He liked "Clue" better. His grades in his forensics classes had not been towering or easy to get and he was not real hot on Applied Logic either. But the content of those courses did not seem to matter too much with the crimes he was called to investigate, where one neighbor shot-gunned another for moving a fencepost three inches to the right or left of an imaginary boundary line, or where one granny woman accused another of stealing her eggs, or where in one memorable case a woman brought complaint against a Wise Woman for causing her cow to go dry.

Fu ny thing about that was that the Wise Woman fessed up and said she was proud of her arts and skills . . .

But if he wasn't keen on forensics and logic and rights of the accused, he was very good on armament. Harris was your true mountain son, sprung from Bloody Sodom, and ever and always a true denizen. Which meant he knew guns of every sort, knives of most sorts, and had a nodding acquaintance with swords. If he was a leetle mite ignorant of the epee, no one had noticed.

"Yukon Gold," he said again—and grinned.

Now if the vegetable had been a Red Bliss, he would have known to look for a male perpetrator. The Red Bliss is employed as a projectile with the "Little David" Stretchelacity Superband which was mounted on a molded titanium Y. This weapon was essentially a slingshot and it re-quired some strength of bicep and forearm to be useful. That let out most of the women Harris knew about, but of course there are always excep-tions.

Russian Banana Fingerling: this potato was favored by women because of its light weight. The male of the species fired the Fingerling in clips of eight or twelve from the Spudsender RX13, but the female of the species was likely to load it into a Colt 0070 "Frybaby," a sidearm convenient for large handbags. It accommodated a revolver cylinder holding six or an automatic clip holding four. Victims of the Frybaby were often impatient young men who suffered groin bruises.

Red Dawn Sweet Potato: fired by Yam-Wham, a light rifle. Rarely if ever used as offensive or defensive weapon. Mostly a ceremonial piece, usually brought out at Thanksgiving.

Idaho Baking Potato: this was the big mother, heavy duty, heavy weight, and heavy damage. Used mostly as an artillery piece, it was com-parable in some respects to a Rocket Propelled Grenade Launcher—which meant that the missile itself had to have an explosive insert. This weapon was manufactured by the Mauser Kartoffelmutter. If this had been the killer's weapon of choice, the victim might have died from bruises without the necessity of a fall from the height. And the noise would have been heard as far as Haywood County.

"But what we got here," he mumbled, "is a good ole Yukon Gold, ammo for your Spudstriker Model 31AB." The Spudstriker was fairly lightweight but well balanced, steady in the hand, accurate, and sported a classy overall design that matched many a female wardrobe.

"So also what we got is a woman murderer and I bet J. D. ain't thought of that yet, wherever he is. He was supposed to call from the hospital but he forgot. Or something. Maybe he got it on with that woman, he's been lonesome so long." He sniggered just a little bit.

Now what kind of woman would use the Spudstriker?

Well, somebody who knew the victim's habits. Because you don't just drive along the road and see a guy standing on a guard rail and say, I think I'll shoot that bird off his perch. You have to watch him and figure beforehand that he did crazy stunts like that pretty often. The reason he did was not important right now, but the fact that the girl knew he did was important.

Why girl? Why not an older woman?

Because the older woman in these counties did not go about peppering potatoes at peculiar people. They had .38s, .44s, .30-.30s, and twelve gauges a-plenty and if they got angry enough to shoot, they wanted to see some blood. That made it seem more worthwhile.

So: we got the girl tracking the guy for some time, getting to know his days and ways. We got a girl who can shoot a Spudstriker with accuracy—which is a little harder than puncturing a tin can with a .22. We got a girl who planned it all out, maybe long before.

So, we got motives: 1. revenge or 2. money. If 2., she was paid to do it. You can't rob a corpse you've shot off the side of a mountain. If 1., *He was her man but he was doin' her wrong.*

Harris was pleased with himself. Hummed a few bars: *Rooty-toot-toot she did shoot Right through that hotel door He was her man But he was doin' her wrong . . .* This detective stuff ain't all that hard, he thought. Easy as finding your ass with your hand in your hip pocket.

*****

96

J. D. Klontz had spent some part of the weekend studying the card that Garnell had received in the hospital. It was mostly ordinary, the firm's logo spelled out in an old-fashioned, slender script and decorated with a half-tint of a Rosebud orchid native to these parts. Quite attractive.

The message was in purplish ballpoint, a blocky handwriting of distinctly masculine cast. The phrase "back in the game" was puzzling. *In the game* was an out-of-date term for prostitution and he knew that Garnell did not fit into that bracket, though she was plenty tough. So tough she would not compromise with circumstance anymore.

Those were his impressions, anyhow.

Monday morning brought him to Florally Yours which, surprisingly, was located on Main Street in West Jefferson. That was way out of the way, but his job was to follow leads. He might have sent Harris to inquire, but then the picture of the deputy trying to formulate sensible questions and following them up with more made him decide to let the man sleep in—or keep on doing whatever he was doing, wherever he was.

So at 11:06 a.m. he entered Florally Yours, accompanied by the friendly jingle of the bell at the door. It was more than a florist's shop, for there were all sorts of other things for sale: vases, glass baskets, statuettes, dried flowers, pet toys, greeting cards, and so forth. He walked to the counter that ran across the back of the store and waited. In a moment a woman entered through a curtained archway.

"Yes sir?"

He produced his credentials and she gave them a curious examination. "I need to inquire about the sender of this card." He passed it to her.

She took it, looked, and passed it back. "Yes?"

"Do you recall who bought the flowers and sent the card with them?"

"Yes, Mr. Klontz. His name was Black. I think Max was his first name, but I'm not sure. I can look that up."

"How did he pay?"

"He paid cash and asked for a receipt. That's how I can look him up. Not many people do that anymore and I had to find this little old receipt pad and write him out one." She searched in a drawer behind her and produced it. "Doesn't that take you back to days of yore?" She handed it across the glass counter that displayed little crystal and china knickknacks of all species.

"Did he write the message himself or did you write it for him?"

"He wrote it with this pen here," she said.

"I'll need to take this from you," he said. "My office will reimburse you, of course."

"Don't worry about it," she said. "I've been trying to sell these purple pens for two years now and nobody wants them." She shook her head in mild despair. "I don't know what he wrote, though. I tried to sell him some of our special greeting cards that my son Jezmund writes for me, but he was not interested."

He judged her to be in her early sixties: petite, hair gray to silver-gray and bunned. She wore a gray, light woolen dress neck-high with a narrow lace collar and a strand of modest pearls below the collar.

"I think this particular gent would want to send a personal message," J. D. said. "I don't think he's the poetic type."

"Not many people are." She sighed. "But I think they would like the sentiments if they would just give the cards a chance. Look at this one. Jezmund designed and wrote it." She picked it up with loving fingers.

J. D. read it aloud: *"How much we miss you, Dad, And the good old times we had. But now you're dead and gone, And I've got to say we're sad. But if you're near or far, We love you wherever you are."* The card was illustrated with an ink sketch of a skull and a gravestone. "Very nice," J. D. said.

"It's honest, isn't it? Not too flowery and made-up-sounding."

"Straight from the heart."

"Here's another one. This is for the loss of a mother." She read in a clear but emotional voice, her engagement with the lines evident: *"O Mom you were our Spring and our high Summer. Now you are gone and life is a Bummer."* She laid it on the counter and reached for another. "This is for a little girl whose older brother died. *"You're sad because your brother died. O how you cried and cried and cried. No more ever will he be there, To break your dolls and pull your hair. We all know how hard it is, But let's do try to buck up, Sis."* She dabbed at her eyes with her wrist. "Excuse me. I get a little wrought up."

"That's okay. They're real affecting," J. D. said.

"Of course, they're not all sad. People send flowers for many different occasions. With the troop draw-down, we get some requests for coming-home displays and messages." She flipped through a little box of 3X5s.

"Here's one: *It's good you're back, With your wife and kids, And not overseas, All blown to bits.*"

"I like that one the best," said J. D. "If you don't mind, I'd like to ask you a little about the fellow that sent the flowers. Did you recognize him? Is he from around here?"

"I recognized him because he's been in before, but I'm pretty sure he's not from around here. I'd guess he comes from up north or maybe out Midwest. Chicago, maybe."

"Why do you say that?"

"I don't know. The way he acts, real bossy, like he owns your soul because he's spending a few dollars at your business establishment . . . I'm not making myself clear, am I?"

"You're doing very well. What did he look like? Did you see what he was driving?"

"He's come in before and sent flowers and one time I saw the message he wrote: RECALLED TO LIFE. I have no idea what that was about. But he doesn't think about it; he just writes it down."

"So he's thought it out beforehand," J. D. said.

"He looks like a man who would be named Max Black, if you know what I mean. Swarthy complexion, small, dark eyes, always looking side to side like he's trying to see around corners. Heavy shoulders, bull neck, shortish. You'd expect him to be wearing a cheap suit, but this was real tailoring, I can tell. I can't place his accent, but it is definitely not mountain. I didn't see what he was driving."

"How many times would you say he's been in?"

"Six or seven, anyhow."

"Always sends flowers? With a message?"

"Yes."

"Is he particular about what kind of flowers?"

"He always asks which ones are in season. I go through the list and he picks out one or two, sometimes three, for the arrangement. Never more than three . . . An odd thing. He asked if we had any pussytoes in stock. Of course, I said no. Those only grow wild and they're not much to look at. He seemed to think the name was funny. 'She'd like pussytoes,' he told me. We wound up with a lily-and-rose combo. Very nice, very dignified, but cheerful too—just what you'd want for someone in a hospital. Do you know who the lady is?"

"I know a little about her and I need to find out a lot more. She's from over in Avery County, I believe. It's a complicated business."

"Police work must be fascinating."

"If I could grow and sell flowers, I'd give it up in a minute. You see too much in this trade."

"You see a lot selling flowers, too," she said. "I've seen brothers and sisters squabble over pennies in funeral home florals for their parents. Right in front of me."

"Hard times."

"No. They were cheapskates or they just couldn't get along and had to argue about everything."

"What else can you tell me about Mr. Black?"

"He said he worked for a removal agency. When I said, 'What do you remove, spots?' he said, 'We transfer personnel from one place to another.' I said, 'A lot of people who leave the mountains get lonesome for them and want to come back. Do you get a lot of repeat customers?' And he said, 'No, when we remove them they stay put.'"

"He actually said that?"

"I said, 'There must be a lot of paperwork' and he said, 'Not on our part. Others take care of all that.'"

"That sounds kind of suspicious, doesn't it, Pearl?"

"It sounds kind of creepy, if you ask me. How did you know my name was Pearl?"

"It suits you—and you're wearing pearls. And I looked you up in the directories. I am a detective. What else can you tell me?"

"It seems like there is a lot more, but I can't put my tongue to it right this minute. I will say that I don't like this Black person. He makes me feel odd, the way he looks at me like he's measuring my height or weight."

"Like for a coffin?"

"Is that the case?"

"*Personnel removal?* Suggests something to me, but he may just have been kidding around."

She gave him a mild, prolonged stare. "I'm just real sure he doesn't kid much."

"You've been extremely helpful," J. D. said. "Here's my card. If you think of something else that might be important, give me a call any time of day or night. Do you mind if I take a few of these condolence cards by Jezmond? I might be able to recommend some people to Florally Yours."

She read the card he had given her. "J. D . . . Are you any kin to the Klontzes over at Frog Level? I used to know a Ralph."

"I'm not from around here originally. You already knew that from my accent."

"People change," she said. "I'm proud to help any way I can. And thank you for taking an interest in Jezmund's work."

12:17 and the sunlight was bright but not too hot and he decided to get a bite to eat up the street at Frazier's. He trudged along, hoping that a slow pace would allow him time to think. Coffee would do him good, he thought. Then he thought, but a beer would do me better.

The nice server with a blonde page boy cut brought him his Highland Gaelic and he said "Thanks" and she said, "No problem, honey," and he tried to think about what he had learned—if he had learned anything.

A first question was why Mr. Black (or whatever his real name was) would come all the way out to Ashe County to choose a florist. Hardly a hamlet so small in the hills here that a florist wouldn't find a niche. And the idea wouldn't be to try to throw an investigation off the track; Florally Yours was easily found; the business was not trying to hide.

Convenience, he thought. If that were the case, then The Black Operation (as he would tag it) was located nearby. Or maybe it was spread out, with several locations, and West Jefferson was near to one of them. Whatever kind of enterprise it was, The Black Operation was limited in scope; a large-scale operation would require a sizable corps, difficult to keep secret. But if the functions were split up—extortion here, land fraud there, bootlegging over yonder, murder just around the corner—each part of it, each cell as you might call it, could be kept small and efficient and the number of employees would be unobtrusive. Not a bad concept, except that kind of organization would need a dependable but invisible communications network.

He would quiz his friends in the Tech Dept about that stuff.

And what was this business of sending cards? "Back in the game." "Recalled to life." The first seemed a greeting to someone who had been ill—or incarcerated. The second seemed vaguely threatening—also slightly familiar, though he knew he'd never he able to place where he had come across it.

He reached into his shirt pocket and took out one of Jezmund's efforts. This one was a condolence for a woman whose husband had deserted her: *Now he's left you, And it's so sad, But you'll get another, Three times as bad.*

Some truth in that, J. D. thought, but he didn't see how the sentiment would condole anybody.

But why flowers in the first place? If Mr. Black had been sending out large arrangements with different kinds of bloom, there might be something to look into. Back in Buffalo, there had been a funeral parlor that relayed messages at wakes by means of a flower code. If the gatherings had included Virgin's Bower and a couple of tea roses and Fringed Orchid, it was a signal that plainclothes cops were in the group of mourners. If irises and lilies and violets were on display, it meant that the widow of the deceased had better receive a memorial donation of some heft or the missing names would be noted and their owners visited by a squad of muscular *paesani* who possessed a more than usual respect for the dead. If there was a great spray of mock orange in the foyer, it intimated that the false bottom of the coffin concealed cocaine by the kilo. Fiori by Gino stocked a whole vocabulary of such *ostentazioni* and the neighborhood kept abreast of it.

The whole thing was a tangle, a puzzle, a maze, and a vexation. Maybe, J. D. thought, I should just give up on this part of the investigation and let Harris handle it.

The thought made him chuckle into his Cobb salad and he checked his iPhone for messages, though Harris had never sent him one. He wasn't sure that good ole boy knew how to use the thing.

His server returned. "Detective Klontz?"

"'Fraid so."

She handed him a small envelope. "Somebody just left this for you at the cashier."

"Who was it?"

"She didn't know. If she'd known who he was, she would've told me. I hope it's nothing bad."

The only writing was his initials, **J. D. K.**, in a blocky style almost like printing. The purple ink he recognized as Florally Yours ballpoint. He opened the envelope to find an ancient, crumbling newspaper photograph of a man and a woman, recognizable Appalachian types of an earlier period, their faces strained with harsh work and harsher religion. You'd know them a mile and a generation away. In fact, they looked very familiar indeed, though he couldn't place where he had seen them. The problem was that the pictures were so old and faded and grainy. He had to peer closely to make out individual features, but when he pulled his head back, the faces came together.

The card sported the Florally Yours logo and a message: RECALLED TO LIFE.

He rose and laid down some paper money and rushed out onto the sidewalk. Nothing here out of the ordinary—no one slithering away furtively or sitting hunched down in a parked car, just local types doing local-type things.

He trotted to the floral shop and pushed inside. Pearl did not answer when he rang the bell on her counter. His senses told him the place was empty, but he called her name five times. "Pearl. Pearl MacReady. Pearl."

He went behind the counter, then all through the place. Deserted. The cash drawer was closed and when he opened it bills and change were still there. Nothing had been disturbed. And nothing in the building moved: dead silence.

He sighed. He would have to be here for a while, keeping the store secure and working with the West Jefferson constabulary when they arrived, putting out alerts and bulletins, immersed in all the routine details that sprouted from a single incident like toadstools from fallen timber.

He sat in a straight chair behind the counter and put the firm's telephone and his own to use. As he talked to the police chief and several of his staff and the fire department and the hospital staff, he pulled out the photograph again. There was a thin brown smudge across the face of the male and it cleared mostly away when he rubbed it.

Then he saw a ray of light. Actually, he saw two Rays, Lawson and Jean, murder victims of a generation past and gone, the parents of Garnell.

It made no sense. These people were not going to be "recalled to life." Perhaps the meaning was not literal. Perhaps they were to return as figures from the past that pointed to a direction he was searching for.

I need to know more, he thought. Hell, I need to know everything.

*****

"Girl, where you been keepin'?"

"To tell the truth," Penny Bright said, "I haven't been keeping. Lately I've just been ducking."

"Run of bad luck?"

"There have been some good things. One was, I broke up with my boyfriend."

"That Loftin dude? I warned you about him."

"No, the one after. Josh Hanley was his name. Maybe. Anyhow, that was what he wrote on the checks he kited."

"Well, it's good to see you anyway. You're lookin' good. You're always lookin' good."

"You're sweet, Lakeesha. You'll never change. It does me good to see you, all dressed up to do business. Smart-looking!"

"Now it's you that's being sweet, Penny. I have to dress like this for the Grove Park desk job, but I plan on stepping up from that slot pretty fast. I get good reports and my grades from my school classes were pretty solid."

"After you got out of Dance, you mean?"

Lakeesha grinned, showing her beautiful teeth. "I guess I just don't have that natural rhythm. I'm a disgrace to my DNA. You were always the dancer. The instructors made us watch you work out. I was a little jealous. But once I entered into business I got over it because this is what I really like."

"Let's have another coffee," Penny said. They were sitting in the small bar in the east wing of Grove Park Inn, going over old times. Sometimes they giggled and sometimes they sniffled. They had been very close at UNCA, rooming together until Penny moved out to be with a guy, Buddy Whazzisface, whom Lakeesha had detested from Day One.

"Not for me. I have to stand behind the desk and they don't give me all that many breaks . . . So what are you up to these days?"

"Still dancin'."

"*Really?* Not many get to do that. What troupe are you with?"

"I hope to be with my own. That's why I got in touch with you. I want to tell you about our idea and then you can decide whether you'd be willing to help me out a little."

"Penny, honey, if I found two dimes in my purse, I'd know I picked up somebody else's."

"No, not money. Let me tell you. We were watching TV and this reality ghost program came on and we came up with an idea—"

"We who?"

"That's my boyfriend, Leroy Leonard. You'd like him, I think."

No I wouldn't, Lakeesha thought. This world would be a happier place if every Leroy was wiped off its face.

"Anyhow, we got to thinking how many places have famous ghosts and how these turn into tourist attractions. But a lot of people are disappointed because the ghosts are not interesting or don't even show up at all. So we thought, Why don't I become a ghost? I've had drama training and voice lessons and dance. I could play the parts of ghosts in places that are supposed to be haunted and they could pay me scale at least."

"I don't know," Lakeesha mused. "Did you think of this idea or did Leroy?"

"I did."

"Then it might work. It's not as weird as it sounds at first. Well, it is weird, but it's supposed to be."

"I just knew you'd see the possibilities. You have a head for business. Would you be willing to help us out?"

"How?"

"Well, here at the Inn the famous ghost is the Pink Lady. You know, the one who fell in the Palmetto Room? Back in the 20s? We looked her up. I am real sure I could play her."

Lakeesha considered. She wanted to help Penny, but she would be taking a risk. If something misfired and she was known to be involved, they might just flat sack her. On the other hand, if it worked out well, she could claim some part of the credit—and she did want to help Penny. She owed her a couple from time long back.

"How would it work?"

"The Pink Lady Room is on the top floor and there's a big balcony there. I would not even have to be seen, or hardly. I could wear long pinkish veils and stuff and float about and sing in my ghost voice. That's all it would take for the illusions. It shouldn't last longer than three or four minutes."

"What would you sing?"

"I'll show you. Let's go to the little girls' room."

Lakeesha checked the time on her iPhone. "I have to be on in ten minutes," she said. "Time enough?"

"Oh, yes."

In fact, it took less. The restroom had a high ceiling at one end and different wall surfaces that helped to make Penny's low warble spooky. It seemed effective to Lakeesha.

Boone River

Wilder than a loon

My huckleberry spoon

Of clay

Saltshaker

Ole Spudstriker

Wherever you're flowing

You're going astray . . .

"I'll get the words right in performance."

"You better," Lakeesha said, "because I have just the setup you want."

*****

It was cooler out here than Penny had counted on. There was a fine, soft breeze and the pines moved against the stars in wonderfully picturesque fashion. From below drifted the sounds of music and diners chatting and chaffing and dancing.

Romantic, Penny thought. When Leroy and I put a little money aside, we'll have romantic evenings under the stars, sipping the bubbly, and I'll teach him how to tango.

She had expansive plans. North Carolina had plenty of ghost houses; there were books full of them. Once she had established herself as a ghost figure, she could go from one to another, from Murphy to Manteo, a tourist attraction all by herself. And if the enterprise were successful, she could put together a franchise. She knew other dancers who would be glad for the work. Oodles of them. And she could make and sell her own videos and CDs. All she needed was a foothold.

She had already chosen her stage name. Her real name was horrible. Penny Bright. It sounded like a program on the Disney channel. But a classy French-type name ought to provide atmosphere. Sofie La Sylphie. She could go a long way with that.

And if she could impress this Senator Rightwang, as Lakeesha called him, there would be free publicity wherever he went. But she had to keep her mind on her work. She had always had trouble remembering the lyrics to songs.

She practiced a few steps, pirouettes and light leaps, and swirled her pinkish veils all about her. Not bad, well, not too bad. She had gained a few pounds these last years, not being able to dance regularly, and it had taken her three times as long as formerly to warm up. But it wasn't like she was doing *Swan Lake*. She only needed to fan about a little, make ghostly music and remain unrecognized in order not to endanger Lakeesha's record.

It had taken her awhile to decide on repertoire. Ghostly tunes were not all that common. "Ghost Riders in the Sky" didn't seem to fit. "Oh how the ghost of you clings" from "These Foolish Things" was nice, but it was only one line. "The ghost of a chance with you" was a phrase she remembered, but she couldn't recall where it occurred.

Finally, in desperation, she turned to opera and settled upon "In questa reggia" from *Turandot* in which the princess recounts how the rape of her ancestress Princess Lo-u-Ling made her resolved to test her suitors with riddles, placing their lives at stake. She recognized that she was no Fleming or von Stade or Netrebko, but all she needed was something spooky and her rendition of the Puccini aria was bound to be spooky. It scared her to sing it; it would scare the people who heard it—all twenty-plus seconds she was going to allow to be heard, anyhow.

It should have worked out. Rightwang—that is, Michaux—showed up on schedule, came into the room and ventured out on the balcony. She kept herself well within the shadows there. She had to wait until he went back inside his room to sing; she was too exposed with him out there. In a short while, he returned to the room, then went out again. When he came back from wherever, he was carrying a can of root beer. He sat down at the desk before the mirror and began writing in a little notebook. Good, she thought. He was concentrating on his work.

Penny sang softly and slowly and with tenebrous timbre: "In questa reggia Tallahatchie Bridge." Oh no.

She tried again. "When Bobby Bean McGooberty pissed off the Waxahatchee Bridge . . ." No, no, no. That was the song she'd warmed her voice with earlier and now she couldn't get it out of her head.

She gave it one last try. "When Guacamole Gottapee walked off the Circumstantial Ledge . . . "

She almost sobbed. She had ruined everything. With the words gone all silly, her veiled, spectral appearance could have no impact. She'd just look goofy; she would look the way she felt.

But when she sneaked around to the window and peeked inside, she saw that Rotwhang was crying, weeping hot tears and guzzling root beer, as if to drown whatever sorrows her singing had conjured up.

Was I that bad? She thought. Or was I that good?

She changed her mind. The ghost-performance was a good idea. Look at the effect it had produced. *Franchise, here we come.*

Then somebody from security had shown up and closed the curtain.

After a while the room went dark and Penny pushed back the glass door and entered. She used the bathroom to change, stuffing her pink veils into a paper grocery bag, making up her face in one of the over-large mirrors with all the lights. Once again she thought, When Leroy and I get a little money put by . . .

Downstairs she did not approach the desk to speak to Lakeesha. Too risky, of course. But she did slip her a thunderous, conspiratorial wink and blew her a sisterly kiss. Lakeesha kept her eyes on her work at the desk, but Penny knew her friend had seen her.

She found her old Honda not in the parking lot but on the roadside farther up the mountain where she had left it as a precaution. She started it up and began taking the hairpin turns that would bring her down to Charlotte Street. She was happy and began to hum and then to sing. "In questa reggia...' O for God's sake. She did remember the words. *Now.*

She had got about a quarter of the way down when something small, white, and bouncy bobbed across the road in front of her. At first she couldn't think what it might be, then realized it was a golf ball. It had come out of the undergrowth on the left-hand side of the road. How was that possible? The course was way over yonder to her right.

Mystification had slowed her car to a crawl.

Then out of the same patch of underbrush dashed a dog, a beagle, making as much speed as his stubby little legs afforded him. He darted off the roadside into the same declivity the ball had taken. Was he in pursuit?

Then out of a persimmon tree on that side swooped a huge crow and it swept across into the same patch of darkness. Once more, she was not certain what she had seen. She stopped the car dead and put on her warning lights.

And then appeared two men. One she recognized as a security guard for the Inn; the other she recognized as personal security for Senator Rightwarp. He had been arranging things in the room before the senator arrived.

The pair of them were brandishing golf clubs and shouting unintelligible words. They were clearly upset with that crow. Or beagle. Or golf ball.

The Silence of the Llamas

by Alan Gratz

Garnell pushed a pea off her mountain of mashed potatoes, watching it tumble into the river of gravy below. Just like Richard Sweatt had fallen to his death from the Beacon Heights overlook on the Blue Ridge Parkway. Only it wasn't a mountain of potatoes that had done him in.

Just the one had been enough.

Garnell smiled at the thought. She had finally killed the third man who'd been responsible for her parents' deaths. The first man, Peter Paul, there had been no art to that murder. She had caught him on the way home from one of those bogus shareholders' meetings and stumbled through a hurried, confused explanation of why he deserved to die before gunning him down. She'd been so close she'd even gotten his blood all over her. Remembering it now, she couldn't believe she hadn't been caught—but when the police started looking into Peter Paul's finances and found out he'd been selling shares of a residential-retail mountain community that didn't exist, they'd had other suspects aplenty.

If Garnell had it to do all over again, she'd do something more creative with Peter Paul. More fitting.

Maybe something biblical. Like locusts.

She'd dropped a chestnut oak on James Woody, the unscrupulous lawyer who'd made a fortune off of buying up cheap mountain land he knew was destined for gated community development, and she'd put a spud in the back of Richard Sweatt, the couch potato real estate agent who'd been trying to get her parents to sell their mountaintop property to him for years.

Three down, one to go. But here she sat at a kitchen table in a safe house recuperating from a gunshot wound in the town formerly known as Sodom, pushing peas around on her plate.

"Eat your victuals," Granny told her. "You're healing up. Your body needs to get strong."

Granny. That was the latest kicker. Everybody called the old woman "Granny," even folks not related to her, but if the pictures in the hallway didn't lie, she really was Garnell's granny. Which made her some kind of relation to Marshall Harris, The Agency man who'd brought her here to lay low and recuperate. And the picture of Marshall in the hall as a boy—why did she remember that young face?

"Granny, I'm dying here. I've got to get back in the game," Garnell told her.

"Now, now. You know what they say: patience is a virgin."

Garnell opened her mouth to correct her, but thought it kind of worked anyway and let it be.

"Granny . . . how long have you worked for The Agency?"

"Oh, let's see," she said, mopping up her gravy with a roll. "Must be going on forty years now. Started up in 1972 as I recall. I was one of the first. Back then it was just make-up and skin care, of course, not all this other nonsense we sell now, too—perfumes and butt-tox injections and whatnot."

Garnell choked on her sweet tea. "Butt . . . *what?*"

"Butt-tox injections, you know, for the wrinkles? Mary Kay sells so many different things now I can't hardly keep track of it all."

Garnell stared across the table at the woman she had just learned was her grandmother.

"Granny, are you talking about the Mary Kay *Cosmetics* Agency?"

"Of course, darling. What other agency would I be talking about?"

"The . . . covert eco-terrorist agency that pays me and Marshall to take out people for crimes against nature?"

"Lord have mercy, child. No. Where did you get such a notion?"

Granny stood and cleared their plates.

"So, wait," Garnell said. "Just to be clear here: this *isn't* a safe-house for a super-secret assassination agency?"

"No, no. Now, if you want to see a good mystery, my program ought to be on."

Granny went into the living room and turned on the television. Garnell followed her in a haze. No Agency? No safe-houses or secret agents or coded messages? But there had to be. She'd seen it all.

"Granny, when I got here, you told me Marshall worked for The Agency."

"Well, not Mary Kay, of course. The other agency."

Garnell sighed. Okay. It was all just a misunderstanding. Granny didn't work for The Agency, Marshall did.

"The *law enforcement* agency, of course," Granny said. "The pigs. The fuzz. The Man. The po-lice. Here now, I can't see these tiny numbers. Find the station with Matlock on it, will you?"

Garnell took the remote as slow and careful as a driver with New Jersey plates coming down Grandfather Mountain. Granny worked for the Mary Kay Cosmetics agency. Marshall worked for the law enforcement agency. But neither of them worked for The Agency. The one she thought she'd been working for for the past three years. But if there wasn't an Agency, who'd been paying her big money to kill people? Why the elaborate lie?

And who had shot her?

The Asheville evening news was on the television, and Garnell tuned in when she heard a name carved into the picnic table of her consciousness.

"At this hour, Asheville police still have no leads in the disappearance of State Senator Andy Michaux."

Michaux was the last of the four men alive who had conspired to kill Garnell's parents. She sat forward and listened.

"The state senator from Mitchell County was last seen with this woman, whom authorities have identified as Gloria Gudger, of Blowing Rock."

Garnell dropped the remote control. The woman staring back at her on the screen was her Aunt Gloria.

What. The. Hell?

"Chairman of the North Carolina state Republican party Bob Snide-son assured reporters once again that state senator Michaux is hiking the Appalachian Trail, though Democratic chairman Rob Bentchild was quick to point out that the state senator's mysterious disappearance comes on the heels of what the national media is now calling the Asheville To-bacco Riot. For more on missing politicians purporting to be hiking the Appalachian Trail, we're joined now by former South Carolina governor Mark Sanford . . ."

"Granny, I need a car," Garnell said.

"Now sweetheart, you don't need to go exasperating that gunshot of yours. I'm sure whatever it is needs doing can wait."

Garnell stood. "Granny. Please. I have to go. It's important."

"Well now, if you're all fired up to go, there's nothing I can do to stop you. Keys to the car are in the bowl on top of the TV."

"Thank you, Granny. Thank you thank you thank you," Garnell said, snatching them up. If her Aunt Gloria was hiding out with Andy Mich-aux, she had an idea where they might be—that little cabin down past Hot Springs on the French Broad where they had always gotten together for family reunions when her parents had been alive.

Garnell did a mental inventory of everything in her backpack and real-ized there was one vital piece missing.

"Granny, do you own a gun?"

"A gun? Oh, heavens, no, child."

"Do you know where I can buy one?"

"Oh. Well, no place left but the Wal-Mart."

Garnell felt her skin crawl. As a dutiful Defender of All Things Good and Local, she had sworn off shopping at Wal-Mart since 1992.

"Nowhere else?"

"Can't think of none."

Garnell cast around the room, looking for anything else she could use. She wanted more time to plan things out, to make sure Michaux got exactly the right justice coming to him—something French? With a ba-guette?—but she'd also learned not to look a gift horse in the mouth.

Or a gift llama, she thought. She picked up a poncho draped over the back of a chair and rubbed it in her fingers.

"Granny, is this llama fleece?"

113

"I—I expect so," Granny said, confused. "My great niece Eustacia made that for me. They've got a llama farm up in Big Laurel, where they—"

"Thank you, Granny!" Garnell ran from the room with the keys and the poncho, then remembered something and ran back. "Granny, if anybody asks you if I asked you about whether you had a gun or not, tell them I didn't ask you anything like that, okay?"

Granny frowned. "Ask me *what?*"

Garnell gave Granny a peck on the cheek. "Just like that. Thanks! You're the greatest."

Garnell hurried down the hall to the front door. Killers three and four, taken care of in one week? She still had questions for Marshall, and Gloria, and Mr. Black, her "Agency" contact, if she ever saw him again, but none of that mattered right now. All that mattered was that she stayed unnoticed and inconspicuous until she could get to her aunt's place down by the river.

Garnell threw the door open and froze.

Granny's car was a bright pink 2010 Cadillac.

*****

In Buffalo, New York, they snow-plowed one side of the street on Mondays, Wednesdays, and Fridays, and the other side of the street on Tuesdays, Thursdays, and Saturdays. If you left your car on the wrong side of the street, they didn't tow it. They just buried it. And if you left your car there all week, they would keep burying it. Snow plow after snow plow after snow plow would heap mounds of dirty brown snow onto your car so that by week's end you wouldn't even know a car was there. All you'd see was an enormous mountain of snow like the ones they pushed together in the middle of parking lots, and you wouldn't see your car again until the spring thaw. Which in Buffalo was sometime around July.

J.D. Klontz felt like that now. Like a car that had been buried, and buried again, and buried again. This case just kept piling it on him, and if he wasn't careful he was going to be snowed in until next summer.

In short, it was time to dig himself out.

Fact: Richard Sweatt had taken a swan dive off the Beacon Heights overlook, leaving nothing but his very expensive Lexus and a few pieces of raw potato.

Fact: Garnell Lee Ray had been shot through the shoulder at the Linville Falls Campground by an unknown assailant, and had been found in a Porta-Potty trying to self-medicate with duct-tape and a binder clip.

Fact: Garnell Lee Ray had later bailed from the hospital before she was discharged, leaving behind nothing but a burned up old Toyota pickup truck and a note that said, "Heal quickly. We need you back in the game."

Fact: Richard Sweatt had once been in business with Garnell Lee Ray's parents, Jean and Lawson Ray.

Fact: Jean and Lawson Ray had been gunned down execution-style in their expensive Yancey County home seven years ago.

All those facts, when put together, added up to one hell of a coincidence—and if J.D. Klontz had learned nothing else from years and years of *Columbo* reruns, it was that there was no such thing as a coincidence. Garnell Lee Ray and Richard Sweatt were connected somehow, he knew it.

That little coincidence turned up another: James Woody, the real estate lawyer who'd worked with both Richard Sweatt and Jean and Lawson Ray just happened to have shuffled off this mortal coil when an oak tree had fallen on him at a railroad crossing in Buncombe County earlier this year.

J.D. was beginning to see the gravity of the situation.

Heh. Gravity. He chuckled at his own little joke as he came down I-26 toward downtown Asheville. *Tree dropped on you—that's sure some way to leaf.* Leave? No, leaf worked, if you said it right. He chuckled again at his own wit. Why wasn't anybody ever with him when he thought of good ones? He thought about calling dispatch just to use them, then thought better of it. Nobody back at the station would get it anyway.

One coincidence had led to a second coincidence had led to a third coincidence: the Rays and Richard Sweatt and James Woody had all once been in business with a man who was now a state senator from Mitchell County, Andy Michaux. And Andy Michaux . . . well, anybody with a television set knew State Senator Andy Michaux had set the Grove Park Inn on fire and then taken a hike.

Garnell Lee Ray was connected to Sweatt, who was connected to Michaux, who had just gone M.I.A. It didn't take Lt. Columbo to figure out Garnell was mixed up in all this somehow, either as a target like the others, or as the one doing the targeting. But Garnell Lee Ray had checked herself out of Gannon Memorial Hospital, and then from the Linville Falls Campground, and J.D. had lost the scent. He had an All-Points Bulletin out for her, but so far there hadn't been a hint of her. Her six degrees of separation with the state senator was all he had left.

That tree's bark was worse than its bite, J.D. thought.

No, the leaf one was better.

J.D. worked his way downtown, pausing at a light straight across from the Asheville Civic Center so a man and his llama could cross the street in front of him.

A man and his *llama?*

J.D. turned off his auto-pilot and really looked around for the first time. There were llamas everywhere. Coming and going from the convention center, walking up and down the sidewalk, sitting on benches and parked cars. In the little park at the end of Broadway, hippies and llamas danced in a drum circle. There was even a llama standing with a tip bag tied around its neck while its owner played a guitar outside Malaprop's Bookstore.

A passing llama turned and spit on J.D.'s unmarked police car.

"Hey!" J.D. said out the window.

"Sorry!" said the llama's handler. "You must be a cop, right? Lorenzo hates authority figures."

Lorenzo Llama, J.D. figured. Forget the Keep Asheville Weird bumper stickers. Asheville was weird enough as is.

J.D. finally made his way to the Asheville Police Department headquarters and went inside. He told the officer at the front desk he had radioed ahead, and she had him take a seat until Detective Milo MacGuffin met him in the lobby.

"Sorry to keep you waiting," MacGuffin said when he eventually appeared. He was at least a foot shorter than J.D. and trending toward portly, with a thick, bushy moustache and a ketchup stain on his tie. He offered J.D. his hand. "It's Detective Klontz, isn't it?"

"Yeah. Sorry. I had no idea the circus was in town."

"This is Asheville. The circus is always in town," MacGuffin said. "But it's worse this weekend: it's the annual Llama Lovers convention."

"You don't mean like . . . literally, do you?"

"Oh. Oh, God no. I mean, well, not officially. But some of these nuts?

I wouldn't put it past them."

As he spoke, two uniformed APD officers pushed men they had arrested inside. Both perps wore colorful llama fleece ponchos and llama fleece satchels, and one of them even had on llama fleece pants.

"Yo llama so ugly, when it entered the ugly contest, they said, 'Sorry, no professionals!'" one of them yelled.

"Oh yeah? Well, yo llama so ugly, when it sits on the sand at the beach, cats try to bury it!" yelled the other.

The llama lovers lunged for one another, but their hands were cuffed behind their backs. They kicked and head-butted each other as the officers dragged them away.

"Yeah, so . . . you're here about the Michaux case?" MacGuffin said.

J.D. laid the whole thing out for him, all the facts and coincidences, including the death of James Woody, as they went upstairs to MacGuffin's office. "It's a weird one, all right. I mean, a tree dropped on you? That's sure some way to leaf, am I right?"

MacGuffin stared at him.

"Leaf? Leave? Some way to leave?" J.D. tried. Still nothing. "Never mind."

"The Michaux case file's there on the table," MacGuffin said, pointing J.D. to an unused interrogation room. "Not much there. Got the video tapes from the Grove Park Inn, too. They're on the cart."

J.D. started with the tapes, watching through them for Garnell. There was a small stack of them, and a machine to play them on. If he could place Garnell at the scene—not even at the dinner, just in the hotel somewhere at the same time—he'd be sure she was behind all this. Maybe go to the media with it to help catch her. If he couldn't . . . well, he was still leaning toward her as his main suspect, but he'd give a little more consideration to the idea that she was a victim in all this just like the others.

He was on the second security tape when he saw something that made him sit up and almost fall out of his chair. *No.* He had to be crazy. He fumbled at the remote to pause the black and white security video and rewind it frame by frame until he could see the face again.

And there it was. He hadn't been crazy. But it wasn't Garnell Lee Ray staring back at him from the television monitor, like he'd expected.

It was Marshall Harris.

Deputy Marshall Harris, of the Avery County Sheriff's Department.

What the hell was Marshall Harris doing in the Grove Park Inn, in plain clothes, a full three counties away from his home jurisdiction, the day State Senator Andy Michaux disappeared?

J.D. stood and fumbled his cell phone from his pocket to dial dispatch.

"Dispatch, this is Avery CID-two. Can you put me through to Avery Patrol-Five, pronto?"

"Stand-by, Avery CID-two."

J.D. stood by.

"Negative, Avery CID-two. No response," the dispatcher told him.

Damn it, Marshall. Where was he? Marshall did this all the time—disappeared with his radio off. He always told them he'd changed the channel looking for a good music station, even after they'd explained to him it wasn't that kind of radio. But suddenly J.D. wondered if Marshall was maybe just a little smarter than he pretended to be. Maybe he turned that radio off when he had somewhere else he wanted to be, and somebody else he wanted to be with.

Rather than be excited that Marshall might actually have a higher I.Q. than a garden hose, J.D. felt a little pit of dread open up in his stomach. If Marshall was smarter than they thought he was, they could all be in a great deal of trouble.

J.D. saw that snow plow charging at him, ready to heap on another wedge of dirty snow.

"Avery CID-two, you still there?"

"Yeah. Yeah, Gladys. I'm still here," J.D. said, punting protocol. "Gladys, can you do a GPS locate for me on Marshall's patrol car, tell me where it is?"

"Sure, hon. Hold on," Gladys said.

J.D. held on.

"I've got him. Well, his car at least." She gave him the coordinates. "You're not gonna believe where he's gotten himself to."

"Where?" J.D. asked. He was almost afraid to know.

"Madison County. Down past Hot Springs, almost all the way to the Tennessee border. The dern fool has gone and got himself lost again, and he's played with his radio again so he can't call in."

Or he's not lost, and he switched it off on purpose, J.D. thought, staring at the plain-clothed and altogether not stupid-looking Marshall Harris on the security tape. He thanked Gladys and hurried to his car.

It was time to make like a tree and leaf.

*****

State Senator Andy Michaux scrambled up out of his deck chair. Somebody on the French Broad River was throwing golf balls at him. Lots of golf balls. The first one had startled him from his Hot Springs reverie, but more and more thundered down on the roof, like Captain Kangaroo being showered with ping pong balls. But how was the man on the raft throwing so many of them? Michaux backed away in horror as the tin roof above him roared and balls bounced up off the deck to land at his feet.

Wait—they *weren't* golf balls. They were wet and white and misshapen. He picked one up. Golf ball-sized *hail*. That's what it was. Hail that filled the yard as it thundered down. Michaux gazed through his binoculars again at the person on the raft he thought had been watching him and realized it wasn't a big man with buck teeth and a beagle at all. It was a big old ugly woman with a beer cooler. A big old ugly *naked* woman with a beer cooler, who was scrambling for the cover of some overhanging trees as the hail beat down on her. As she rolled on the raft to grab for the bank, Michaux got a clear shot of her wrinkled butt crack. He pulled the binoculars away before he saw anything worse.

What was wrong with him? Why was he so jumpy? And why was he seeing beagles and ravens and golf balls everywhere? Andy Michaux was not a superstitious man. Religious, yes, but not superstitious. Those were two different things. Superstitious people believed in omens and magic and ghosts. Religious people believed in prophecies and miracles and holy spirits. It was different. But if he had been a heathen, he would be very scared right now that something very, very bad was going to happen to him. And soon.

Andy Michaux stumbled back inside the cabin, definitely not scared. Not for the first time he wished there was a television in the little cabin, so he could hear another human voice. Whenever he was not-scared but lonely (yes, that was it, he was just lonely) he would turn on Fox News and always have a friendly face there to tell him something he wanted to hear. Lately Gloria or Marshall had been there to talk to him, but they were both gone from the little cabin, which was unusual. He hadn't thought about it until now, but it was almost like one of them was always there to watch him.

Did that mean he'd been kidnapped? They'd certainly taken him away from the Grove Park Inn like he was being kidnapped—a bag tied over his head and tossed into the trunk of a car. But Gloria said that was for his protection, to get him away without being seen. And Marshall Harris was a deputy, after all. He drove a cruiser. Sheriff's deputies didn't go around kidnapping innocent people. Jesus. They only kidnapped the bad guys.

Michaux definitely hadn't felt like a prisoner the two weeks he'd been at the cabin. Did prisoners get good views and good food and good sex? And he could come and go from the cabin as much as he wanted to, even though there wasn't much place to go. Just the river and the woods and the little barn with the llamas. Gloria and Marshall had cars, but they never took him anywhere with them.

But two weeks was two weeks. It had been fun, and relaxing, and, he had to admit, he'd begun to understand what all those environmental nuts were talking about when they started to foam at the mouth about preservation at public hearings. But he was a state senator, God damn it. He was an important man. He might be able to take two weeks off from the world, but how could the world take two weeks off from *him*? Raleigh had probably ground to a halt without him there to lead them. Certainly the Senate Prayer Group was lost without him there, and he'd always been the one to choose the titty bar for Senators' Night Out.

Yes, it was time to get back to the real world. When Gloria and Marshall came back, he would tell them he was ready to go.

In the meantime, he went back to the book he'd found in the cabin's little library. Vacation home bookshelves were always hit and miss, and this cabin's selection was no exception. There was one Harry Potter novel (book six, *Harry Potter and the Half-Blood Prince*), ten books about the care and feeding of llamas, and one book called *Esperanto por Komencan-toj*. As he wasn't a satanist and didn't give a fig about llamas, that left him with *Esperanto for Beginners*. He'd been studying the language now for two weeks, and he congratulated himself on his progress. Mexicans made up two percent of the Mitchell County population and almost fifty percent of his voting base. Now he'd be able to talk to them the way George W. Bush did.

Michaux practiced his Esperanto, repeating the English translations after each phrase the way the guide book told him to.

"Saluton! Hello. *Mi nomigas Senatano Michaux. My name is Senator Michaux. Bonvolu sango miaj folioj antau mi revenigi.* Please change my sheets before I return."

The hail had stopped, and Michaux heard a car (*auto*) drive up outside and went to the window (*fenestro*) to see who it was. He expected to see Gloria's Subaru or Marshall's police cruiser, but it was neither. It was a pink (*rozkolora*) Cadillac. One of those make-up saleswomen. What were they doing all the way out here? Michaux watched as a red-headed woman in a multi-colored poncho got out of the car. A Mexican! A perfect opportunity to practice his Esperanto.

Michaux met the woman at the door. "*Saluton!*" he said. "*Mi nomigas Senatano Michaux. Bela vetero ni estas hav, cu ne?*"

The woman whipped a shotgun out from under her poncho and pointed it at his face.

"*Merd'!*" Michaux said, and he threw his hands in the air.

*****

"Inside," Garnell told Michaux. She backed the state senator into the cabin. "Who else is here?"

"N-nobody," Michaux said. "Gloria's in town buying groceries, and I don't know where Marshall went. *Um, ni estas sole.*"

"Marshall?" Garnell asked. Did he mean Marshall Harris, the man who was some kind of distant cousin once-removed from her? The man who'd picked her up in Marshall (the town) and taken her to the "safehouse" with Granny in Sodom? No. It had to be someone else.

Garnell poked at Michaux with the end of the shotgun, pushing him farther back in the room.

"*Bonvolu. Mi havas familion. Mi estas tro sufice morti,*" Michaux said.

"What the hell are you saying?" Garnell asked.

"I'm speaking your language. Esperanto. Aren't you a Mexican?"

"I—no," Garnell said, dumbfounded. "What makes you think I'm a Mexican?"

"Well . . . you're wearing a poncho. And you have a shotgun."

"I'm not . . . I'm *white*, you idiot! And Mexicans don't speak Esperanto!"

Michaux frowned. "Isn't Esperanto the Mexican word for Spanish?"

"That's *Español*, idiot!"

"*Merd*," he said, casting a disapproving look at the Esperanto book open on the table. "So what country *do* they speak Esperanto in?"

"They don't speak Esperanto in any country! It's a made-up language! Now can we get to why I have a shotgun pointed at you?"

Michaux backed into an end table, knocking a lamp to the ground with a clatter. "Is this about oil-drilling in the Smokies? The EPA clean-water standards we repealed? The death of the damn snail-darter?"

"Those would have been good enough reasons, but I've got a better one. You killed my parents."

She'd expected Michaux's eyes to go wide at that one. Expected him to realize who she was and go down on his knees, begging her forgiveness. Instead he just looked awkward and swallowed.

"Um, I'm afraid you're going to have to be more specific," he said.

Garnell hefted the shotgun, aiming at his face. "Outside," she told him.

Michaux stumbled out onto the porch and down toward the river, but Garnell grabbed him by the shirt and turned him toward the llama barn. He started to ask why, but a shotgun barrel jammed in his back made him shut up.

Garnell wasn't going to have him ruin this for her.

She hummed the Rascal Flats' song "Walk the Llama Llama" as they went.

At the gate she pushed Michaux into the field where the llamas grazed. There were four of them, two adults and two crias, all white with black patches or black with white patches, and they came up to Garnell and Michaux curiously, their little heads bobbing on their long woolly necks.

"Hello, Dolly Llama," Garnell said, scratching one of the adults under the chin. "Hello Llamadeus. *¿Cómo te llamas, llamas?*" she asked the two young llamas.

"What did you ask them?" Michaux asked.

"I asked what their names were," Garnell told him. "In *Español.*"

"Oh. Well, that one's Rama Llama Ding-Dong. And that other one is Barack O'Llama," he said bitterly. "Just because Palin doesn't rhyme with llama doesn't mean . . . wait a minute. How did you know the names of the other two?"

Garnell aimed the shotgun at Michaux again, then lowered it at his crotch. He squealed and dropped his hands to cover himself like a soccer player protecting his nads on a free kick.

"Drop 'em," Garnell told him.

"They dropped when I was eleven," Michaux said.

"*Your pants.*"

Whimpering, Michaux did as he was told. He started to step out of his pants and underwear, but Garnell told him to leave them around his ankles. "Now lay down. On your back."

"But there's llama poop all over the—"

Garnell fired the shotgun in the air, making Michaux jump and the llamas scatter. He quickly laid down on his back like she'd told him.

Garnell reloaded the shotgun one-handed with a *chik-chik* and sat on Michaux's lap, straddling him. With her free hand, she pulled the llama poncho off over her head.

Underneath her, she felt him rouse.

"Really?" she said. "What are you, thirteen?"

"I'm sorry," he said, closing his eyes. "I have a thing for Mexican maids."

"I told you. I'm not Mexican. I'm Garnell Lee Ray."

His eyes finally *did* get wide with recognition then. "Ray . . ."

"As in Jean and Lawson Ray," she said.

"You . . . *you* shot Peter Paul. And dropped a tree on James Woody. And pushed Dick Sweatt off a mountain!"

"Not so much push as potato, but yes. And now for the last of the gang of four."

"Wait!" Michaux said. "I—I did you a favor! Your parents were awful people!"

"I know. But they were *my* awful people," she told him, and she smothered him with the llama fleece poncho.

*****

Marshall Harris knew there was trouble as soon as he saw Granny's pink Cadillac out in front of Gloria's cabin.

"No. No no no no no," he said, running inside. "Granny?" he called. "Garnell?" Either one of them here right now was not good. That stupid Esperanto book Michaux had been reading was out on the table, but otherwise there was no sign of him or anybody else. Marshall hurried out back to the porch and the yard that led down to the river. Still no one. And Michaux wasn't in the river, either. At least not right here at the cabin.

There was only one place left to check. *The llama barn.* Marshall shuddered at the thought.

The past is the past, Marshall reminded himself, reciting the words of his therapist. *The past is the past, and this is now.*

Marshall drew his service pistol and stalked toward the llama barn like Perseus sneaking up on the Gorgons. Llamas were his own personal demon to slay. *Fear is the mind killer,* he told himself. *Fear is the little death that brings total obliteration. I will face my fear.*

He was just about to turn around and run away when he saw Garnell, and all his fears of llamas went loping away. She had just finished posing the dead state senator, his pants around his ankles, on the back of a llama like he'd been mounting it from behind.

"Garnell!" Marshall cried. At the sound of his voice the llama ran off and the dead body of Andy Michaux flopped to the ground. "Garnell, what are you doing?"

"Finishing the job," Garnell told him.

Marshall hurried over, his fear of llamas hovering on the periphery of his consciousness like . . . well, like the llamas that hovered uneasily nearby.

"No, no, no, no. You weren't supposed to kill this one. That's why she brought him out here, to hide him. She *needed* him. And what are you doing with the body?" Marshall asked.

"I'm setting it up to look like State Senator Andy Michaux died doing what he loved: screwing nature."

"Damn it, Garnell! You and your stupid 'clever murders'!"

"It is clever!" Garnell said. She held up a colorful poncho. "I smothered him with a llama poncho! Forensics will find llama fleece in his windpipe, like he snuffed it with his face up a llama's ass."

Marshall snatched the poncho from Garnell and held it close to her face. "How many red, orange and purple llamas have you seen? It's *dyed*, Garnell, and every fiber forensics finds will be dyed too!" He rubbed the poncho between his fingers. "And this isn't even llama fleece! It's alpaca! You can tell because alpaca fibers are thicker than llama fibers by 10 micrometers!"

"How do you know so much about llamas?" Garnell asked.

"You should know that more than anybody," Marshall told her. One of the llamas took a step closer, and he shied away. "But we're not talking about me and llamas right now. We're talking about your stupid stunts."

"How do you know about my 'stunts'?"

"Because I'm always the one who has to come behind you and clean them up! The tree you dropped on James Woody? I had to play the fool and get out there with a chainsaw and start hacking at it so they wouldn't see where you'd cut it. Richard Sweatt? I had to eat that damn raw potato so the feds wouldn't find it. And now I'm going to have to fix this, too. Why the hell couldn't you have stayed at Granny's where you were safe?"

"Oh," Garnell said. "The 'safe-house.' For an agency that doesn't exist. Does it, Marshall? That's right. I figured it out."

"Oh, did you?" Marshall said, finally losing the last of his patience. "Did you *really*, Garnell? You finally figured out there is no secret eco-terrorist organization in Avery County that can afford to pay you *fifty thousand dollars a hit* to take out back country lawyers and real estate agents? *Of course there isn't!* And it only took you four years to figure this out? Damn it, Garnell, you've been used. All this time, you've been used as a one-woman assassination service. And I was sent to work for the Avery County Sheriff's Department just to make sure you didn't get caught. *The Frickin' Avery County Sheriff's Department!* I have three degrees, damn it. Three! And one of them is in comparative literature from Appalachian State! But what am I doing? Driving around in a squad car playing Sancho Panza to your Don Quixote!" Marshall spun and ran his hands through his hair, trying to figure out what to do now. "Oh, you should have stayed at Granny's!"

"Why, Marshall?"

"Because then none of this would have happened!"

"No, why did you hide me away? Why were you trying to protect me? I know we're related somehow, but—"

"You don't remember? The big family reunion here when we were kids?" Marshall remembered. He relived it every night before he went to sleep, recounted it over and over again in regression therapy with Dr. Closter, and thought of it every time he saw a llama. "I remember it like it was yesterday," he told her. "You wore blue, the llamas wore gray. Blankets. It was kind of chilly. We hid behind the hay bales where no one but the llamas would see us, and we kissed. My first kiss . . . so perfect . . . but then your brother and sister jumped out, laughing at us. It startled the llamas." He put his hands to his ears. "They screamed. The llamas. They were so frightened they screamed, and your brother and your sister just laughed and laughed, and the llamas kept screaming. I can still hear them, Garnell. Can't you? Are the llamas still screaming, Garnell?"

"Um, no," Garnell said. "I don't know what you're talking about. I just went inside after that and got some ice cream. So, if there isn't really an agency, who had me kill all those people? And why was my Aunt Gloria hiding Andy Michaux at her cabin? *And who shot me?*"

"A car!" Marshall said. They both heard it. A car crunching on the gravel driveway. Marshall hurried to the edge of the llama pen to see who it was, and couldn't believe his eyes. It was *J.D. Klontz,* in an unmarked car! Marshall looked back wildly at the state senator lying in the muck. There wasn't time enough to clean up this one.

"Go," he told Garnell. "You have to go. It's Detective Klontz."

"No," Garnell told him. "I need you to tell me what's going on!"

"Later, later," Marshall said. "We can't let J.D. catch you here." He pushed her out of the pen, toward the far side of the house. "Double back around and take off when he comes out here. I'll keep him busy."

Marshall looked one last time into those root beer colored eyes that had so enraptured him in his llama-scarred youth and gathered up his courage. To her surprise, he took Garnell in his arms and kissed her for the second time in their lives. Here, in the eyes of no one but God and the Dolly Llama. It was tender, and magical, and tasted faintly of gravy.

As he pulled away, he watched those root beer colored eyes for some sign of the spark he felt.

"I love you, Garnell Lee Ray," Marshall said.

"Okay," Garnell said.

Inside the cabin, J.D. called Marshall's name.

"Go," Marshall told her, and she ran. "Good night, good night!" he called after her. "Parting is such sweet sorrow, that I shall say good night till it be morrow."

Garnell disappeared around the other side of the cabin just as J.D. came outside and saw Marshall.

"God damn it, Marshall, what are you doing all the way out—*is that State Senator Michaux?*"

"Him? Oh, yeah, I think so," Marshall said, reverting to the foolish persona he had modeled after two of the greats: Shakespeare's Falstaff and Don Knotts's Barney Fife. "I was just wrapping the body up in this here llama poncho to keep it warm for the coroner." He worked the poncho under Michaux's down-turned face and tied it in a fat knot at the back of his head.

"Marshall, stop! How many times have I told you not to contaminate the crime scene?" J.D. stopped when he heard a car peeling out on the gravel driveway. He ran to the edge of the pen to see around to the front of the house. "It's that pink Caddy! Come on. We've got to—"

When J.D. turned around, Marshall had his gun pointed at him.

"Anon, anon, my dear Detective Klontz," Marshall said. "This day's black fate on more days doth depend: This but begins the woe others must end."

Pink Clouds

by Annette Saunooke Clapsaddle

A non? How long you been sniffing this llama shit?" J.D. demanded, certain Marshall Harris had finally gone completely obtuse.

"I thought for sure a *Yankee* would know the reference better," Harris smirked.

And there it was, the look of clarity in Marshall Harris's normally dumbstruck eyes. He stared confidently at J.D. Klontz. Klontz had been the fool. The dead state senator, Garnell, the enormous pink Caddy, and the dumbass deputy he couldn't shake. He should have seen it.

"What's your plan now? You gonna leave me here with Michaux and the flies? Dispatch already knows I was coming to find you. They know where I am."

"Don't worry. We've got it all worked out."

"We? Who you tangled up with? Don't tell me . . . Garnell Ray?"

"I guess you could say that." Marshall glowed like the Brown Mountain Lights with the memory of Garnell's lips against his.

J.D. ran it all back as he stared into Marshall's cold, black Glock 22: Marshall eating evidence, Garnell's effortless escape from the hospital, and the Grove Park video. Just how many of the bodies was Marshall responsible for? Possibly more than even he knew himself.

J.D. needed a distraction. There was no evidence of another human being for miles, not way out there. No one would come looking for him for hours—maybe days, knowing his office. If only he could call Pecker or had thought to bring Mr. Pibb. The whole damn place was nunnery silent except for those . . . llamas?

Ahhh . . . the llamas. J.D. and the boys had always harassed Marshall about how he dealt with livestock. You would have thought he was the city boy the way he danced around animals during calls. No saving kittens from trees for him. *No sir.* He'd make like that tree and leaf. J.D. chuckled to himself. *Man that never gets old.* Okay, so those goofy-looking sheep-wannabes would have to do.

"Must be feeding time." J.D. looked past Marshall signaling to a potential herd of llamas on the move. Marshall craned his neck around, phantom llama screams filling his head. Llama . . .

"Nooo!" Marshall yelped, forcing his palms over his ears. J.D. seized the opportunity and lunged for the gun, forcing Marshall over a bale of hay and onto the senator. J.D. grabbed the barrel of the gun and tore it from Marshall's hand.

Standing over Marshall, who had assumed a fetal position on top of the senator, J.D. smiled at his deputy. "Alas poor Marshall, he is already dead; stabbed with a white wench's black eye; run through the ear with a love song." J.D. struck Marshall hard across the jaw with the gun. His body practically liquefied onto the corpse beneath.

*****

Garnell rolled down the driver's window of the Caddy and let her arm hang limply over the side. She tapped her fingernails against the door, beating time to "That's the Night the Lights Went Out in Georgia."

Thank God the radio works. Garnell had maneuvered the pink eyesore onto the highway and headed east toward Linville Falls. She had no place else to turn. The address Marshall had shoved into her hand as he pushed her out the gate was familiar enough, a campground she knew all too well.

"Ask for Dawn," he had called to her as she cranked the car.

Shit. Not that crazy bitch. Well, at least I can bring her a vehicle back. Might not be her style, though.

The car, however, provided an efficient cover for her return to Linville. No one would expect a murder suspect to be selling Mary Kay on the side. Beyond that, the car's contents provided ample disguise essentials. About ten miles down the road, Garnell pulled the Caddy off onto the shoulder and climbed into the backseat. Granny had five boxes of unopened Mary Kay products ready for delivery. Inside, Garnell found Mary Kay nail lacquer (in shades of *Eat Your Heart Out Red* and *Pussytoe Pink*), Mary Kay Weekender Lip Pencils (*Romantic Getaway Scarlet* and *Love Affair Rose*), Mary Kay Deep Bronze liquid foundation, and a collection of plain, solid-colored drapes used for seasonal color analysis. Garnell wondered briefly if she'd be an autumn or a summer. The rearview mirror was not conducive to her experiment. She opted for the white headscarf, winter, as the others had unidentifiable stains.

Garnell twisted her auburn locks into an unforgiving knot, draped the scarf over her head, and tied it snugly against the back of her neck. She knew she should ditch the thick glasses, but would be blind if she did. With her hair pulled firmly from her face, the fat lenses functioned as a set of pint glasses serving up her russet eyes. Her face was a root beer float.

Garnell smeared five tubes of the tawny foundation over her face and body, wherever her creamy skin peeped through. Unsure how to use the other products, she tucked a couple of samples of each into a Mary Kay gift bag and crawled back into the driver's seat with it. She noticed the sky had grown a dull, sterile gray. There was little definition between it and the dullness of the roadway. Billboards filled the horizon advertising fast food exits, adventures in the Army, and a giant pair of glowing WCU catamount eyes—or was that a UNCA bulldog? Garnell felt as if she had hitched a ride on one of Fitzgerald's big pink clouds and was willfully being pushed around by a Gatsby character. She certainly had lost control of her fate long ago.

As she passed through Spruce Pine, Garnell re-evaluated her plan. Getting past Daniel would be a challenge, especially in a mammoth pastel gas-guzzler. She opted to stash it at a Parkway overlook and enter the campground through the woods, circumventing the campground entrance and most likely, Daniel. As usual, a song took over her thoughts, this time, Survivor's "Eye of the Tiger."

*****

"Where the hell is he?" Ruby demanded. "I thought you were bringin' him with you this time." Ruby was dressed neatly in a Chanel skirt suit with a brown faux fur collar and wore oversized Louis Vuitton sunglasses, transforming her into a brown squirrel from the neck up.

"Press is still too hot. I was afraid we'd get stopped before we made it here," reasoned Gloria. Gloria self-consciously adjusted her own over-sized sunglasses, Prada . . . last season's Prada. *How embarrassing.*

"How much does he know?"

"Ahh, nothin'. He's spent his career practicing the art of knowin' ab-solutely nothin'." Gloria liked her men this way. They felt grateful when she played the demure role every so often to spice things up.

"So he doesn't even know about me?" Ruby had taken great care not to intertwine her name with her aunt's in public; a connection with Gloria would be unexpected.

"Nope. Hasn't had time to figure anything out, anyway. I've been keeping him busy, if you know what I mean."

"And Harris?"

"I think his dumb cop act is sinkin' in a little too much." Gloria con-sidered, for the moment, taking on a second lover if Harris kept up his simplemindedness, though things were complicated enough. "Has your sister been in touch with you?"

"No, I don't expect her to."

"You sure the information you got on her is right? I'd hate to move forward for the wrong reason."

"Nothin's ever certain, but I got it from a reliable source. We're movin' forward and as quickly as possible." Ruby felt a tiny pang of what she could only theorize must be the feeling of a conscience. It was too foreign to be sure.

*****

Penny scrounged through her hemp knapsack to produce the last dime of her admission fee into Cherokee's Annual Powwow. Lakeesha had al-ready paid and waited for her on the other side of the gate, smiling at the ticket taker awkwardly.

"Would have thought these things were free," Lakeesha complained.

"Consider it a business investment . . . Be sure to save your receipt."

The ticket taker forced a smile and fastened a nylon bracelet around both Penny and Lakeesha's wrists. "You're good for the weekend."

"So I guess you have some sorta plan, 'cause I can smell the frybread and I know where I'm headed," Lakeesha informed Penny.

"We'll have time for frybread later. Right now we gotta concentrate on talent recruitment."

"Yeah, so what you lookin' for? Dancers for your troupe? You weren't real clear on the phone."

"No. For *So You Think You Can Haunt?* That's what we're calling our reality ghost program. Well, it's between that and *Specter Detector*. Anyway, you know how so many of these local stories have Cherokee ghosts in 'em. Well, we need a couple of folks to help us out. Thought we should get us some real Cherokees to make it all authentic and what not."

Lakeesha scanned the crowd. "Shouldn't be too much of a problem here."

"No, I'm not worried about getting the adults; it's the kids that'll be tricky."

"Kids? Whatcha need with kids?"

"Little People. Best stories out there. All Little People supposed to be runnin' around the woods. Playin' tricks on people. Hidin' your shit. Kid hauntings are always freaky. It's kinda like Cherokee's own version of Children of the Corn. I'm tellin' you, Lakeesha, this place is ripe with ghost stories. We've really lucked out."

"You think parents are just gonna let you borrow their kids?"

"We might have to hire the parents to get the kids. But we've got a bigger problem anyway."

"What's that?"

"Not really supposed to talk about Little People, from what I hear. We'll have to be careful when we do auditions." Lakeesha looked worried. "We'll figure it out as we go. This schedule says that the Little Miss Cherokee pageant is this evening; let's go check out the contestants."

"Can I get an Indian Taco first?" Food always calmed Lakeesha's anxiety.

"Yeah, but hurry up. We're on the clock."

Penny positioned herself backstage after the pageant results were read. She comforted a young girl who had just lost the crown to her "know-it-all" cousin and was weeping into her fancy dance shawl.

"I told you to go with a traditional dance," her mother chided, busily gathering her daughter's accessories. "But nooo, you couldn't just listen to your mother." The mother stopped her sorting abruptly and looked up at Penny, who was near tears herself. "And who in the hell are you? Get away from my daughter."

"Oh . . . Yes, ma'am. I just wanted to say that Miss Kendall here did a fine job. See, I'm a dancer myself and . . ."

"That's nice. Let's go, Kendall."

"Ma'am if I could just talk to you for a second about an opportunity I have for her."

"Opportunity?" The mother eyed Penny carefully.

"Yes, a job. No, more like a dramatic role for her."

"Here." The mother handed Penny a small card.

"What's this?"

"Her agent's card. Call him."

Kendall and her mother almost knocked Lakeesha over as they disappeared into the crowd.

"How'd it go, Penny?"

"Well, I have a contact now."

"She didn't really look like the Little Person type to me."

"No, but her momma would make one hell of a Banshee."

Lakeesha nodded in agreement. "So what's next? Bunch of kids over there at the carnival rides. Want me to go check it out?"

Penny was feeling defeated. She hadn't fully prepared herself for the hard sell and needed to rework her approach. Lakeesha was antsy. "We staying for the concert? We should at least get our money's worth."

"Naw. Mingus Mill is our next stop," Penny informed Lakeesha. "They say if you knock on the door at night, somebody knocks back."

"Where's that?"

"Not far, just past the Visitor's Center as you enter the National Park."

"Oh, that place with the big water wheel on the river. They got a store that sells grits. I saw on the sign."

"No, on past that. This place is kinda tucked back in the woods. Old place. Doesn't operate any more."

Lakeesha sighed. "I ain't knockin' on no door in the middle of the night. And I especially ain't knockin' on no door in the middle of the woods in the middle of the night."

"We have to try it out before we can sell the experience. I mean, maybe it just knocks back on its own and we won't have to hire any knockers."

Lakeesha grinned mischievously. "Won't be the first knockers you bought, will it, Penny?"

Penny rolled her eyes. "Come on. We need to get us a room before we go on up. I'm sure as hell not planning on sleep at the mill." She paused and turned back toward Lakeesha. "And for the record, they just look big because my waist is so tiny."

*****

Daniel Puckett and Nurse Genevieve sipped coffee and listened to old Dee Dee Sharp recordings. Daniel had never been much for seeking out female companionship, but after the empathy he had shown Garnell at the hospital, Genevieve could not help herself from her own pursuit. Most men that Genevieve met never made eye contact with her. She was like nurse Rachel in that way, but for a much different reason.

Daniel was not typical of the men she encountered at the hospital, though. When it became clear that he was of no greater relation to Garnell than landlord, Genevieve took the opportunity to make her move. She found his home address on the information sheet he filled out for Garnell and drove over after her shift at the end of the week. Genevieve found it romantic that Daniel lived in the woods. A real hunter, gatherer type. Genevieve arrived in uniform, not the modern scrubs she had taken to wearing after the birth of her first grandchild, but the uniform that had hung in her closet since the seventies, pristine white, form-fitting, low cut. She borrowed a push-up bra from Rachel's locker, not that Rachel would miss it seeing as she rarely wore a bra.

Daniel felt indebted to Genevieve for bringing Garnell home from the hospital. Though she had made far less an impact on him at the hospital than Rachel, or even J.D. for that matter, he recalled her fondly upon hearing of her successful cover for Garnell. It was as if they had formed a partnership long before they knew each other and Garnell was the linch-pin.

"I just don't know where that girl has gotten off to. I'm plumb worried about her."

"Probably got spooked. I mean if someone shot me, I wouldn't want to go back to the place it happened." Genevieve poked around the camper trailer with no obvious purpose.

"Well, you do have a point there," Daniel conceded. "I just thought she'd tell someone. I guess I could try to find Dawn Reindeer to ask her, but she's probably off pilfering in the woods again."

"Maybe Garnell left you a note," Genevieve offered, digging through the stack of catalogs and envelopes on Daniel's makeshift kitchen table. "Looks like you haven't looked through your mail lately."

Daniel started for the stack quickly, unsure if his *Playboy* was scheduled to arrive this week or next.

"What's this?" Genevieve held up a simple white card with bold purple writing. "A weird sort of advertisement. Doesn't even say the business name."

"Let me see," Daniel reached for the card but Genevieve was already reading it aloud.

"RECALLED TO LIFE." Genevieve squinted. "That's all it says, RE-CALLED TO LIFE. All in bold letters. How strange."

"Ahh, probably just another Viagra ad. Once you get my age, they put you on some sort of mailing list." Daniel smiled nervously.

"Oh, honey. I really doubt you need anything like that." Genevieve blushed and tucked a strand of wiry gray hair behind her ear.

Daniel swallowed hard. "Well, how's about we just step into my berth and see." Genevieve smiled as Daniel closed the curtain behind them.

*****

"Come on baby, just give me one little . . . Oh!" Dawn had spent the last hour attempting to coax an ornery raven from its perch. She needed a feather to complete her latest remedy . . . love potion, really. The raven, not much on love, swooped down, pecked her forehead, and flew out of the camper into the woods.

135

Dammit! I'm gonna have to get Daniel to build me a trap.

Dawn set her "cunjuring" journal on the kitchen/living room/bedside table and concentrated her efforts on evening dinner. Her fiancé, no, *her lover* (that sounded more natural) had promised to try out her home cooking for the first time ever that night. Usually the couple took picnics of bologna sandwiches or granola (depending on who packed the lunch) or they made a quick trip through the drive-thru, as Dawn's *lover* felt strongly that restaurants were too impersonal.

Dawn stood over her creation. The pinto beans looked like dried leather clinging to the bottom of a large aluminum pot. Fried potatoes and onions burned in an over-sized cast-iron skillet next to the beans. *I hope I don't get accused of destroying evidence*, Dawn smiled, checking on her last hope: golden, moist cornbread steaming in the oven. *He's liable to handcuff me after the first bite.* She not so secretly hoped he would.

Dawn's relationship progressed much faster than she had anticipated. She rarely took a shine to local men, having had her fill of traditional domesticity growing up. She was the oldest of eight children, with an alcoholic father and a mother particularly adept at disappearing acts. She usually fell for the Patagonia type, Appalachian Trail hikers with trust funds. Perhaps she loved them because they loved her so much, at least for the four days they stuck around before remembering their original objectives.

This man was different. There was something mysterious about him. Maybe it was his line of work. Maybe it was his independence. He wasn't needy. She hadn't even seen him cry yet, something she dreaded everyday from the other men. He had proposed with no sentimentality, as if they were making a business transaction, but followed up her agreement with enough corporeal passion to make up for it.

Tap, tap, tap.

Dawn wiped the cornbread steam from her face. "That damn bird," she muttered. "Won't leave me alone, won't let me touch him. Must be male." Dawn grasped a plastic Wal-Mart bag with her left hand and slung open the hollow trailer door with her right. "Gotcha!"

"Get your damn hands off me!" Garnell flailed at the bag. "Crazy bitch."

"Oh, Garnell. I'm so sorry, hon. I thought you were that raven."

"Just get back inside before someone sees me."

"What are you doing here?" Dawn stepped back to her stove, pretending to salvage an unsalvageable supper. She had thought she had shed Garnell for good. "You look . . . different."

"Yeah, nevermind that. I brought you something."

"You best have brought me my Subaru."

"Not exactly. I think you'll like this ride better."

"Where is it?" Dawn peered out her tiny window.

"I've got it parked outside. Didn't want anyone to know I was here."

"Why are you here?" Dawn felt uneasy.

"Marshall Harris told me to come here."

"Marshall Harris? The deputy, Marshall Harris?"

"Yeah. I mean, I think he is an actual deputy. Not too sure what to believe."

"Why would my Marshall send you here?"

"Your Marshall?"

"We're engaged . . . He didn't tell you?" Dawn looked pissed.

"No. He sure left that nugget out." Garnell sat down on Dawn's bed and rubbed her face. "Why do you think he would send me here? Not exactly the safest place to go considering this is my last known residence."

"I guess cause he was supposed to be comin' here tonight. You hidin' from something?"

"Just tryin' not to get shot again."

"Maybe you should stop doing things to get shot."

"What are you talkin' about?"

"Takin' things . . ." Dawn shook her head. "I mean like how you took my car and all."

"I told you I brought you one back. In fact, I better go get it. You heard about that state senator gone missing, right?"

"Yea, somethin' 'bout it."

"Well, I know a little too much and I don't need state officials on my tail. I need to get out of here. Daniel will be making the rounds soon enough. I'm just gonna grab some clothes."

"We have to wait on Marshall. I mean, don't you think he would want you to wait on him?"

Garnell considered her options. The camper trailer tucked in the forest seemed to simultaneously smother her slowly and expose her to the outside world, unprotected by street lights and telephones. She was trapped in a borderless world, like framed art on display for any gazer that happened along.

"This was a mistake, Dawn. I have to go."

"Then I'm coming with you. I know where you can go where no state officials will go. Hell, they probably don't even know how to get there."

Garnell dug through Dawn's piles of clothes for a change of underwear. "Where you got in mind?"

"Cherokee. I've got some contacts there."

"Cherokee? You sure?"

"Yeah, Smokies are great for disappearing. Just ask Eric Rudolf. Besides, this weekend's the powwow. I was goin' over for that anyway. I'll just leave Marshall a note. This supper's done for anyway."

An hour and a half down the road, Garnell silently wondered if Dawn knew Marshall's history, his feelings for her. If so, this trip was a huge mistake and Garnell's first instinct might have been right all along. Her shooter might have just ridden shotgun next to her in the ridiculous Caddy for the past one hundred miles.

"You know Cherokee is federal jurisdiction," Garnell felt compelled to mention. "Crimes, felonies like . . . say . . . murders are handled by the FBI."

"Even better," smiled Dawn. "You should be really safe there then."

"And you?"

"Me? I'm just here to help you . . . and of course Marshall. He obviously feels like you need my help."

Garnell felt uneasy, but she was too far in now and needed to stay with Dawn if she was going to try to contact Marshall again. Garnell maneuvered the Caddy through a throng of PETA protesters hovering at a downtown bear zoo.

"I just can't believe they have those majestic animals in a cage," Dawn shook her head. Garnell thought back to the Ziploc bags of dead lizards, tupperware containers of claws and feathers, and the tanned deerskins all proudly displayed in Dawn's musty, tin can trailer.

"Just tell me where I need to park up here. You're sure you don't want to go find a room tonight or something first?"

"No. I told you I have people here. We'll stay with one of them."

"Family? You from here?"

"Not exactly. Friends I've made over the years."

"You think they'll let us stay at their house tonight?"

"Oh, no," Dawn said. "I don't know anyone who *lives* in Cherokee. Not well enough to crash at their house, anyway. I know lots of folks who come into town for the powwow, though. They're probably staying at a camp ground. Wouldn't mind us sharing a tent with 'em, I'm sure."

Garnell was already sick of Dawn's odor. The mix of absent deodorant, campfire smoke, moldy tobacco, and some scent she would never be able to identify had assaulted Garnell's nostrils like noxious gas. Now she was going to be stuck in a tent for God knows how long with this stink bomb, wannabe powwow princess.

"Here. We're gonna park here." Garnell pulled the pink land yacht into an already overflowing parking lot and squeezed it into a makeshift space, partially landing in the adjacent mulch bed. Dawn checked the finishing touches on her braided pigtails and applied a fresh coat of lipstick she had scavenged out of Garnell's goody bag. Garnell reapplied bronze foundation to her face, tightened her knotted hair, and smoothed the head scarf. "Let's just get us a place for tonight, grab some food and get out there. Too many people for me."

"Sure thing," said Dawn. "We'll get you settled at someone's campsite, and I can come back in the morning to explore."

Garnell wondered what getting "settled" really meant. It suddenly occurred to her that as far as she was concerned, her career had ended with a dead state senator in a pile of llama shit. The four men responsible for her parents' deaths were dead. After her conversation with Marshall, she felt confident she could walk away from the The Agency with ease . . . if an agency even existed. Settling down was a different matter all together. She would never rest easy until she knew who shot her and had the opportunity to return the favor.

Dawn practically dragged Garnell across the street and through the admission gate. "I'm buying your ticket. My treat."

The fairgrounds were bubbling with shrill voices and baritone drum beats. Vendors called out, and the loud speaker buzzed with static-charged announcements. Dense thickets of primary colors dotted the gravel landscape and waved with the motion of the drum. There were men with bare chests and women draped in heavy wool blankets standing side by side. Feathers bobbed in all directions and tiny cones made from Skoal cans jingled on the legs of young children. It was a beautiful abstract of human motion, and that was just the white people. The Indian competitors wouldn't return until after dinner recess.

As Garnell and Dawn made their way through vendor booths, Garnell began to feel glares grow into whispers. Those whispers grew into giggles. Giggles grew into full out laughter by the time they circled the exhibit hall. Dawn seemed completely oblivious. "Did you notice that, Dawn?"

"What? Those baskets? Yeah, they're pretty incredible, you know, the patterns . . . "

"No, the way people stared at us. I think they were even laughing at us."

"Oh, I'm used to that. It's cause we aren't from here."

"They're not laughing at anyone else, and I'm pretty sure there are lots of tourists here . . . Oh!" Garnell froze at her reflection in the cotton candy trailer. "Shit. I didn't realize I looked like a . . ."

"Moon Pie!" Dawn shouted across the dance grounds. "Ohhh, girl. You best get over here right now and give me a hug." Dawn had spotted one of her powwow pals from across the crowd.

Garnell shook her head. Moon Pie, or whatever her name was, looked like Dawn's twin sister, silly grin and all. "Dawn, I gotta get this shit off my face. No wonder those people were laughin'."

"Why? I think you look the best I've seen you . . . healthy." Dawn frowned, but let it drop and turned to greet Moon Pie properly.

"I'll find you later," Garnell said as she headed for a bathroom.

She dashed into the ladies room adjacent to the exhibition hall to avoid eye contact with anyone else. She sat her glasses on the mirror ledge and pulled out brown paper towels from the dispenser until it was empty. She ran the towels under the excessively hot sink water. The soap dispenser sputtered hapless bubbles, so her resolve to scrub the bronzer off was futile. Her face burned from the rough towels and blistering water.

"Lady, you okay?" an elderly woman timidly questioned while washing her hands in the next sink over.

"I'm fine," said Garnell. "Soap's out and I can't get this stuff off my face."

"Oh . . ." The lady, a short, portly women with gray hair and dark, aged skin looked nervously at her. "Here," she said, handing Garnell a packet of salt from her purse.

"Uh . . . thanks."

"It's for your face. It will scrub the paint . . . makeup off."

"Really?" Garnell rubbed the salt over her face, filling in the creases with detailed effort.

"Now wash it off and you should be good to go."

Garnell splashed her face with cold water and patted it dry with a kleenex, also provided by the elderly woman. She eyed the results in the mirror.

"Let me see," the woman asked. Garnell faced her full-on, like a teenager on prom night.

"Much better." The woman smiled and started to turn back to her own sink, but stopped suddenly.

She looked closely at Garnell, as if inspecting for dents. She leaned in closer and squinted into Garnell's eyes. Those eyes looked so familiar. Though set in a much matured face, they were the unmistakable root beer eyes of an infant she had known well.

The elderly woman stepped back and adjusted her glasses. "Oh my . . . are you? No. Can't be. Yes, yes. Is that you, Garnell?"

Was her name already on the news? Garnell reached for her glasses, preparing for a swift retreat.

"Lord, child. It's been so long. I haven't seen you since you left as a baby, except for those pictures your folks sent back."

"I'm sorry," Garnell said. "Do I know you?"

"I'm sure you don't remember me. You were just a tiny thing when you were adopted. But I'd know those peepers anywhere. Even as a baby they were stunning."

Adopted. The word lodged in Garnell's throat before being thrust outward by a gasp. How did this lady know her name?

"Yeah, that preacher man and his wife, the Rays, right? Yes, they adopted you." The lady saw the confusion on Garnell's face grow. "Oh, honey. I was told it was an open adoption. I thought you knew."

"Knew what?"

"That you were born here. That you were adopted. Shouldn't pay it no mind now. I mean now that you're all growed up and all." Garnell thought she might vomit in the toilet behind her.

"Come on, sweetie. You look like you need something to eat. I'll buy you a hotdog and tell you what I know if you want."

Garnell nodded and followed the woman outside. What she was about to tell Garnell would change everything. Garnell couldn't stomach the hotdog, but watched intently as the woman sipped a black coffee and reminisced.

By the time the elderly Cherokee woman finished recounting the last few decades, Garnell had learned the following truths:

1. The Rays were not her biological parents.

2. The reason for her adoption amounted to Lawson Ray's desire to polish his façade as a pillar of the Christian community and adopt a poor, underprivileged, orphan of color. Preferably Ethiopian.

3. Lawson Ray had initially considered using the Christian World Adoption service.

4. However, adopting from a third world country took too much time and red tape when he could easily pass off a Cherokee child for his purposes.

5. Thus, Lawson Ray filled out the paperwork and selected a child from the Cherokee Children's Home.

6. Garnell was born with jaundice and dark hair.

7. Eventually the jaundice subsided and in two months Garnell's hair had turned fiery red.

8. Lawson attempted to return Garnell to the children's home when neighbors started gossiping that she was the product of one of her mother's extramarital affairs . . . a bastard.

9. The children's home refused, citing what amounted to an expiration date on their responsibility.

10. Later investigations found that the biological mother was not actually enrolled in the Eastern Band and the father had never pretended to be native of any sort.

11. Lawson Ray took up drinking shortly thereafter.

Garnell had never been the daughter the Rays, especially Lawson Ray, had wanted. She was as free-willed as her adoptive mother, but never wild enough to evoke sympathy from her adoptive father's fellow parishioners.

Garnell was a mistake two times over, rejected by one family and resented by the other. Garnell wondered if this had anything to do with her being shot. She also wondered if she would have avenged her parents' deaths had she known about the adoption. She wondered if anyone else in her family knew the truth. Her siblings had never mentioned it to her, and surely they would have brought it up in the heat of an argument at least once. There was no more hurtful insult than to insinuate that one was adopted . . . though perhaps in her family it would be a compliment.

Garnell thanked the woman for the information and decided to take a walk around the grounds to clear her head before returning to the drum circles to seek out Dawn and Mud Pie, or whatever her name was. The scent of buttered popcorn mingled with sweet cotton candy and carnie sweat. Sawdust played hide and seek between her socks and shoe laces. The cool evening air chilled her newly-exfoliated skin and she felt young again. Garnell heard the cheers of the pageant crowning and recognized a band starting to warm up on the main stage. They began their set and Garnell hummed along with their first song, "Cherokee People."

Then she stopped to listen to the words straining through the drone of the base amplifier. For once she reckoned her father had been right about something. *I'm sure not Cherokee because I sure as hell wouldn't be proud of dying.*

Altered States

by Gene Cheek

Little Law, aka Lawson Junior, aka The Accident—*damn he hated those names, hated anything that reminded him that he was his Daddy's son*—lay on his back almost in the geographic center of the fourteen acres that made up Raven Ridge. Fourteen acres doesn't sound like a lot of land to someone from say, Kansas. You couldn't park the machinery it took to farm a Kansas farm on fourteen acres, but here in the Blue Ridge Mountains fourteen acres that doesn't run seven straight up and seven straight down is a lot of ground. Raven Ridge was gently rolling pasture land surrounded by hard woods and views . . . the views . . . well it was the kind of view that people paid for.

Little Law lay there surrounded by big bluestem and long hair sedge grasses and the white and the electric blue flowers of white snakeroot and Appalachian gentians, and exhaled the blue smoke from a joint, "Indoor Trainwreck" he believed it was called. Good shit. Above him was that luminous blue sky that Carolinians have been crowing about for centuries.

He remembered, as he starred up into the cloudless sky, the story he'd heard old man Bale tell a long time ago about this October sky. He'd walked up on the porch at Campbell's store—a ten-year-old boy with a dime in a dirty hand and a mouth watering for Mary Janes—just in time to hear Bale say, "You'uns won't believe it if I tell it to ya. It was tolt to me for the truth by a retired Baptist preacher what lives over in Leicester, said he'd swear on the King James that it was the gospel. This preacher says ever year all the retiring Baptist preachers are brought down to Raleigh during the dog days." Without cracking a toothless smile, the old man went on. "There's this secret room down in the belly of the Cap'tal Building, underneath the Office of Tourism, where all them retired ministers, hired by the state now mind ya, prays for picture-perfect-postcard-days just like this one. He said—this retired preacher—that it takes six weeks for the prayers of a Baptist to reach the ears of God, and that's why we got this here sky in October and no other time. If I'm lying, I'm crying, and I ain't sheddin' a tear."

Inside Little Law's head a Teddy Thompson song began to fight its way through the haze left by the Trainwreck he'd just smoked. "I like to live in an altered state," the song went. Little Law loved that song. He loved it because it was about him. He lived in an altered state and he'd been crying on the inside all his life, suffering first at the hands of that good for nothin' piece of shit excuse of a father of his, and then by the pure T shame of his street-walking excuse of a mother, and now at the hands of his sister.

The day his altered state reached its zenith was that day eight years ago when his mental state went to Hell and never made the return trip. He'd just turned fourteen, was skipping school, and had been standing on the little back porch amongst the rain-soaked cane back chairs fixing to light up a fatty when he'd heard their voices coming from the bedroom.

"I hope you at least have the goddamn common sense to try and hide this . . . this . . . this . . . whatever the hell it is you're doing—from Ruby and Little Law," his Mama had screamed in a rage.

"I can't place trust in Ruby or Law to do the right thing here, Jean. Ruby is just like you, sneaky and conniving and doesn't care one iota what happens to anyone but her. Little Law, well bless his heart . . . if they put his brain on the edge of a razor blade it'd roll around like a BB on a four lane highway. You just remember what the combination on this old safe is in case something happens to me. It's my Mama's birthday, left, right, left. One of these days someone is going to try and take Raven Ridge away from us, and I don't think that day is far off, and I don't think they're gonna give much of a shit how they go about it. Garnell is the only hope for this place. I hate that's the truth, but it's the truth nonetheless."

When that conversation ended and Little Law watched them drive off down the driveway completely unaware that he'd been standing on the back porch, he moved. He wasn't as dumb as everyone thought. He went to the family Bible, opened it up and read "Verna Manson Law, beloved Mother, born on April 22, 1918. The Accident did the math in his head, 4—22—18.

He'd called Ruby, told her he'd found something important, and that she better come quick.

"What did you find, Law?" she'd asked him.

"Never mind, I ain't saying over the phone. You just get here before they get back."

When she got there he'd handed her the will and she'd read it out loud. "It is with a sense of sadness that my wife, Jean Ray, and I, Lawson Ray, name our adopted daughter Garnell Lee Ray as the executrix of this, our last will and testament. We do so with the hope that the twisted gene that has found its way into the Ray bloodstream, and therefore bypasses Garnell, will give her the wisdom and sense to do what is right for Raven Ridge."

"Well isn't that a fine howdy do," Ruby had said to no one in particular. Little Law was the only one there at the time so he assumed she was talking to him, ass—u—me he'd thought and grinned.

"I don't want you to say a word about this to anyone, Law, do you hear me? I'll take care of all this. Mama, Daddy, and our fine red-headed step-child of a sister, I'll take care of all of it. Do we understand each other here, Law?"

She asked it in such a way that Law had little doubt she meant every word. He shook his head in the affirmative and said, "Can I have twenty bucks?"

Back in the present, The Accident remembered why he was here today at Raven Ridge. Ruby was coming to meet him. It was that damn will he'd found in the safe that started all this.

It wasn't enough that the two living, breathing, steaming piles that called themselves parents had done everything in their power to screw up his life and everyone else's while they were alive. No, they had to leave a will and a letter describing who and—why the who—was to be the executrix of their mountain top Shangri-La.

*****

Ruby Jean Law had known early on that her sister was not her sister. One look at that red hair and those freckles was all it took to convince anyone with even a tiny morsel of brains that that branch didn't belong on her family tree. Ruby Jean Law had a lot more than a tiny morsel of brains. Not only was she the smartest woman she knew, she also had plans, big plans. Come hell or high water she was going to be something big in these mountains, and Raven Ridge was the means to that end.

She also knew that neither her Mama nor her Daddy were people you wanted to tie off to in a storm. Her Mama, with her wandering eye and serpentine body crawled or wiggled her way in and out of every bedroom in two counties. It would have been one thing had she tried the least little bit to keep her trysts secret, but she did not. She would flaunt them all over town and stand right in front of her husband, God, and her children and dare any one of them to say anything about anything. "I will slap the taste out of all y'alls' mouths in a New York minute, and if you don't believe me . . . TRY ME!"

Her Daddy, the holy-rolling head deacon at the First Baptist Church had more than a taste for whiskey. He had a wandering eye of his own and hands that got way too friendly and frisky when tuckin' in his daughters. Her hatred of him had grown out of her fear of him, and now with her impatience for the "good life" growing, she saw him as the dime holding up a dollar. *"The twisted gene that has found its way into the Ray bloodstream."* Every time she thought about those words it made her hate him all the more. *I'll show you twisted soon enough, you son of a bitch*, she thought.

Her husband to be, the honorable Dr. Christian Williamston had broken off their engagement, though no one knew that yet. It didn't matter. She didn't love him anyway, but being a doctor's wife brought certain comforts and respect that she had counted on. A Brooks and Dunn song ran through her pretty but twisted head: *You should a kissed me, cause you're damn sure gonna miss me now that I'm gone.* Ruby smiled. This sudden change of heart came upon the doctor as a result of a recent episode. "Ruby," he'd said. "I have a friend who is a psychiatrist in Raleigh. I want you to go see him. I talked to him and he told me he'd make whatever time was necessary to see you."

"What . . . just because you walked in and found me naked on the floor, now all of a sudden I need to see a shrink?"

"You weren't just naked on the floor, Ruby. You had smashed every picture in our apartment along with every other glass or porcelain object you could find, and were lying, and bleeding I might add, in the middle of it all. I put almost a hundred stitches in you that night. You need help. If you don't get it, I'm afraid of what you might do to yourself . . . or . . . to someone else. Please go to Raleigh, see my friend. Maybe he can help you with this . . . this . . . whatever it is."

She'd just screamed, "Screw you, screw you, and screw everyone else while we're at it! I don't need your friend poking around in my head." And with that she'd stormed out and gone to stay with her Aunt Gloria. Good old Aunt Gloria.

No one knew what was in her head, or for that matter what she was capable of. She was capable of things that no one who "knew" her could have imagined. That docile, sweet innocent, doting school girl act was just that, an act. Underneath, just below the skin, was a surface hotter than the sun. Should she get caught doing what she had planned—which would never happen by the way—the press that would surely follow would be like those interviews with a mass murderer's next door neighbor. "I can't believe it," they would say. "She was the sweetest, kindest person you'd ever want to meet, and she'd give you the shirt off her back."

Ruby Jean Law believed one thing. It was a dog eat dog world, and if she had to act this way or that to be the biggest dog on the porch, then so be it, she'd do it, no questions asked. When acting this way or that wasn't enough, and action was needed, she could bring more action to the party than Carter had little liver pills. When The Accident found the will those many years ago, action was needed, and action she took. She hired a crooked disbarred Yankee lawyer of Italian descent—and she suspected former mafia ties—who now worked as a "Private Investigator." He lived near Shatley Springs in Ashe County.

When they first met he'd introduced himself as Max Black.

"Bullshit, Max Black. What's your real name?"

With the question and the tone, Ruby set the table early that she wasn't someone to screw with.

"Anthony . . . Anthony Ghirardelli."

She immediately put Guido, as she called him, on the payroll and set him to work, trying to figure out how they could get her Mama and Daddy committed. Lord knows they were both as crazy as shit house rats, but proving that turned out to be a mite more difficult thing than just knowing it.

Local big-wig real-estate developer Andy Michaux had done some of the work for her. She had pulled into the driveway one day and seen the developer standing on the front porch kissing her Mama in broad daylight. When Michaux heard and saw her car, he pushed Jean Ray away like she had Mad Cow disease and headed towards his car, clearing his throat and harrumphing all the way.

"Afternoon Mr. Michaux. It's a fine day for pressin' the flesh, ain't it?" Ruby said as she passed him.

Michaux never looked up. "Yes . . . well . . . yes . . . good God," were the only words he could find.

Ruby, once inside the house, which is where her Mother had fled to, confronted her.

"Mama, are you having an affair with Mr. Michaux?"

Her Mama broke out in a Betty Davis laugh. "An affair? Why Ruby, you make it sound like he and I have feelings for each other. Why of course we're not having an affair. He comes over, we bump uglies, then he goes his way and I go mine."

With the look of a woman who could care less what her own daughter, or anyone else, could or would think, she leaned in and looked straight into her daughter's eyes.

"Does that answer your question, dear?"

She made that last word slide and twist out of her mouth, and then without waiting for an answer, Jean Ray turned and walked away.

If her Mother had been trying to shock her, if she had been looking for some tell-tale sign that her words were having some effect on her daughter, she walked away disappointed.

The next day Ruby handed a handwritten note to Guido.

"Here. Type this up and send it to Michaux, and for Christ's sake don't write it on your own typewriter. Go some place like over to the library at App State and write it there, and don't mail it from here, go to Wilkesboro and mail it, and don't write the address out with your hand, type it out, too, and wear gloves. All this forensic bullshit you see on NCIS isn't make believe."

The note read:

Dear Mr. Michaux,

I have pictures of you and the wife of a prominent Baptist deacon in . . . shall we say . . . compromising positions. I'm not sure the "holier than thou" clients of a right-wing nutjob such as yourself—and feel free to correct me if I'm wrong here, but it was those folks that got you where you are today—are going to understand these pictures, nor are they going to believe that she had merely gone flat and you were pumping her up. Meet me at the Connemara Farms goat barn (That's Carl Sandburg's home in Flat Rock just in case you really are as dumb as I think you are) two weeks from now at 6:00PM. COME ALONE.

A concerned citizen from The Agency.

Thus The Agency was born. A complete and total fabrication from the twisted mind of Ruby Jean Ray. The members were herself, the disgraced, disbarred, and possibly at one time connected—*hell, for all she knew he was in The Witness Protection Program*—bullish looking Guido, and her not so bright, pot-head, totally unaware of what was going on brother, The Accident, and working—unbeknownst to her, really—as a gopher and all around "yes" woman, was her Aunt Gloria. Aunt Gloria was Jean Ray's younger sister. For reasons known only to Gloria, she had wanted Lawson "Babe" Ray for her own, had dated him first, but being younger and not as "worldly" she was not ready to "put out" and her sister was. Suddenly, ZZ Top popped into a tiny space empty of the evil that otherwise filled Ruby's head. What were the words she was looking for? *Who's that girl that lives on a hill, she won't . . . but her sister will.*

I wonder if ZZ Top knew Mama?

Aunt Gloria had hated both her parents ever since. It was a useful sort of feeling for Ruby to have around.

The rest of Ruby's plan had been a piece of cake, really. She met with Michaux, showed him a few pictures she'd had photo-shopped by an expert in Greenville, SC—and like most men in his position—he folded. The developer's estimation of himself was much larger than the real thing as he was one of those folks that if you could buy him for what he was worth and sell for what he thought he was worth, a sizeable profit could be made. When Michaux failed to talk sense into her Mom and then by default into her Dad, and Michaux's pals—the snake-in-the-grass real estate lawyer, and the real estate agent—failed as well, Ruby had come to her wit's end and decided she had no other choice but to kill her parents herself.

Guido had volunteered to do the job. "You can't kill your own Mom and Dad . . . it . . . it's not right."

"*Well you stand over there and watch,*" Ruby had replied.

A year almost to the day after Little Law found the will, Ruby drove back to the house on Raven Ridge. After pleasantries of sorts, her mother headed into the kitchen to get Ruby a glass of ice tea. While her Mother stood at the refrigerator, Ruby walked up behind her and with a little nickel-plated .22 pistol she'd pulled from her purse, shot her Mother in the brain stem, and then stood back to watch her dissolve into the floor.

As her mother lay dead and bleeding on the floor, Ruby poured herself the tea, and slid her Mama's body out of the way so she could close the door—*no use wasting energy,* she thought—and waited for her Father to come home. When he pulled into the driveway, Ruby walked to the front door and stood behind it. With the pistol raised, she waited for her Daddy to walk in. As he turned his back to close the door, she shot him dead.

The .22 nickel-plated pistol had been purchased by Guido from some desperate crack-head who had stolen it. Guido had filed down the serial number and Ruby carefully wiped it down with a kitchen towel. On her way home she stopped at a long ago abandoned farm house she knew from her childhood and dropped the pistol down the well. When she heard the splash, she got into her Prius—Ruby was conscious of the environment, at least to the degree of being seen as conscientious—and drove away.

*****

Garnell Lee Ray—which wasn't even her name now, not in her head anyway—was now a motherless child. Had she not been a murderer, too, that thought might have crushed her right then and there on the sawdust covered ground, but the world (or was it Ruby?) had given her bigger fish to fry. Billie Holliday began to sing in her head, and she joined in: *God bless the child who has his own.* The sudden urge to scream was overwhelming. All those years, all those connections to some things and some ones, were now meaningless, less than meaningless, they were all lies.

What kind of mother gives up her child? She could never abandon her own flesh and blood, never! Except for that once upon a time thing back in college, Garnell had never seen herself bounding toward motherhood with open arms. From the effort she had seen her Mama make—correction, the woman she once thought of as her Mama—and the results she'd seen garnered from that effort, a sister whose self-absorption knew no bounds, a brother whose self-doubt knew no limits, and her . . . the task seemed to be impossible.

She knew that other mothers had somehow found the capacity needed for the daunting task of raising children. Her friends—what few there had been in high school and college—had seemed to be covered in that mother's blanket of protection and love, even if she herself, Ruby, or poor old Little Law were not.

Luck of the draw, she thought, not only is my family the shits, now they're not even my family. Billie Holliday faded and she now sang along to Albert King: *If it weren't for bad luck, I'd have no . . .* " Seemed appropriate at the moment, she thought to herself. She was sure if it wasn't for her ever growing bad luck, she'd have no damn luck at all.

As she rounded the corner of the funnel cake booth she saw Dawn Reindeer and Mud Pie or whatever her name was sitting on a hay bale.

"There you are. Well, you look a sight better now that you got that war paint off your face. I was just telling Moon Pie that Marshall should have been here by now."

"*I love you, Garnell Lee Ray,*" Marshall had said.

What was that all about, and what was the twinge in her heart she'd felt when he said it?

*****

Marshall Harris tried to sit up but his head, the inside of his head, was on fire!

Lying on the ground, he fell back in time. It was 1989. He was the boy standing in the shade and shadow of the big black walnut tree watching the red-headed freckle-faced girl play hop-scotch with her friends. She was the most beautiful girl he'd ever seen, and that blue dress set that

152

head full of auburn hair on fire.

She was a small thing, with small features, but even from a distance and with no more competition than a game of hop-scotch going on, it was obvious to Marshall Harris that she had more spunk than you could stuff in a gunny sack.

He did not belong at the Ray family reunion on the llama farm outside the small town of Marshall. He had no family here, nor anywhere else that he knew of. He was just a twelve year old hired hand, someone to walk behind a plow and pick up rocks and carry them to the fence line, or to gather eggs, or milk the cow, or muck the barn. He'd been eight-years-old when Jimmerson Harris and his wife Thelma Ray Harris came to the Presbyterian Children's Home in Black Mountain and adopted him. That had been four years ago—seemed like a lot more.

He'd been an old man in the adoption game. Folks wanted babies, sweet smelling baby-powdered babies that they could cuddle and snuggle. No one wanted an eight-year-old boy, especially one as big as he was. He'd have to be able to work from can to can't just to make feeding him a break even proposition. Marshall could work all day, day in, day out.

His adoptive family had moved down to Marshall from Spillcorn the past year, so this was his first reunion. They had made the move so that his adoptive father could take a job as a gravedigger for the Marshall Cemetery. That just meant more work for him around the Harris's four-acre spread. He didn't mind the work really. Not working gave him time to think, and he did mind thinking. *Where did he come from? Did he have any brothers or sisters, and if so, did they wonder about him as much as he wondered about them?*

That kind of thinking led to nowhere but the blues and crying spells behind the barn. He was sick of thinking about what might have been instead of what was, and he was damn sure tired of crying. His only escape from work was school, but he had the feeling that if it weren't for laws and regulations about the education of a child, he'd be splitting wood instead of conjugating verbs.

He could remember no other home but the Presbyterian Children's Home, and no other family save the girls and boys around him. He reckoned Ms. Abigail Gore, his house mother at the home, was the closest thing to a real mother he had ever known, or was likely to know.

Mrs. Harris made no effort to impart any particular motherly skills on him with the exception of feeding him, making sure he washed, and patching the patches on his jeans and the elbows of his old flannel shirts. It was alright though. He managed. School kept him interested and oc-cupied for one-hundred and eighty days—give or take—and books—any book kept him occupied year round.

He had a pen flashlight he guarded with his life, and he saved every penny he could find or earn, to keep that flashlight in AAA batteries. When the lights went off in the Harris house Marshall's world expanded greatly. He floated the Mississippi River with Huck Finn, an orphaned boy who reminded him of him thanks to Mark Twain. He fought ren-egade Indians and desperados right here in the Blue Ridge Mountains alongside the Sackett clan thanks to Louis L'Amour, and he went to war with the 101st Airborne via Cornelius Ryan.

He was a good student who liked challenges, so he took to learning quickly. It was something he could excel in, all through his own efforts, and that gave him the sense of pride he needed to keep going and not simply fold up and quit.

Later that afternoon at the Ray's family reunion, while the grownups were churning away on Ice Cream makers, he found himself in the barn alongside that pretty red-head, Garnell Lee Ray as she had introduced herself. Well not really an introduction as much as it had been a challenge.

"I'm Garnell Lee Ray and I'm ten years old and I'm stronger than ev-erybody I know. You're pretty big. I guess you think you're stronger'n me. Well, you ain't, so git over yourself." He just shook his head up and down.

They were in a corncob fight with some of the other kids. They were squashed down behind some hay bales when the urge just overtook him, and he leaned over and kissed her full on the mouth. "I love you, Garnell Lee Ray." Before she could do anything but look at him with a blank dumbfounded look on her face, a corncob from the other side smacked one of the llama's right square on the ass—and the llamas, all the llamas, not just the one that was hit, went to screaming. A God-awful sound like a banshee's wail from hell.

That's the last thing Marshall remembered. Next thing he knew he was sitting in the backseat of the Harris's green wood-grained 1979 Pontiac station wagon getting yelled at. He never heard a word they were yelling.

All he could think about were those screaming llamas and that kiss flush on the mouth.

That was the first and last Ray reunion he ever attended. He never saw Garnell Lee Ray again, not close up anyway. His adoptive father lost his job at the cemetery a short time later and they moved back to Spillcorn.

It wasn't until he came back to Marshall in 2004 that he heard the name Garnell Lee Ray again. By then he was 6'2", weighed 195, and was an undercover agent for the North Carolina State Bureau of Investigation.

*****

Andy Michaux had been as corrupt, self-serving, and diabolical as anyone who'd ever achieved his level of success as a real estate developer, and those facts alone made him stick out on the SBI's radar screen like a pimple on a virgin's forehead. When an anonymous tip and a copy of a handwritten blackmail letter which had been sent to Michaux came to the attention of the bureau, he moved up "with a bullet" on the radar screen. You couldn't blackmail someone as well-known and wealthy as Michaux without attracting the attention of the bureau.

When confronted with the letter Michaux denied everything. When presented with the two options that the SBI proclaimed as the most logical outcomes, he acquiesced.

Option one had been to go on denying his knowledge or involvement, in which case the bureau would simply set up around the clock surveillance on him and also be at the rendezvous point with men and camera. Or option two, which was to not show up at the rendezvous and have this "Agency" release the pictures. Andy came up with option three—admitting the affair, but having nothing to do with the SBI's investigation.

Even without Michaux's help, everything went fine early on in the investigation. The connection was made between Ruby Jean Ray, Michaux, a real estate agent, and a prominent real estate attorney. Together the bureau considered these people to be the main players in this "Agency."

The whole thing seemed to center on fourteen acres of prime land in Madison County called Raven Ridge, which was owned by Ruby Jean Ray's parents. Ruby wanted control of the land so that she could, along with Michaux, the real estate agent, and the lawyer, develop the land and make a fortune.

One thing stood in the way of this plan—well two things, really—Mr. and Mrs. Ray. They were not about to sell their land, nor were they interested in turning it over to their daughter. When the Rays were found brutally murdered in their home, the whole Raven Ridge thing went to number one on the SBI charts. After the Rays' murder and the members of what the bureau considered to be The Agency started dying off in weird ways, the bureau came to the conclusion that maybe they'd missed someone when it came to this Agency thing.

*****

Marshall Harris knew the SBI had missed someone, Garnell Lee Ray, but she was not really a member of The Agency, merely its pawn. Garnell had been used by someone or someones, to start tying up the loose ends. That's how Marshall saw it. The bureau didn't know about Garnell, not yet. Marshall hadn't been cleaning up Garnell's crime sites as a member of the bureau. He had been cleaning them up . . . well . . . because he loved her. He didn't know why he loved her, but he did. He could not bring himself to turn her into the bureau, not yet, not until he figured out who was behind it, and how on earth, please God, he could save Garnell, if not from prison, then at least from lethal injection. He had to at least try.

Dawn Reindeer and Garnell together—that was an unfortunate accident. He'd met Dawn at The Old Farmer's Ball contra dance at Warren Wilson College. She was a helluva a dancer; he was, well, not so much. The attraction he felt for her was purely one of a physical nature. He wasn't sure he had the skills or the tools to be anything more than someone's lover. He cared for her, but his own weakness when it came to matters of the heart stopped him from walking out on that limb and trusting. It had always been easier to keep those few people who made their way into his life at a safe distance, at least that had been the case until he came across Garnell again. *What was with her? What was it with him and her?*

He'd been sent back to Madison County seven years ago. That had been during his first year with the bureau. He'd originally been sent because of corruption in the county, including both the Tax Collector, who had a little pot growing thing on the side, and the local sheriff. Those issues had been resolved, but he had stayed on for one thing then another.

The dumb redneck act had been just that, an act. Along with Barney Fife and Falstaff, he'd based his act on his adoptive father Jimmerson Harris. A dumber man, or one with less common sense than Jimmerson Harris, had never been born. It was an easy role, one he suspected anyone who lived in these mountains could have played. The "civilized world" had taken these people for granted for centuries; they sound dumb, therefore they must be dumb. That was a long way from the truth, and any Yankee or Floridian who came here to trade these good old boys out of their land could attest to that fact, if they'd only known, which most of them did not.

When this business concerning The Agency and Michaux became the number one priority, he had no idea Garnell was involved. It wasn't until her parents were killed, and he attended the funeral out of respect, that he even knew she was in the area. He found out she worked as some kind of map maker and figured she traveled a lot doing her job. Of course, she wouldn't have known him from Adam's housecat—as the funeral confirmed. They had only stood face to face lo those many years ago as boy and girl, yet he would know her anywhere. How or why he could not say, and how in God's name he was going to get himself and her out of the mess they were now covered up with was beyond him.

His trip back to that ill-fated llama farm had been the final act of a desperate man and now the chickens were gonna come home to roost.

*****

When he was finally able to move, Marshall could barely lift his head. It pounded with each breath and with each blink of his eyelids. What was that smell, where the hell was he, what had happened? He looked around. He was laying half on and half off another man wrapped in a damn Mexican poncho. The half of him that was laying off was in llama shit, which explained the smell. *What the hell? Where am I?* Then came the question *. . . Oh God, who am I?*

Pandemonium

by Linda Marie Barrett

A
s he stared into the sun, the shock of amnesia sending his unte-
thered mind racing towards a full-blown panic attack, a shadow
accompanied by a lovely low humming crossed over his face.
He looked into beautiful brown eyes that reminded him of someone
else, someone he couldn't remember at the moment, but whose connection to those just above his face comforted him. The eyes blinked, long
white lashes fanning out against furry white cheeks. A leathery black nose
wrinkled, and then more humming. He reached towards the face and it
retreated, clucking, then came back and sniffed at his fingers. Another
face appeared, large brown eyes similar to the first pair, but this one had
ginger-colored hair and was smaller, more delicate. Marshall craned his
head towards the second face and it hummed in response, a "hmmmmm
. . ." like the sound of hummingbird wings. Another pair of eyes, and
then another, came into view, all of them brown, liquid, gentle and in-
quisitive. Marshall rested in their gazes, his heart easing, and he closed his
eyes. A girl's face—root beer colored eyes, a spray of freckles across a pert
nose, soft, pink lips, thick auburn hair that he yearned to curl around his
fingers—formed in his mind. Garnell. Like a flash of lightning across a
storm-darkened summer sky, he remembered. Remembered everything—
what, where and who he was—and why he was lying on top of this very

lumpy corpse that was throwing his back out. He opened his eyes and rolled over and off Michaux. He stood up among the herd of llamas and, for the first time since that traumatic day when he kissed Garnell and was scared unconscious by their screams, felt no fear of them. The relief that came from being cured of a phobia so deep-seated he'd despaired of ever conquering it almost brought him to his knees. He let out a long, full breath that took with it any remaining burdens.

"Oh, my God!"

Marshall turned to see Gloria tearing across the pasture, her high heels sinking into the dirt and causing her to nearly stumble as she made her jerky progress toward him. She fell to her knees beside Michaux, twisted his head, and stared into his dead face.

"Andy! Honey! No! You can't leave me! I need you!" She cried out, grabbing his shoulders and attempting to shake some life into him. "We need you! Oh, Andy! No! No!"

She looked up at Marshall, her face a mess of teary makeup. "What in God's name happened here?"

Marshall wanted to spare Garnell, but to protect his role with The Agency, he had to tell some truths. "Garnell killed him and ran off when Detective Klontz showed up. Klontz saw Michaux lying here, and he suspects I'm working with y'all, or at the very least, with Garnell. We've got to get a move on before more police arrive."

"What about Andy? Do we just leave him here?" Gloria lay Andy back down and began to unknot the poncho beneath his neck and cover his face with it.

"Give me that," Marshall said, taking the poncho. "Leave him be. There's nothing we can do for him. I'm going to look for Garnell. You'd best lay low until we find out what Klontz knows and what he intends to do about it."

They walked over to where they'd parked their cars in the drive to the barn. Gloria leaned over to look in her car's sideview mirror and wiped off her mascara-stained face with the backs of her hands. Frowning, she extracted a compact from her purse, snapped it open, and brushed foundation over her cheeks. Then she took out another compact and brushed on some blush. A tube of lipstick came out of the purse next and then a small hair pick, which she used to tidy up her teased-out Shania Twain-inspired hairdo. She examined herself in a small hand mirror and seemed satisfied with the results. She turned to Marshall. "I've got to go meet Ruby and fill her in. She said Garnell was going to be a problem and, honey, she sure was right. Garnell needs to be stopped. I tried to argue against it, but now that she's killed Andy . . . " Gloria choked back a sob before continuing. "You be careful. Garnell might try and kill you, too."

Marshall gave her a quick hug and a reassuring smile.

"I'll talk to her, Glory. Don't you worry 'bout me."

As soon as he got into his car he made a call to the SBI to see how quickly they could get Klontz off his ass while he dealt with Garnell and put an end to the agenda of The Agency.

*****

Little Law fumbled in his pocket for his bag of weed. He'd resupplied at the headshop on Lexington Avenue just that morning. He'd been at the used bookstore picking up the latest George R. R. Martin to take his mind off his sister's hysterical rant over his fuckup with Garnell (okay, okay, so he'd failed to take her out; he'd done some major damage, and if she hadn't managed to get medical attention so quickly, she'd have died, so it wasn't like he'd completely fucked up) when it occurred to him that he'd used up his stash before breakfast during his wake n' bake. Lucky for him, the Squid Shoppe's mantle-shaped neon sign beckoned and he'd set himself up with a bag of "sengin' n' bangin'"—a primo blend of ginseng and marijuana popular among the older crowd as a potent all-natural Viagra substitute—to help him stay alert, and some "Highland Gale" for when he was in the mood for a totally mind-blowing high. Which was now. The inner voices that kept telling him he was a no-good-loser-worthless-piece-of-shit-Accident were talking so fast and so loud he couldn't get high soon enough.

Little Law packed a few buds of the Gale into his pipe and fired up. He heard the sound of a car popping and grinding gravel under its tires as it made its way up the road to Raven Ridge. Ruby had finally arrived. She'd told him over the phone that he had another assignment and she'd be coming by to give him details. Tonight was Halloween and she'd implied his job was to deliver the ultimate treat to his adopted sister. Maybe he did fuck up last time, but he'd get it right tonight.

Ruby stepped out of her Prius and slammed the door shut. Her eyes were pinched and her mouth pursed like she'd swallowed a lemon. Law heard the inner voices again, this time louder, more shrill, like an angry woman's voice. The Gale was letting him down. He inhaled harder and deeper and pushed a growing sense of paranoia and doom to the left, then to the right, just the fuck out of the way.

Then he realized that it was Ruby who was saying the bad shit and he tried to chill. He watched her lips move, framing the words, "Are you even listening to me, you moron?!!"

He coughed and whimpered at the same time. "I hear you. What's on for tonight?"

Ruby slung her Coach bag back over her shoulder and narrowed her eyes at him. "I just told you the whole plan, you no-good Accident. You're going to shoot the fuck out of our goddamn enviro-bullshit-fake-sister at that pagan to-do that's going on in front of the courthouse. You can't screw up again, Law. You have to kill her. If you don't get a kill shot, then keep shooting till you do. No running away this time. You hear?"

Law nodded, trying not to scream at the giant pink praying mantis walking up behind his sister. It looked like it was going to crush her head between its mandibles. He'd seen a praying mantis spear a hummingbird through the chest with its spiny leg and proceed to make a meal out of it. It was the most violent, creepy thing he'd ever seen in his life, except for the thing his dad had done to him that one time when he'd been drinking too much of the Maker's Mark and going on about Samson and what he'd like to do to Delilah if he had his hair back and didn't have to hold up those goddamn pillars. But Law didn't want to think about that because it made the voices start up again. He wondered if Ruby was about to be impaled. His heart beat so hard he was sure Ruby and the praying mantis could hear it. He wondered if praying mantises could sense fear. He grew even more frightened.

"Law, you okay, honey?" the praying mantis asked him, bending its head to the side and fixing him with its terrifying compound eyes. He was going to pass out. The mantis sounded just like his Aunt Gloria. He started backing away as it moved on its spindly hind legs towards him.

"Oh, hey Aunt Gloria," Ruby was addressing the creature.

Law rubbed his eyes and looked again. The praying mantis had turned into Aunt Gloria in a pink designer suit and oversized sunglasses. Jesus, he swore to himself, this was so not a good high.

"Uh, I better get going, Sis. I'll call you after." He stuffed his now-cold pipe in his pocket, but not before tapping out the charred remains of the dreaded Highland Gale onto the ground. That shit was too powerful even for him, and that was saying something. "Bye, Aunt Gloria." He backed away from both of them, then turned and ran to his car.

Gloria and Ruby stared after him. "Ruby, darlin'. There's something just not right about that boy. Too bad, cause he's cute as a button."

"He'll take care of Garnell tonight at that witchy gathering in Asheville," Ruby replied, watching her brother stare at his car door for a long time before getting out his keys and driving away. He looked drunk, but she knew better. Stoned as hell like he always was.

Addiction ran in the family, but Ruby was in control of her own cravings. She liked freaky sex and cutting, but she made sure she didn't go there more than once a week. That prude of an ex might have had a problem with her tastes, but once she came into big-time money she wouldn't have to go all Junior League and pretend to actually desire a normal upscale family life. Freed from the need to marry into money, she could satisfy her wildest imaginings among the swinger set the UPS driver who delivered to her medical office had enigmatically hinted was thriving in Asheville. Behind the locked doors of downtown offices and condos, the traditionally married heterosexual couples everyone admired in church, rotary club, and city council meetings were banging the hell out of whatever they could get their hands on. Men on men, women on women, piles of men on piles of women—it was all happening and she wanted in. She doubted that most men were turned off by a little blood and scarring, anyway. Ruby was all about finding her own kind, and judging by the kinds of people she'd seen walking around Asheville on a Friday or Saturday night, they were out there. As Asheville's tourism guides proclaimed to one and all, "Asheville: Any Way You Like It."

She looked back at Gloria, who seemed lost in her own thoughts as she gazed out over the multi-million dollar view that would allow Ruby to never have to work another day in her life. "After he finishes off Garnell, we'll have Little Law take care of Klontz. And then we'll move ahead with the sale of Raven Ridge. Nothing can stop us now."

Gloria nodded and wiped a tear from her eye as she thought about poor Andy lying dead in a pile of llama shit, an undignified end for a man for whom she'd felt strong feelings for such a long time. He may not have been the sharpest knife in the drawer, but he sure as hell knew how to use his assets. She felt warm between her legs and wriggled against her tight Chanel pants. She glanced over at Ruby. "Honey, we needed Andy to make sure this deal would go through. Without him, we may run into some trouble selling this land to those developers planning on building a theme park devoted to a 3-D experience of the Rapture. Andy just loved the idea, bless his heart. But I'm not sure how the county commissioners will like it. Too many of them turned tree-hugger lately, not like in the old days when they'd be begging for a prison or a Wal-Mart. Nowadays everyone's concerned about run-off, erosion, increased traffic on rural roads, all those silly city things I don't pay no mind to. Andy had a way of convincing people to see his side. He had a gift and he worked it. If he could make Parks to Putts a statewide success, imagine how easily he could have helped with 'Rapture at Wolf Laurel'?"

Gloria sighed and pulled out her hand mirror, reapplying her lipstick before she spoke again.

"I'll call Max and see what he suggests. That man has a plan for everything. In the meantime, I trust you and Law can take care of Garnell and that detective. I've invested a lot of Walter's money in this venture and I want to see some return. Now I really do need to go to my mani-pedi appointment over at the Grove Park Inn. You call me." She air-kissed her niece and sashayed back to her car.

Ruby watched her drive off, clenching her fists so tightly her fingernails drew blood from her palms.

*****

Garnell drove the pink Caddy towards Asheville. Dawn and Moonpie had pretty much abandoned her and she was feeling very unsettled. She'd killed the last of her parents' murderers and she didn't have that sense of closure she'd hoped for. In fact, she felt a little let down. Any satisfaction from avenging her parents withered away when she found out she wasn't blood-related to them, and, even more humiliating, that they'd tried to give her back to the adoption agency. They didn't deserve what she'd done in their memory, what she'd risked on their behalf. If it wasn't for her, Ruby and Little Law would have long ago sold that property to developers, and now she felt no connection to the place, not a good one, anyway. She didn't want to see Raven Ridge ruined, but she no longer wanted to make it her home. That dream had died in Cherokee.

So the big question still remained: who the hell shot her? It wasn't Michaux. The person who shot her wasn't that stout and she couldn't imagine Michaux ever deigning to wear a hoodie. Was there someone out there who still wasn't finished with her? She touched the wound on her neck and shivered. She'd ask Marshall if he had any leads.

Which brought her to the other subject that was causing her distress. What to do about Marshall's declaration of love? The kiss was really hot, she had to admit, and totally unexpected. Marshall had spent years trying to help her and she'd been completely unaware of his actions, of his very existence. When she thought about it, with the exception of the father of her baby, no one else had ever told her they'd loved her. She believed only Marshall meant it.

The sun was disappearing behind the mountains as she neared Asheville. The leaves had changed color more slowly this year, and it was just now, at the end of October, that the fall foliage had reached its peak. Reflecting the shimmering light of the setting sun, the mountains were ablaze in shades of red and gold. She'd lived here all her life and still the sight of the mountains in the fall never ceased to take her breath away. Clicking on the radio, she heard Cyndi Lauper's "Time After Time." The song turned her thoughts back to Marshall, to his protectiveness and the longing in his voice when he spoke about his feelings for her. She sighed.

It was far too soon, and way too crazy, and he was a bit too weird-looking for her to contemplate a relationship with him, but there was a part of her, and this brought to mind the image of the Grinch's small heart growing three sizes in that Christmas show she used to watch with her family every year, that warmed to him. When he said, "I love you, Garnell Lee Ray," she'd been shocked. She cringed when she remembered her lame response: "Okay." But what could she have said? "Thank you, I had no idea"? She was such an idiot when it came to men.

All this confusion made her plans for tonight even more important. Garnell might be a cynic and an assassin-for-hire, she might roll her eyes at Dawn's fanatical embrace of Native American spirituality and dismiss her father's Baptist ravings about an all-powerful, punishing God as outright lunacy, but she was a devoted Wiccan and she would not ignore the holiest night of the year just because she was in danger of being arrested for murder. No, on the first of the Greater Sabbats she would join her fellow Wiccans around the bonfire in front of the courthouse. She hoped the Samhain rituals would cast off the bad mood she was nursing and help her start the pagan new year with a clean slate. No more killing. No more Agency or whatever it was she'd been working for. She was free of that shit. Fuck Klontz and his suspicions. They had nothing on her, nothing they could prove anyway. And maybe Marshall would back her up on her assertion of Michaux's accidental asphyxiation from ingesting llama hair while attempting to force himself on said llama. Bono's heart-wrenchingly passionate voice singing "I Still Haven't Found What I'm Looking For" snapped her out of her reverie. She lifted her own voice to sing with him as she turned onto I-240 and took the first exit for downtown Asheville.

*****

Marshall chucked the fake Billy Bob teeth he'd been sporting since he took the Avery deputy job, and raked his fingers back through his hair so he didn't look like the bumpkin he'd pretended to be for two years. It was amazing how bad teeth, bad hair and bad posture (the forward shoulder slump he'd affected, which he had to counter with almost an hour of stretching every evening so he didn't develop nerve damage in his neck) could transform a person and deflect attention away rather than towards. He was going to save Garnell tonight and take their relationship to the next level. He'd talked to Dawn, broken up with her in an awkward, mercifully brief phone conversation, and then headed into Asheville, where he suspected Garnell already was. He'd found out from his research on her that she always took part in Asheville's *Samhain on the Square*, and he believed her life was in danger. Gloria's words, "She needs to be stopped" alarmed him. He knew how Gloria and Ruby and their partner Max Black stopped people and that sure as hell wasn't going to happen to Garnell.

165

The SBI let him know they'd contacted a very irritated Klontz and told him to back off on his investigation of Garnell. The man was as one-track minded as his beagle and although he'd agreed to step aside, neither the SBI nor Marshall were convinced he'd stop investigating. Klontz seemed to have a sixth sense where Garnell was concerned and he was probably on her tail right now. Marshall needed to get there first, before Klontz made things more complicated. If Marshall could prove that Garnell was merely a tool of the conspirators making up The Agency, the SBI promised immunity for her. She'd have to testify against them, but when she found out she'd been duped by her own sister and aunt, she'd probably be a very willing witness. The alternative was life in prison, and he knew she didn't want that. Nor did he. He wanted to share his life with her, and with that goal in mind he headed into Asheville.

*****

J.D. swore as he ended the phone call with the SBI. This was just the kind of officious rank-pulling bullshit he thought he'd left behind in Buffalo. He was too old and too pissed off at everyone lying to him to let this one go. The only pleasure he'd had lately was plowing that Glock into Harris's jaw. "Oh, what a tangled web we weave, when first we practise to deceive!" Allude that, Harris.

Everyone involved in this investigation was pretending to be something they weren't: Garnell and her Brown Mountain Lights research, Harris the dimwitted deputy who didn't know how to work his radio, Dawn Reindeer—Native American, my ass—even that kindly old vet at the campground, Daniel, had something to hide. A background check revealed he'd served a 10-year prison term for the production, distribution and sale of moonshine which he'd tried to pass off to J.D. as innocent ole "branch water." Hell, from what J.D found out, Daniel "Crackerjack" Puckett was a local moonshining legend and the subject of an Emmy Award-winning documentary on his family's multigenerational involvement in the moonshining trade. J.D. was pretty sure the campground owners had no idea they'd hired a convicted felon to manage their family-friendly campground, and it was on his shortlist to let them know. Improvise or die, Daniel.

After leaving the unconscious Harris behind, J.D. had pulled his car into a blind and waited to see who would show up next. He watched as Gloria Gudger—wealthy widow, possible kidnapper and murder accomplice—arrived, then observed her and Harris leave shortly after in separate cars, both of them in a hurry. He set off in a stealthy pursuit of Harris's vehicle. He'd soon gotten the call from the SBI, surely a result of their mole calling in and reporting on J.D.'s encounter with his jaw after seeing the state senator lying dead on the ground.

Mr. Pibb squirmed on the seat next to him, sighing as he settled in between a stack of paperwork and the swiveling arm of J.D.'s laptop. He usually didn't bring Mr. Pibb along on assignments, but the beagle had been acting funny lately—coming home after dark sweaty and exhausted, the pads on his paws worn and caked with mud, and his appetite like that of a much larger dog, only to be gone in the morning when J.D. awoke. He didn't know what the dog was into and wanted to keep an eye on him. He was glad he'd kept Mr. Pibb in the car when he confronted Harris, as Mr. Pibb might have run off in pursuit of the pink Caddy. He stroked Mr. Pibb's little beagle head like a worry bead and considered his next actions.

SBI agent or no, Harris had been covering up something, and not just Michaux's dead body. When J.D. saw what he believed was Garnell driving off in the pink Caddy, his instincts told him there was a connection between the two of them that went beyond professional association. (Was Garnell in the SBI, too? Garnell was the real puzzle in this whole investigation). No man of military inclination—soldier, cop, G-man, whatever—spouts Shakespeare in the middle of a crime scene unless they are head over heels in love. It was like a secret code between men who otherwise would not show the weakness or vulnerability of affection, an admission that however bad the shit going down, they couldn't stop thinking about the women they love.

Okay, so he got that. Garnell was one of those women who could be a real looker if she ever wanted to take the trouble. But she was also involved in, and possibly responsible for, multiple murders. If Harris was trying to cover up for her, he was aiding and abetting. J.D.'s curiosity about Harris's motives was also born out of the shock of finding out how incredibly wrong he'd been about Harris all this time, and his desire to get the real measure of the man behind the fool he'd put out there for everyone to ridicule. J.D. was angry about the deception, but more than that he was curious, and for someone who'd been conducting investigations for most of his adult life, curiosity was by far the stronger motivator for going around the SBI's order that he back off.

J.D. believed Harris was on his way to see Garnell, and J.D. intended to follow Harris and find out what was going on. To justify to the feds, should they sweep in and give him some chin music about his continuing involvement, he'd already come up with a reason that couldn't be denied: a crime had occurred in his county, and he would not rest until he found out who killed Dick Sweatt.

*****

Garnell parked the pink Caddy near the square and made her way through the jostling crowd to join the growing band of Wiccan celebrants. Some had already disrobed while others came in elaborate dress—low-cut, bosom-flattering velvet gowns with sleeves that draped past heavily-jeweled fingers, LOTR-inspired hooded elvish cloaks, long ornately-embroidered tunics, mantles of fur pelts, wizard hats, gnomish boots, faerie slippers, torques and tiaras. If you could imagine it, someone had fashioned it and wore it proudly. There was no rule on dress at this gathering and the permit allowed no dress at all. Garnell, like a few brave others, preferred to be skyclad. Perhaps because she was a solitary practitioner and not a member of a coven, she felt that being naked was the most pure and direct way to worship, and she also felt, if she was honest with herself, a little thrill knowing that her father, were he still alive, would have been appalled. And probably turned on, if he was honest with himself, which he wasn't. Ever.

She greeted Rowena, the High Priestess leading the gathering's rituals. Rowena was a seemingly ageless woman with creamy white skin, long flowing brown hair, a heart-shaped face, and an amazing body (Garnell couldn't help but notice since Rowena was unclothed). Garnell took off her own clothing and unbound her hair, letting it fall in thick waves down her back and across her breasts. She took a thick lock of hair and draped it over her neck to cover up the slowly healing bullet-wound. She was slight, but curvy, and when she looked up after arranging her hair just so, she noticed that Rowena was checking her out, too. She smiled coyly but reminded herself that this was NOT Beltane, and flirtation was really not cool at Samhain, a much more somber occasion.

She folded her clothes and placed them in a pile near the garments of Rowena and a few other skyclad men and women. She kept on her glasses and made her way past a small group of brightly dressed cronish types to join the circle forming by the bonfire. Two men were building up the fire with split logs of oak and ash stacked up on a trailer parked nearby. Woodsmoke curled up into the crisp autumn air and wafted across the large expanse of field between the courthouse and the fire department, which was keeping an eye on the bonfire, too. The sun had finally set and a full-moon, the Hunter's Moon, rose up behind the neogothic majesty of the Jackson Building, stone gargoyles ringing the base of its penthouse. The weather was perfect for this Samhain ritual gathering—Garnell could sense strong magic in the air.

A group of boys sat by the circle and balanced African drums between their thighs. They were waiting for Rowena's cue to begin, but for now they were joking around with each other, laughing and gaping at some of the costumes and naked flesh. One boy took a long appreciative look at Garnell and nudged his friend, who blushed scarlet when he saw Garnell looking back at them. She smiled, amused by their interest—they had to be half her age—then turned her back on them as the man on Garnell's left took her hand, and the young woman on her right reached for her other hand. The circle was now actively forming and the crowd began to hush. Rowena paced around the closing circle, urging people to join the blessing or observe in respectful silence. She took her place across from Garnell, and winked at her. Garnell felt the heat of a blush cross her face as she bowed her head. The drummers began to beat their drums slowly, their rhythm increasing as Rowena's voice grew louder, directing listeners to connect with the Divine within and to the spirits of the land, water, and sky. She called out to the spirits dwelling inside the rock and soil that formed the mountains visible in every direction; she called out to the spirits living in the rivers and springs that nourished the soil, the plants and the animals that drank from them; she called out to the spirits dwelling among the flowers and trees that also nurtured life and brought beauty and comfort. Holding a crystal wand in her hand, Rowena traced a spiraling pattern from above her head to the ground at her feet. She spoke to the dead, honoring those who had come before, and invited them to the circle, too. She undid the boundaries between the living and the dead, the animate and inanimate, the earth and the cosmos. All were welcome to the gathering.

Those in the circle lifted their faces to the sky and repeated the sacred prayers Rowena offered in her low, melodic voice. As Garnell looked up, the moon seemed to vibrate with an almost audible celestial hum, and she felt power grow. The drums beat faster and her heart matched their pace. Sweat trickled between her breasts and a feeling so strong, so visceral and needful that it almost obliterated her sense of self began in her stomach and threatened to emerge as a shout. She squeezed the hands of those on either side and let out a deep breath.

A young woman in a skintight red dress and buttoned up black leather boots walked counterclockwise within the circle waving a stick of burning incense that smelled of myrrh and frankincense. Simultaneously, a young man in loose black clothing, his hair dyed black and his lips and fingernails painted a matching dark red, walked clockwise outside the circle sprinkling salt onto the ground. Garnell looked over at Rowena, whose eyes glowed with sparks reflected from the bonfire. The spirits had been summoned, the circle set, and the power from outside and within the circle now spiraled from the ground towards the sky.

A raven swept through the circle and knocked the stick of incense out of the woman's hand. At the same time, a beagle called out, its tortured bugle-call interrupting the focus of the group and causing everyone to turn towards the source of the sound. Garnell felt a prickling on the back of her neck. Blinking, she turned and saw deep in the crowd, among the shadows cast by the fire, the street lights, and the moon, a hooded figure staring at her. She couldn't see the face, but she thought she saw the glint of something metal and baton-shaped in the person's hands. Was this person holding a rifle? How could they have gotten past the police, who rimmed the square to keep out protestors, the Baptists standing on vegetable crates shouting out Bible verses and dire warnings about the Satan worshippers practicing their witchcraft and bringing the Devil into their midst? One oily-haired man in a cheap suit was thumping his Bible and exhorting the group of kids openly laughing at him, "You must not worship the LORD your God in THEIR way, because in worshiping THEIR gods, they do all kinds of detestable things the LORD hates. They even BURN their sons and daughters in the fire as SACRIFICES to THEIR gods!"

Garnell looked around to see if anyone else had noticed what she was noticing, and then she saw another person staring at her, this time a familiar and welcome one. Marshall? Was this really Marshall? Standing taller than most of those around him, his shoulders back and his curly hair no longer in the unflattering sidecombed style he seemed to favor, he was quite handsome. She knew she was staring but she was astonished by his transformation and she felt an almost irresistible urge to run to him. Sweet Jesus, she thought, the look in his eye was enough to set her skin on fire. Was that awe or naked desire or both? He was looking at her slack-jawed, yet his eyes were riveted. She suddenly remembered she wasn't wearing any clothes, and she felt a wave of self-consciousness. She nodded to show she'd seen him and then pointed with her chin to the hooded figure way back in the crowd.

Marshall followed her gaze and saw the hooded figure, too. The figure had a gun in his hands and was raising his arms to aim the gun at Garnell, who was now transformed into HIS goddess, a woman whose beauty had stunned him speechless, but not deprived him of the ability to act. With a speed years of training and exercise had honed, Marshall covered the fifty yards between him and the sniper in less than four seconds. The sniper must have heard the commotion as Marshall slammed his way through the Wiccans because the sniper suddenly whipped his rifle in Marshall's direction and began shooting.

Garnell screamed, and the whole square devolved into pandemonium.

[*Exeunt.*]

by Tony Earley

First, once he hit Asheville, Detective John Daniel "J.D." Klontz of the Avery County Sheriff's Department lost Harris (Marshall's extensive counter-intelligence training as an S.B.I. mole had included a weekend seminar in evasive driving taught by Kyle Petty at Lowe's Motor Speedway—he simply disappeared in traffic almost in front of Klontz's eyes), then Klontz couldn't find a place to park. It was Halloween, leaf season, the weather warm, the moon full, not to mention a Friday night, and every joker in the deck and nut in the forest and dull knife in the drawer, it seemed to Klontz, had decided en masse to come to town and make his life miserable. Yankee leaf peepers in antediluvian Town Cars, and soul-patched hipsters on Italian scooters, and unwashed off-the-gridders in ragged-out Volvos, and cryptographically-inked Latinos in day-glo Civics, and socially conscious Episcopalians in silent and appropriately-stickered Prii, and inexplicably angry rednecks in straight-piped F-150s crept and honked and optimistically turn-signaled, incrementally stretching the shoe sizes of their carbon footprints block by ozone-depleted block. Only the skatepunks, weaving almost invisibly in and out of the traffic in their uniformly tea-length, goth-black t-shirts, displayed any real mobility. Klontz briefly thought about flashing his shield and commandeering a skateboard. He thought about switching on his blue light, but realized it wouldn't have done any good. If there had been anywhere to pull over, he would have done so himself. Eventually he tossed the keys of his unmarked Intrepid to a bewildered valet at the Radisson and warned the kid not to mess with the radio. He had no idea where to look for Harris, but, once he heard drums beating in the distance, he instinctively set off at a jog down Spruce Street. The unmistakable *pop pop* of gunfire caused him to lumber into the first sprint he had attempted since retiring from the force in Buffalo. When the initial pops were answered, as if in call and response, by a chorus of pops in a truly frightening number of pitches and timbres, Klontz drew his own Glock and began knocking people out of the way with his free arm as he ran.

On reaching the courthouse square, Klontz crouched behind a trashcan and tried to figure out what the hell was going on. Hundreds of tourists and retirees and banjo frailers and people who hated Carolina and people who hated Duke and B&B owners and free-range turkey farmers and collectors of rare 78 rpm blues sides and cloggers and naked witches and Labradoodles dragging leashes and stout women in flannel shirts furiously scrounging around in their fanny packs for Subaru keys fled screaming and barking in radiating waves away from what seemed to be a firefight, chaotic even by firefight standards, going on in the middle of the square. The ground was littered with left behind bolo ties and half-eaten gluten-free pastries and the zipped-off legs of nylon hiking pants and pictures of the Dalai Lama and tiny statues of the virgin of Guadeloupe and ratty-looking but prohibitively expensive hemp messenger bags and fashionable but increasingly cliched rat pack fedoras and Earnhardt t-shirts (Sr. and Jr.) and crystal Wiccan rosaries and environmentally indefensible Warren Wilson brochures and iPods and iPads and iPhones (many of them 4G) and bottles of homeopathic de-lousing shampoo and pine tree-shaped automobile air fresheners recently worn as medallions and spilled containers of free trade coffee and take-out boxes of vegetarian fusion entrees that had looked good on the menu and the occasional Mountain Dew bottle half-filled with tobacco spit. Klontz winced as an older gay couple in matching Rockports and travel vests trampled a gaunt vegan who didn't have the strength to run away. The detective scanned the area for shooters and found them everywhere he looked. The weird thing was that the shooters, maybe thirty white guys in cheap suits, seemed to be shooting indiscriminately at each other. Usually, so far as he knew, people engaged in firefights tended to be organized, more or less, into identifiable teams. But this was like watching a football game where all 22 players ran around tackling each other randomly. The APD officers on the scene, their service weapons extended combat-style, spun around like flak-jacketed weather-vanes, shouting, "Drop your Weapon! Drop your Weapon!" but nobody paid them any attention.

When Ruby Jean, wearing one of Little Law's hoodies, spun away from Garnell and opened fire on Marshall, she hit him only once, in the left foot, despite getting off 14 rounds. (Little Law, famished, had stopped off at the Denny's in Spruce Pine, where he polished off a Grand Slam, two pieces of cherry pie and six glasses of chocolate milk before falling asleep in his car. When he woke up, he couldn't remember what it was that Ruby and Aunt Gloria had wanted him to do, so he drove back home, fired one up and watched the last half of "Lawrence of Arabia" on AMC.) Because Ruby was using a .22 (shooting anything larger made her flinch) Marshall's wound, while extremely painful, proved to be neither life-threatening nor, ultimate-ly, crippling. He drew his own weapon and dispatched Ruby Jean easily, two shots, center mass. (Marshall had been number one in marksmanship out of 183 recruits in his top secret SBI mole class. He would have shot her in the head, but that would have been showing off.) The bloodshed might have ended there had not one Dr. Perry T. Parton, Professor of Hermeneu-tics at Mars Hill (emeritus) decided that the panic and confusion caused by the initial exchange of gunfire provided as good an opportunity as he would ever have to rid the world of a few hairy-pitted, Satan-loving Wiccans. He whipped his 9mm Sig Sauer out of his pants and emptied it in the general direction of the rapidly unraveling dance circle without managing—miracu-lously some might say—to nail a single witch. A nearby drummer, however, took one in the bongos and dropped without repercussion. The situation deteriorated even further when the Baptist protestors and the Pentecostal protestors, restrained until that moment behind separate barricades, began exchanging fire. The long-dormant feud between the two Protestant camps, Balkan in its longevity and rancor, had its genesis in irreconcilable doctrinal differences: the Pentecostals considered the Baptists uppity in their aversion to unknown tongues, while the Baptists believed the Pentecostals to be, well, nuts. Nobody could say later which denomination fired first.

Peeping up and down from behind his trashcan like a whistle pig with a death wish, Klontz scanned the square for Marshall until he discovered the former colleague he had so grossly underestimated rolling around on the ground. Harris was clutching the calf of his left leg with both hands and appeared to be trying to blow on his foot.

"Marshall!" Klontz shouted through the din of gunfire and Wiccan curses and surprisingly fluent Baptist imprecations and yet-to-be interpreted Pentecostal jibberings. "Marshall Harris! Are you alright?"

"'Tis not so deep as a well, nor so wide as a church door," Harris yelled, "but 'tis enough, 'twill serve. Ask for me to-morrow and you shall find me a grave man."

"Hold on. I'm coming over."

"Don't worry about me, Klontz," Harris said. "They have made worms' meat of me! Find Garnell!"

"A plague on both your houses," Klontz sighed, frantically searching the square for the sylph-like assassin. He spotted her dragging herself away from the bonfire. She crawled behind the flatbed holding the firewood and collapsed onto her belly. A handful of thoughts chased each other through Klontz's brain like teenagers down a waterslide: she's hit; she's naked; why is she naked? God, she's hot; and Jesus, J.D., what's wrong with you?"

"You see her?" Harris called.

"I got her," Klontz yelled, mentally computing the distance he would have to travel across the open square to reach Garnell. "She's been hit."

"Garnell!" Harris screamed. "Garnell! Answer me!"

"Marshall!" yelped the hard-bodied hit-girl. "Somebody shot me in the ass!"

"Go to her, Klontz!" said Harris. "O, that I were a glove upon that hand that I might touch that cheek!"

"I don't want that Yankee pervert anywhere near my ass," Garnell yelled.

"He's a peace officer, honey! That's almost as good as a first responder!"

Klontz watched Garnell reach around and palpate her wound. She briefly appeared to faint. That wasn't a good sign. "Hang on, Garnell," he called. "We'll get you out of here."

He put the knuckles of his left hand onto the ground. He had been an All-Big East defensive tackle at Syracuse. He had once beaten a double team and dropped Doug Flutie onto his pretty little head. He could do this. "One," he whispered to himself. He raised himself into a three-point stance. "Two." A bullet pinged into the metal trashcan he was hiding behind and whirred angrily away. He lowered himself back to the ground. "Okay," he said. "One."

"Klontz!" Marshall yelled. "Don't forget to crouch! Run in a serpentine pattern!"

"Three!" Klontz grunted, and lit out across the square, crouching, to be sure, but on a more-or-less Point A to Point B heading. A hand-loaded, hot Baptist hollowpoint passed within inches of his head with a deafening, supersonic *crack!* but he somehow clambered behind the trailer beside Garnell in one piece. He holstered his weapon and looked at her ass—not for the first time, certainly, but for the first with even remotely legitimate justification. Her left cheek was, for lack of a better word, fine, but in the right cheek a jagged, irregular wound, probably from a ricochet or a piece of shrapnel, bled profusely. As his large hands rotated uncertainly over Garnell's nether regions as if playing the intro to "Good Vibrations" on a stolen theremin, the syllables of the word *harassment* constantly italicized themselves in the detective's brain into any number of new and disturbing emphases.

"If you lay one finger on my ass," Garnell growled, "I will gut you like a pond-raised trout."

"I've got to stop the bleeding, Garnell."

"Sure you do. Next thing you'll tell me is that I've been snake-bit and you have to suck the poison out."

Someone scurried up and dropped down beside Klontz in what can only be described as an intoxicating nimbus of woman-scent: coconut shampoo; conditioner with traces of lavender, patchouli, lemongrass and sandalwood; Deseo Forever, a Jennifer Lopez perfume. "You better let me take over here, J.D.," Nurse Rachel de la Fuente said.

"Nurse Rachel? Is that you?" Garnell asked, trying to swivel around and see behind her. "Don't let Officer Klutz here touch my ass."

Rachel placed her hand in the small of Garnell's back and pushed her gently down onto her stomach. "You need to lie still, Chiquita," Rachel said softly. "You're losing a lot of blood."

"Rachel," Klontz stammered, inhaling deeply. God she smelled good. "I mean, Nurse de la Fuente. I mean, what are you doing here?"

She shrugged. "Sometimes you just gotta get out of Avery County, you know? We'll talk later. Right now, we've got to keep our little one here from going into shock."

Rachel whipped off her Vanderbilt Nursing School t-shirt, folded it into a compress, and expertly applied it to Garnell's bleeding buttock. Klontz had seen some beautiful things in his time—the Little Pigeon River slipping invisibly at dawn beneath a river-shaped coverlet of mist, a black thunderhead wild with lightning looming behind Grandfather Mountain, the 32-point comeback of the Bills against the Houston Oilers in the 1993 AFC playoffs—but he had never laid eyes on anything as even remotely magnificent as Rachel de la Fuente's breasts. Klontz would remember the moment he saw them swelling gently with Rachel's breath against her black, lacy, tastefully sheer, front-loading bra as without sound, when in fact he was at that moment buffeted by the overwhelming cacophony of what the media would later dub as the "Great Asheville Witch Hunt": the boom and crack of previously concealed registered handguns fired in anger, the screams and spells of wounded witches, the death cries and invocations of stricken fundamentalists, the earnest pleadings of community activists and peace facilitators, the background hound-pack wailing of every siren in Buncombe County. But Klontz heard none of it. He felt his throat tighten. He thought he was going into anaphylactic shock. "My God," he choked. "Rachel."

"Hold on, cowboy," Rachel said. "Stop staring at the ladies for a minute. We need to help this girl."

"I'm sorry."

"Don't worry about it," she said. "I get that a lot. Hold this."

Klontz placed his hands on top of Rachel's and pressed down. She slid her hands from beneath his and moved to take Garnell's pulse. The warmth of Rachel's skin flooded him with optimism. He felt suddenly that he could do anything. He didn't feel old anymore. As he leaned his weight into the compress, he was sure he could keep Garnell Ray from bleeding to death. So he could arrest her.

"I told you not to touch my ass," Garnell said, but all the fight seemed to be leaking out of her with her blood.

Klontz also discovered that since Rachel's arrival on the scene he had lost interest in Garnell's ass as an ass. Now it was just an ass, albeit an ass with a bullet hole in it.

"I don't like this pulse," Rachel said. "It's fluttery." She stared at Klontz for a long moment. With the back of her bloody left hand she brushed a ringlet of hair off of her forehead. "J.D.?"

He raised his eyes from her chest. Then he raised his eyebrows.

"Would you be nice to me?"

"Excuse me?"

"If you were my man, would you be nice to me?"

Klontz suddenly realized he wanted to be Rachel's man more than he had ever wanted to be anything. He knew then that Rachel de la Fuente was why he had moved to Avery County. Why he had never looked very hard for his wife. He probably could have found his wife if he had looked for her very hard. He was a detective, after all. He nodded stupidly, but with conviction, a lifetime's worth of promises contained within the inarticulate gesture. Yes, Rachel de la Fuente. I will be nice to you. Yes. I will be your man. If we make it out of this square alive, the first thing I will do is spend a month's pension taking you to dinner at the Eseeola Lodge in Linville. The rainbow trout, he had heard, was supernaturally good.

"Okay," she said. "Then you can be my man."

"Jesus," Garnell said. "Get a room."

"Why don't you have a man already?" Klontz asked.

"I had one, but he was no good. He drove a Mercedes with slick tires."

"Real estate broker?" Klontz asked.

"Time share salesman."

"Oh God, Rachel. I'm so sorry."

"Yeah, well. What are you going to do? You know?"

From behind a nearby recycling bin, a naked woman scuttled toward them in a low crouch, her hands covering her head, her breasts—good ones, but not in the same league as Rachel's—swinging rhythmically beneath her in what Klontz judged to be approximately 4/4 time. Wait a minute, thought Klontz, those look familiar. The woman dropped behind the trailer. She lowered herself all the way to the ground and stared into Garnell's eyes. And her ass, Klontz thought. Why did that ass seem so familiar? The woman gently brushed a strand of Garnell's auburn hair behind the younger Wiccan's ear. "Oh, Sweetie," she said. "You took one for the team, didn't you?"

"Please make that big cop let go of my ass," Garnell said.

The High Priestess sat up and looked coolly at Klontz. "Hello, J.D." she said.

"Rowena?" Klontz said, his mouth agape. "What? . . ."

" . . . Am I doing in Asheville?" she asked. "Gaia led me here."

"Who?"

"Gaia. The goddess. After all those years of living so many lies in Buffalo, she called me home, to Asheville, to the land of the sky. I lived here thousands of years ago. Before the Cherokee. I was one of the ancient ones. Although at the time, we weren't the ancient ones yet. We were just 'the ones.' And Asheville wasn't Asheville, of course. It didn't have a name. We called it 'the place with no name.'"

"But I thought you were a Catholic," Klontz said. "I thought *we* were Catholic."

"That was one of the lies," Rowena said. "Now I'm done with patriarchal oppression in all its forms."

"So now you're a . . ."

" . . . Wiccan, J.D. A follower of Wicca."

"And that means you're a . . ."

"Witch. Yes."

"And a . . ."

"Lesbian? A woman who loves women? Yes. I'm not ashamed to say that. Not anymore."

"Which explains the . . ."

"Subaru? Yes, J.D. The Subaru."

"But we lived in freaking Buffalo," Klontz almost shouted. "I thought you wanted it for the all-wheel drive! How was I supposed to know you were a lesbian? I thought you wore those flannel shirts because you were cold-natured!"

Rowena briefly touched Klontz on the cheek. "Oh, you poor man," she said.

"J.D.?" Rachel asked. "Who is this naked person?"

"I'm—was—his wife. And who are you?"

"I'm J.D's woman."

Klontz swallowed and said, "Rachel, Rowena. Rowena, Rachel."

"Charmed, I'm sure," said Rowena. She took a long, obvious look at Rachel's chest. "You always were a breast man, J.D."

"He's a good man, is what he is," Rachel said. "And stop staring at the ladies. It's rude."

"He's still a *man*," said Rowena. "And if you don't want people staring at your boobs, then maybe you ought to put on a shirt."

"You're one to talk. You don't even have on *pants*. And the shrubbery could stand to be cut back a little bit. You know what I'm saying?"

"Oh, great," Garnell moaned. "A cat fight in the middle of a gunfight." Moments before Klontz would have had to separate the two women, Daniel, the watchman from the campground, appeared out of nowhere and collapsed flat on the ground beside Garnell, his face close to hers. He began to weep and stroke her hair, oblivious to the bullets *pocking* and *thwacking* into the firewood above them. "Oh, my Garnell. Oh, my sweet baby girl. Somebody done went and shot you again." He looked at the bloody compress Klontz held to Garnell's wound, at the pool of blood in which Klontz knelt. He stared beseechingly into Rachel's face, then into Klontz's. "Klontz, please tell me my girl's going to make it."

"We need to get her to a hospital," Klontz said.

"It's only a flesh wound," said Garnell.

"She's lost a lot of blood," said Rachel.

"I'm getting better."

"Garnell?" Harris screamed from across the square. "Garnell, are you there?"

"I'm here, Marshall. I'm right here."

"Garnell, I have heard the mermaids singing each to each. They will not sing for me."

"He's switched to Eliot," Klontz said. "That can't be good."

"Modernism is often a sign of shock," Rachel said. "Particularly early modernism."

"When the tide pulls out, and the moon goes dark, I'll build a fire on the point for you," Garnell sang in a clear, perfectly-pitched, surprisingly strong voice. The effort seemed to exhaust her.

"Garnell," Daniel said. "Listen, sweetie. I need to tell you something."

"Is that Jan and Dean?" Marshall yelled.

"Beach Boys," Garnell whispered. "Please tell him it's the Beach Boys. Off *Imaginary Songs, Volume II.*"

"It's the Beach Boys, Harris!" Klontz yelled. "Hold it down, will you?"

"Sorry!"

"Garnell, listen to me," Daniel said.

"Hey, everybody!" Nurse Genevieve said, running up and dropping to her knees beside them. "I was hiding under a bench when I saw y'all over here. What's all this shooting about, anyway? I've never seen the like."

"The Baptists and the Holiness are trying to kill each other," Daniel said, sitting up and wiping his eyes.

Genevieve blushed extraordinarily and touched her hair when she saw Daniel.

"How do you know that?" Klontz asked.

"All the Baptists are wearing blue suits and all the Holiness are wearing brown suits. You're not from around here, are you?"

"Genevieve, if I'd known you were coming to town, we could have ridden together," Rachel said.

"I'll be damned," muttered Klontz. "Blue suits and brown suits."

"It was spur of the moment," Genevieve said. "Tops is having an end of the season sale. I was looking for something light, you know? Summery? With a little height?"

"Like an espadrille?" Rachel asked.

"No, not exactly. I'm too dumpy for espadrilles. More like, oh, really, I don't know what I was after. So I just ended up getting another pair of Danskos." She reached into a shopping bag and pulled out a utilitarian shoe in a leopard skin pattern. "I guess I just wanted to buy some shoes."

"Ooo," Rachel said. "I like. Very sexy."

"They're not too much for work?"

"Not at all. I wear the tiger stripes all the time. Nobody says boo."

Genevieve blushed again and held the shoe toward Daniel. "Danny?" she said.

"It's an attractive shoe," Daniel said. "For a clog. Look, you'uns, sorry to interrupt, but I really need to talk to Garnell."

"She won't be able to hear you," a woman said, stepping out from behind the front of the trailer clutching a pink Charter Arms .32 revolver. She was wearing one of Little Law's hoodies, goldenrod-colored capris, a matching Hermes scarf tied over her face and expensive pumps whose lustrous color fell somewhere between raw umber and espresso. "She's about to get on her little broom and fly off to witch heaven."

"Aunt Gloria?" Garnell said.

"You went too far when you killed Andy, Garnell," Gloria said. "You tried to make him look like a llama-fucker, Little Missy, but let me tell you something. I knew Andy Michaux, and he was no llama-fucker."

"Take it easy, Gloria," Klontz said. "There've already been enough people shot here tonight."

"You shut up, Detective Snowbird," said Gloria. "This is between me and my naked little niece."

"But he helped kill Mama and Daddy!" Garnell said. "And Mama was your sister!"

"Oh, sweetie. Let's face facts. They weren't the nicest people in the world, now were they?"

"I love your shoes, hon," Genevieve said. "Are they Manolo?"

Gloria looked down and lifted one foot off of the ground. "No, Louboutin. You don't think the toe is, I don't know, a little square?"

"Oh, not at all," Genevieve said. "If you had any more point there, you'd have to have more of a heel to keep the proportion. And the color is just right. You have to admit that."

"Thanks, sug. I was thinking about putting 'em on Ebay. Now maybe I'll wait." She pointed the pink pistol at Rachel's chest. "That's a lovely bra," she said. "Sexy, but not too, I don't know, slutty. Very feminine. Victoria's Secret?"

"No, Chantelle. I got it on closeout at Nordstrom's in San Antonio."

"Chantelle," Gloria said wistfully. "I wish we had a Nordstrom's."

"When were you in San Antonio?" Genevieve asked.

"Don't you remember? Last spring? When I went down for my Abuela's birthday party?"

"Oh, that's right. I forgot all about it. How old was she again?"

"Oh, for God's sake," Rowena spat. "Would you listen to yourselves?"

Gloria pointed the pistol at Rowena, closed one eye and sighted down the barrel. "Now, look here, Witchypoo," she said. "You need to mind your manners. And shag carpeting went out with the Carter administration, if you know what I mean."

"Aunt Gloria," Garnell said. "My ass is killing me. If you're going to shoot me, I wish you'd go ahead and do it."

"Oh, that's right, Sweetpea. I got sidetracked for a minute. Let's start over. Like I said, Andy Michaux was no llama-fucker."

Daniel raised his hands. "Look here," he said. "Instead of killing Garnell, why don't you shoot me instead?"

Gloria said, "Wha . . ." and then blinked twice at Daniel, her eyes suddenly uncomprehending. When she reached underneath her right armpit with her left hand, the hand came out smeared with blood.

"Oh, dear," she mumbled. "I'll never get this out of Little Law's hoodie." Then she collapsed dead onto the sidewalk.

"Garnell!" Marshall yelled across the square. "I'm sorry about your aunt!"

Garnell sniffled. "I love Marshall Harris to death," she said. "But he's about to shoot my whole family. I'm not going to have anybody left after this."

"No," Daniel said. "There's another."

"What do you mean?"

Daniel drew in and let out a long, deep breath. "Garnell," he said. "I'm your father."

"Daniel, I don't understand. You're . . . You're my *daddy*?"

"Well, not exactly, sweetheart. I'm your biological father. Your daddy, God rest his soul, awful as he was, was your father. I was only there at your conception, although I've tried to be a friend to you since."

"Then who was my . . ."

" . . . Biological mother? Oh, she was just a sweet little thing from Sodom. She loved me with all her heart, but I left her behind. She never should have turned her back on me."

"What happened to her?"

"It's a sad story. After I broke her heart, she had a number of failed marriages, grew morbidly obese and eventually blew herself up cooking methamphetamine in a mobile home outside Kingsport. I'm sorry."

"Just my luck," Garnell said. "I'm having that kind of night."

Dawn Reindeer stepped suddenly over Gloria's body and squatted down beside Klontz and Garnell and Rachel and Rowena and Genevieve and Daniel. In her hand was a compact, but lethal-looking Detonics

Combat Master .45 with custom Tritium sights. "OK, folks," she said. "The party's over. Keep your hands where I can see them."

"Jesus Christ, Reindeer," Klontz said. "Put down that weapon before you accidentally shoot somebody."

"The name's not Reindeer," she said. She reached into her peasant blouse and pulled out a gold badge suspended on a lanyard. "It's Brenda Ball-Wacker, ATF."

"Oh, shit," said Daniel.

"Oh, shit is right, Puckett. If you'd stayed close to home and just sold hooch to your hillbilly pals, we wouldn't be having this conversation. But hauling to Virginia and Tennessee? Well, that's interstate, Puckett. That's federal. And that's me. I'm afraid you're going to bill hard time."

"Please don't take my new daddy away, Dawn," Garnell whimpered. "I just got him."

"Back up a minute," Rowena said. "Your name is ballwhacker?"

"*Ball-Wacker.* No 'h.' My mother was a Ball and my father was a Wacker. Ball-Wacker. It's hyphenated. She nodded to Rachel. "I like your bra," she said. "Victoria's Secret?"

"Chantelle."

Agent Ball-Wacker nodded and let out an appreciative whistle. "I'm looking forward to strapping one on again," she said. "Look at me. I'm flopping around all over the place. It's disgusting. A peasant blouse at my age. Fucking Asheville. How much did something like that set you back?"

"It was on closeout."

"She got it at Nordstrom's," Klontz said. "In San Antonio."

"She was down to see her Abuela," Genevieve said. "Last spring. I remember now because I pulled a double shift."

"There's a Nordstrom's in Alexandria," Ball-Wacker said. "Never shopped there."

"Oh, Daddy," said Garnell. "I don't want you to go prison."

"And I don't want you to go to prison, either, darlin'," Daniel said. "But we did the crime, we'll do the time. That's the Puckett way." He turned to Klontz. "That is, if you still plan on arresting my baby girl."

"I've got no choice, Daniel," Klontz said. "She's killed four people. It's hard to overlook something like that. I'm sorry."

"I understand, Detective, I really do, but I have to say it's a cruel irony for us to wind up locked down in separate prisons so soon after our belated reuniting."

"That's too bad," Agent Ball-Wacker said. "Maybe you can Skype."

Genevieve covered her face with her hands and began to cry. "And what about me? I don't even know how to Skype and I'm afraid to drive on the Interstate. How am I supposed to get my conjugal visits?"

Agent Ball-Wacker shivered. "Brr," she said. "That's a mental image I didn't need to see."

"What's that?" Rachel asked, pointing at the roof of the courthouse, where a figure, clutching what appeared to be a J.W. Gallagher custom African mahogany cut-a-way guitar with an ebony fingerboard, bone saddle and Sitka spruce top, stood silhouetted against the dark, autumn sky. On one side of the figure sat a beagle and on the other side perched a large bird. The figure raised his arms and held them there. One by one the guns in the square stopped firing; the curses and moans and anguished cries of the wounded and the frightened and the angry fell silent; the glossolalia of the spirit-filled skittered away like leaves before a chill wind. Even the wail of the sirens ceased. The dead, of course, lay already still.

"A king of shreds and patches!" Harris cried hysterically. "Save me and hover o'er me with wings you heavenly guards!"

"Wait a minute now. Everybody hold what you got," Daniel said. "That ain't no ghost! That's Doc Watson!"

Garnell pushed herself up on her elbow and stared skyward.

"What's Doc Watson doing on the roof of the courthouse?" Rachel asked.

"And how in the world," Klontz said wonderingly, "did he wind up with my beagle and my bird?"

"He's one of the ancient ones," said Rowena. "Of course, when I knew him he wasn't ancient. He was just one of the ones. That's what we called him. 'One of the Ones.' He lived in a crystal cave whose entrance has been closed by the gods to human eyes."

"I'm sorry, lady," Agent Ball-Wacker said. "I gotta call bullshit."

"I can't bear to watch," moaned Genevieve, covering her eyes with her hands. "Is somebody looking after him? He's standing so close to the edge."

The figure slowly lowered his arms, lifted his face to the full moon and strummed a G chord so profoundly resonant that it filled the valley from the Beaucatcher Cut all the way to the Cracker Barrel at Exit 44. Everyone who heard that chord ringing out felt the hollowness inside them fill with joy and hope and peace and understanding and felt, maybe for the first time, that they were capable of loving their husbands and wives and children and partners and pets and friends, and even their enemies, in the manner in which all living things, they suddenly understood, deserve to be loved. Or something like that. Before the ring of that G chord died away, it was easy for even the most hard-hearted among them to imagine the souls of the dead, and there were many, pausing to listen as they lifted away from their corporeal bodies and traveled into the uncharted realms. Men in blue suits and men in brown suits looked at each other and nodded, as if to say, "That right there, that's what a good guitar player'll do for you."

Rachel touched Klontz's hand and nodded. He lifted the bloody compress. Everyone leaned over and stared at Garnell's ass.

"I don't believe it," said Klontz. "The bleeding stopped."

"It's a miracle," said Genevieve.

"A Samhain miracle," said Rowena.

"Oh, *please*," said Rachel, crossing herself.

"Thank you, Doc Watson," mumbled Daniel.

Agent Ball-Wacker shook her head. "I have got to get out of North Carolina."

"Y'all hush," said Garnell. "I think he's about to sing."

Afterword

by Charles F. Price

Okay, I admit it, I shot myself in the foot with a Spudsender RX13. I blew the literary opportunity of a lifetime. If I'd said yes, I would've soared from anonymity into stardom, would've become fixed in the authorial firmament along with Faulkner, Fitzgerald, Hemingway, John Jakes, Jacqueline Suzanne, and Gene Hackman.

How could it have been otherwise? No less a giant of letters than Brian Lee Knopp besought me, *me*, at the faltering tag-end of my heretofore scarcely noticed career as a novelist, to contribute to his brainchild, a collaborative serial novel involving a dozen of Western North Carolina's most distinguished writers, a veritable pantheon of fabled names—Brian Lee himself, John P. "Pat" McAfee, Susan Reinhardt, Vicki Lane, Tommy Hays, Wayne Caldwell, Fred Chappell, Alan Gratz, Annette Saunooke Clapsaddle, Gene Cheek, Tony Earley, and Linda Marie Barrett (that's something of a *nom de plume*, by the way; I leave you to guess who it is but can't resist offering a hint: She's a goddess of physical and spiritual beauty, possessor of deep but serene wisdom, a vision of DELETED BY THE EDITOR).

How could I have been so foolish? Brian Lee Knopp, the literary sensation of the hour, seeking out my superannuated and forgotten self to take part in what would assuredly be the most acclaimed book of the coming year, at least in the area between Old Fort and Franklin if not in the nation as a whole.

I mean, look at my career. Come on, speak of bad luck. I write *Hiwassee*; Charles Frazier writes *Cold Mountain* and Jeffrey Lent writes *In the Fall*. I write *Freedom's Altar* and my publisher puts a picture of a graveyard on the cover as if to foretell its sales figures; I write a book I call *My Burdens At Last I Lay Down* and my publisher retitles it *The Cock's Spur* and puts a picture of a rooster on the cover THAT HAS NO SPURS; I write *Where the Water-Dogs Laughed* about logging and Ron Rash writes *Serena*; I write *Nor the Battle to the Strong* about a neglected period of the American Revolution and it is, no doubt deservedly, as neglected as its subject.

And why did I say no to Brian Lee? After reading the above, you probably already know.

I'm STUPID.

I told myself, okay, so you've bombed five times in a row. At least you've got your integrity.

Integrity, shmegrity. Take it to the bank and see what that'll get you. But I had it, and I clung to it with a death-grip. There was this sequel, see? A sequel to the non-selling Revolutionary War book. I was going to write an equally non-selling sequel. That's the way my mind works. Hey, if it really hurt cutting off that finger, let me see what'll happen if I cut off my dick.

It happened that Brian Lee approached me just as I was girding my dickless loins to complete the sequel which I had begun some years earlier but had allowed to languish for two years because I got a wild hair up my ass about these two Hispanic serial killers who murdered thirty-two Anglos in Colorado Territory back in 1863 and I had researched and written a 630-page novel about them called *Blood Offerings* and then a 300-page nonfiction account called *Season of Terror* but nobody wanted to publish *Blood Offerings* (NOTE TO PUBLISHERS WHO MAY BE READING THIS: IT'S STILL AVAILABLE) but although the first publisher to whom I sent the manuscript of *Season of Terror* returned it with the suggestion that I take a remedial writing class, a university press has been perusing it for eighteen months now; it's been peer reviewed twice and re-read a number of times whenever the editors decide to come to work, which seems to be about one week in four, not counting holidays, and a few more reviews are scheduled, including one by the Press's Board of Trustees ... Well, you get the picture.

About the sequel—I had almost finished it, figured I had two or three chapters yet to go when Brian Lee entreated me to do a chapter in the serial novel. Wrapping myself in my toga of misplaced writerly virtue, I declined. Graciously, he accepted my decision. Then I sat down to finish the sequel and hit a writer's block the size and bulk of the Grand Coulee Dam. Not one puny word could I write. And while I peered haplessly at my computer screen Brian Lee and his justly acclaimed cohorts temporarily laid aside their literary *gravitas* to contribute—each within an astonishingly brief two weeks' time—the wonderfully zany 6,000-word chapters that make up the inventive and hilarious novel you've just enjoyed, whose title recalls the 1969 national bestselling spoof *Naked Came the Stranger* and the 1996 mystery thriller parody *Naked Came the Manatee. Naked Came the Leaf Peeper*, as you know, far from sneering at our ways, turns out to be a sly yet affectionate homage to all that makes our mountains special—and peculiar.

Of course I knew nothing of the content of Brian Lee's project while its writers were beavering away. I was gazing into CPU infinity and finding it—infinite. But soon the fates, to repay me for bypassing my chance at greatness, began to wreak retributive havoc. My wife Ruth is a native of Colorado: she was suddenly called there to address a family problem and I tagged along to help if I could (I never can). Also, I hoped to tidy up some details for *Season of Terror* (hope really does spring eternal, even in the face of all evidence to the contrary). While clambering around in a ravine beside Colorado Highway 115 between Cañon City and Colorado Springs, looking for the grave of one of the victims of my aforementioned serial killers in a place called Dead Man's Canyon, I popped a muscle in the calf of my right leg. Said calf instantly swelled to the amplitude, firmness and rigidity of the barrel of one of those old World War Two 81mm mortars. It bled internally creating a sort of nauseous rainbow of bruise colors. It still isn't back to normal. And of course it was so stiff and sore that I couldn't have written anything even if I knew what to write—the leg wouldn't fit under my computer desk.

So there you are. I said no to Brian Lee and thus rejected what must have been my final opportunity for lasting fame. As it is, nobody except

Ruth and Rob Neufeld (God bless him!) and my cat Salem even knows who I am. My mom and dad and sister and our dog Sandia used to know, but they're all dead. And I'm old. My moment has come and gone. I remember hearing Winston Churchill on the radio—when he was prime minister the first time. I got my draft card the same month the Hungarian Revolution broke out; I and Emöke B'Racz are probably the only two people in Western North Carolina who even *remember* the Hungarian Revolution, and I'll bet Emöke was just a toddler. I remember when Robert Frost was alive. Hell, I even remember seeing the last living Pony express rider on an old snowy black-and-white TV program.

Yes, because I failed to take part in *Naked Came the Leaf Peeper*, my life is now drab and sere and scarcely worth the living. It is as inutile as a used condom or an expended shotgun shell. Which reminds me, not only am I myself antiquated, even my arsenal is out of date. Many of the contributors to *Naked* are unnervingly conversant with all types of automatic and semiautomatic weaponry as well as the latest in fancy-dancy wheelguns. What have I got? An 1847 Mississippi rifle. Cap-and-ball revolvers. Under duress I might be able to load and fire one time in two or three minutes. How would I fare against a foe armed with, say, Tony Earley's 9 mm Sig Sauer or the hand-loaded hot Baptist hollow-point bullets that go zipping through the night in his astounding *tour de force* of a climactic chapter, peopled as it is by every conceivable Western North Carolina stereotype, oddball, weirdo and zealot, that left me weeping with helpless laughter even as I felt ineluctably crushed by the terrible awareness of my own deliquescence and well-deserved obscurity.

—Charles F. Price—
October 2011

Acknowledgements

We are unspeakably grateful to Emöke B'Racz and her Mala-prop's Bookstore/Café for great books, big dreams, bigger laughs, best coffee, and all the support we needed to undertake and complete this collaborative project. Happy 30th Birthday to the best indie bookstore in the South!

We are profoundly indebted to our editor Linda Barrett Knopp, our copy editor Maria Fire [mariawriting @gmail.com], and our superb readers: Charles Frazier, Ron Rash, Elizabeth Gilbert, Steve Almond, Sarah Addison Allen, Lucy Doll and Ruth Price.

Finally, we blush to think about how our esteemed cover artist Julie Armbruster didn't hesitate to donate her time, talent, and beagle worship to our cause [www.juliearmbruster.net].

Contributing Authors

Linda Marie Barrett

Linda Marie Barrett is the pen name of Linda Barrett Knopp, General Manager and co-owner of Malaprop's Bookstore/Café. She is the author of a fantasy series set in Ireland that blends historical fiction, urban fantasy, and the erotic world of faerie. She has an MA in Russian Literature and Slavic Linguistics from Cornell University, where she was awarded Olin and National Resource Fellowships. She is also a poet and has published her translation of Marina Tsvetaeva's "344" in *Graham House Review*. She loves all things Irish, as well as fluting, dancing, gardening, and hiking the mountains of western North Carolina.

Wayne Caldwell

Wayne Caldwell, a native of Asheville, is a product of Enka High School. His academic training happened at Chapel Hill, Boone, and Durham. Since 1976 he has worked in the family's furniture and interior design business, Ambiance Interiors. He is the author of prize-winning short stories and two novels, *Cataloochee* and *Requiem by Fire*, the latter of which won the 2010 Thomas Wolfe Memorial Literary Award from the WNC Historical Association. "Rattlesnakes" is forthcoming in *27 Views of Asheville* from Eno Publishers. A poem, "Woodsmoke," recently appeared in *Appalachian Heritage*. In his spare time he works up firewood.

Fred Chappell

In 2004 Fred Chappell retired after 40 years in the English Department of the University of North Carolina Greensboro. During this period he published 26 books of poetry, fiction, and critical commentary. Various awards have been conferred upon him, most recently (2010) the John Tyler Caldwell Award. His wife Susan and his son Heath have made gratitude one of the healthier parts of his life. For five years he served as Poet Laureate of the state and in that capacity visited some 250 or so schools, colleges, universities, retirement homes, churches, and other venues. His latest book is *Shadow Box* from Louisiana State University Press (2009); latest fiction, *Ancestors and Others: New and Selected Stories* from St. Martin's Press (2009).

Gene Cheek

Gene Cheek is a blue-collar son of the South born on March 2, 1951, in Winston Salem, North Carolina. He has lived an unremarkable life with the exception of his children, grandchildren, and his own peculiar childhood. He lives and works in the Blue Ridge Mountains of North Carolina. He is the author of *The Color of Love, A Mother's Choice in the Jim Crow South*, and the co-author of *Butter My Butt and Call Me a Biscuit* and *You're The Butter on my Biscuit!*

Annette Saunooke Clapsaddle

Annette Saunooke Clapsaddle grew up in Cherokee, NC and resides there with her husband, Evan, and their son, Ross. She holds degrees in American Studies from Yale University and the College of William and Mary. As assistant to Principal Chief Hicks, Annette produced *Cherokee Elders: Our Greatest Generation* and a series of children's books including: *The Elder Tree, True Blue,* and *What Wonders.* Recent publications include: "It All Comes Out in the Wash" from *Appalachian Heritage Quarterly,* and "Camouflage" from *Night is Gone, Day Is Still Coming.* Annette teaches English and Cherokee Studies and coaches basketball at Swain High School.

Tony Earley

Tony Earley is a native of Rutherford County, North Carolina, and a graduate of Warren Wilson College in Swannanoa and The University of Alabama in Tuscaloosa. He is the author of four books, including the novels *Jim the Boy* and *The Blue Star.* His fiction and/or nonfiction have appeared in *The New Yorker, Harper's, Esquire, New Stories from the South, Best American Short Stories* and many other magazines, periodicals and anthologies. He lives in Nashville with his wife and daughters, where he is the Samuel Milton Fleming Professor of English at Vanderbilt University.

Alan Gratz

Alan Gratz is the author of a number of novels for young readers, including the teen mystery *Something Rotten* (a 2008 ALA Quick Pick for Young Adult Readers) and its sequel *Something Wicked*. His short fiction has appeared in *Alfred Hitchcock's Mystery Magazine*, and he is the author of a handful of episodes of the A&E true crime show "City Confidential." A native of Knoxville, Tennessee, Alan now lives in beautiful Mitchell County near Penland, North Carolina.

Tommy Hays

Tommy Hays' latest novel, *The Pleasure Was Mine*, has been chosen for numerous community reads, including the *One City One Book* in Greensboro and Greenville, SC's *Amazing Read*. The novel was read on National Public Radio's "Radio Reader" and was a Finalist for the SIBA Fiction Award. Hays has written two other novels —*Sam's Crossing* (Atheneum) and *In the Family Way* (Random House), a selection of the Book-of-the-Month Club and winner of the Thomas Wolfe Memorial Literary Award. He is Executive Director of the Great Smokies Writing Program at UNC Asheville.

Brian Lee Knopp

Brian Lee Knopp is the author of the bestselling memoir *Mayhem in Mayberry: Misadventures of a P.I. in Southern Appalachia*, which was featured on C-SPAN Book TV and UNC-TV, nominated as a 2009 Finalist for the SIBA (Southern Independent Booksellers Alliance) Nonfiction Award, and excerpted in *Now & Then: The Appalachian Magazine*. He is a former criminal defense investigator, private investigator, and professional sheep shearer with an MA degree in English Literature from the University of Texas at Austin. His book reviews and essays have been published in several regional magazines and local media. He teaches writing at UNCA/Great Smokies Writing Program and at Warren Wilson College.

Vicki Lane

Vicki Lane is the author of *The Day of Small Things*, as well as the critically acclaimed Elizabeth Goodweather Appalachian Mysteries from Bantam Dell —*Signs in the Blood, Art's Blood, Old Wounds, In A Dark Season*, and *Under the Skin*. Vicki draws her inspiration from the past and present of rural North Carolina where she and her family have tended a mountainside farm since 1975. Visit her website vickilanemysteries.com for more information.

John P. McAfee

John Patrick "Pat" McAfee is the author of two novels, *Slow Walk in A Sad Rain* and *On Rims of Empty Moons*. His poetry has appeared in several anthologies and magazines. A retired drama director, wrestling and soccer coach, McAfee currently lives in Hendersonville, NC with his artist wife, Elizabeth McAfee. He spends a lot of time as a beach bum down at Cape Lookout National Seashore and refuses to do anything constructive with his life. Oh, and he enjoys power lifting, hasn't a clue why, he just does.

Susan Reinhardt

Susan Reinhardt is a mother of two and a syndicated columnist who focuses on humor and human interest. She is the author of four humor books, including her bestseller *Not Tonight Wait Til I'm a Size Six*. Her work, *Don't Sleep With a Bubba*, was a *January Magazine* Book of the Year. Susan can ride a unicycle and do tricks on a trapeze. She enjoys public speaking, stand-up comedy and impersonating Sarah Palin. Her delights are her children, her mama and being in love. She enjoys Southern fiction, humor being tops. Her favorite book is *A Confederacy of Dunces*.

Cover Artist

Julie Armbruster

Julie Armbruster has been exhibited in solo and group exhibitions in galleries throughout the East Coast and abroad, including the School of Architecture in Venice Italy, 80 Washington Square Gallery in New York, and Rebus Works in Raleigh, North Carolina. Often seeking shows in alternative spaces, her work has been exhibited in skate shops, bars, music venues, tattoo parlors, restaurants, and record shops. A New Jersey native who has lived most of her life in New York's Hudson Valley, Julie received a Masters in Painting from NYU in 2004 and studied abroad in Italy and Germany. Following grad school, she moved to Asheville, where she maintains a studio in the Wedge Studios located in the River Arts District.